The Papal Secret

Stan Miller

Strategic Book Publishing and Rights Co.

Copyright © 2012.
All rights reserved by Stan Miller.

Book Design/Layout by Kalpart. Visit www.kalpart.com

No part of this book may be reproduced or transmitted in any form or by any means, graphic, electronic, or mechanical including photocopying, recording, taping or by any information retrieval system, without the permission in writing of the publisher.

Strategic Book Publishing and Rights Co.
12620 FM 1960, Suite A4-507
Houston TX 77065
www.spbra.com

ISBN: 978-1-61897-063-3

Also by Stan Miller –

The Kruger Millions
The Dead Sea Conspiracy

This book is for my children, Alana, Marc, Karen, Russell, my grandchildren, Doron, Yoni, Ashleigh, Megan, and Chloe, and my lovely wife Cherrie, my best friend and inspiration.

And to my extended family of children and grandchildren, Ari, Jo-anne, Talia, Liora and Sammy; Paul, Tracy, Rachel and Zac, for bringing me so much happiness.

Prologue

Berlin – 1938

In 1933, Hitler became chancellor of Germany and a year later commander-in-chief of the army. His first objective was to rearm Germany in preparation for his conquest of Europe. It was a great year for the German people, so it seemed, but it unleashed a storm over Europe in which over fifty million people were to die.

So began the implementation of his social theories and the final solution of the Jewish problem— Hitler's dream of total annihilation of the Jews. The world's darkest hour had begun— the monstrous atrocities of the Holocaust.

Samuel Grossman and his wife Gertrude knew little about politics, but it was common knowledge among Jews that all was not right in their homeland. Nevertheless, they continued with their lives in the hope that the gossip among some of their Jewish neighbours was over-exaggerated.

When they heard the doorbell of their little jewellery store ring they looked up in alarm and then smiled when they saw it was Mrs. Klinsman, one of their Gentile customers, and a friend. She was looking for a diamond ring her husband had promised her and she had come in to choose one she liked. She was examining a selection in a tray under the glass counter when a commotion outside drew their attention to the window.

Outside, across the street, they saw a Nazi officer dressed in a black uniform wrestling with a woman. She was trying to protect her two children from the man in black who was shouting at them. From inside the shop, they heard the officer screaming at the mother.

"I'm taking one of your children. Which one is it to be?"

As the mother was clutching her daughter at the time, the Nazi officer took that to mean that the boy was to be sacrificed. He withdrew his revolver and without further thought shot the boy in the head in front of his mother. Afterward, he calmly

Stan Miller

replaced the revolver in his leather holster as if he had drawn it merely to admire it.

Suddenly he looked up and saw the Grossmans peering out of the shop window. Without any hesitation, he began walking toward the store.

Mrs. Grossman called her three-year-old son to her side. "Please say the child is yours, Mrs. Klinsman," she begged. She had already discussed this eventuality with her husband. Too many of their friends had been taken away and sent to concentration camps, and the Nazis had no sympathy, even for children.

The Nazi officer burst into the shop. He walked up to Mr. Grossman and said, "You have a very nice store."

Grossman remained silent.

The Nazi officer turned to the customer. "And who are you?" he asked.

"I'm Mrs. Klinsman and this is my son," she answered. "I am here to purchase a ring."

The officer stooped down to have a closer look at the boy. "Ah, what beautiful blue eyes he has – the true sign of an Aryan." He looked at the woman. "What piece have you chosen?" he asked, with a smile on his face.

She pointed to one of the rings under the glass counter. The officer removed his revolver once again and struck the glass top with the butt of the gun. The glass shattered. With his gloved hand, he delicately brushed away the fragments of glass and extracted the ring Mrs. Klinsman had shown him and handed it to her with a click of his heels. "This is for you, madam," he said, "with the compliments of the Third Reich. Now you and your son had better be going," he added. "I have business with these Jews."

"Wait!" said Mrs. Grossman. "I have a present for the boy." She opened a drawer and brought out a wooden box. It had been set aside for an eventuality like this. She opened the box and withdrew a golden crucifix inlaid with ivory. She slipped it onto a gold chain and fastened it around the boy's neck. It was one they had specially prepared. Behind the cross was engraved a small emblem which looked like an upside-down horseshoe. She and her husband knew it to be a secret sign resembling a *chai*, the Jewish symbol of life. It would help identify their son as a Jew one day when the horror was over.

"Remember us," she whispered in her son's ear.

"Seize them!" the Nazi officer barked at his men.

Chapter 1

Rome – May 2010

The heavy rain that had fallen all night stopped at the first light of dawn. The sun made its first appearance at midday when the thick cloud began to dissipate. The streets were wet with rainwater and there was a chill in the air that still belonged to winter. However, the weather did nothing to deter the thousands of tourists from swarming into Saint Peter's Square to visit the Vatican.

Tony Stendardi, attorney at law, raised his coat collar against the cold air as he left his fashionable office suite situated on Via Nazionale on the other side of the Tiber River. He had never visited the Vatican; not because he was Jewish, he told himself, but merely because he was averse to crowds in public places. Instead of crossing Saint Peter's Square and walking past the 85-foot red granite obelisk standing in the centre of the piazza, he skirted the inner edge of the Colonnade, marvelling at the symmetry of design in which the inner column of each row concealed the other three. The columns towered above him as he walked toward the bronze doors where the colonnade joined the north portico.

He was pleased he didn't have to walk to the other side of the square to the main entrance under the *Arco delle Campane*, the Arch of Bells, where the largest throng of people was gathered to view the eighteenth-century clock in the belfry. He went directly to the smaller gate, where he was stopped at the security desk by an officer of the Surveillance Corps.

"*Documenti, per favore*," the guard said as he held out his hand.

Stendardi handed him the document and reference number giving permission to enter, faxed to him by Vatican security beforehand. The guard consulted his clipboard to check if the name matched the daily visitors list and, after ticking the appropriate place, directed Stendardi to pass through the electronic scanner. When it remained silent, the guard smiled and let him pass through.

"*Entrare,*" he said, and stepped smartly aside.

Stendardi crossed the Courtyard of Saint Damasus, the central element around which the three wings of the papal residence are built, and carefully negotiated the five steps leading into the Sistine Palace. His heart was beating rapidly as the time grew closer to his audience with the pope. He had gone over in his mind a hundred times what he would say, but like an actor stepping onto the stage for the first time, he was convinced he'd forgotten his lines. He was escorted by a Swiss Guard to the second floor and allowed time to admire the lavish decorations and wooden ceiling of the *Appartamento Nobile* where the pope received delegations and other important visitors.

Stendardi was ushered through the hall into an unadorned reception area outside the pope's private study, and told to wait for the general secretary of the Pontifical Commission for the State of Vatican City to appear. The usual practice was to first submit any matter that was to go before the pope to the president of the Pontifical Commission for approval, but on this occasion, the general secretary had approached the Holy Father directly. He decided discretion was the wisest option so that the deputy secretary, Cardinal Vittorio Albertini, would not be able to interfere in what seemed to be business of a personal nature.

Stendardi did not have long to wait before a tall, thin man emerged from the office. The cardinal looked at him with piercing eyes as if trying to look into his mind. Stendardi clutched the folder he was carrying tightly to his chest as though there was the possibility of the cardinal possessing x-ray vision; the documents inside were for the pope's eyes only.

"His Holiness will receive you now, Mr. Stendardi," said Cardinal Pollini with a smile.

The office was plain and neat, without a single sheet of paper out of place on the large wooden desk. A large crucifix hung on the wall behind the pope's desk, but Stendardi's gaze was fixed on the imposing figure dressed in a white cassock sitting on the other side of the desk.

Pietro Bandini, now Pope John Pietro I, enormously popular within the church and with the College of Cardinals, had been elected to the seat of Saint Peter by an electoral process that had been one of the quickest in recent history. In spite of his kind disposition, Bandini realised that, as pope, he had to tinge his humility with a little bit of toughness in order to deal successfully with the political infighting that sometimes occurred within the ranks of the Holy See. The pope had many advisers concerning matters outside theology, but the man he loved and respected the most was the General Secretary of the Pontifical Commission, Cardinal Angelo Pollini. That is why he had agreed to a meeting with the man who now stood before him.

"Forgive me for not rising," said the pope, "but my joints have been troublesome lately. I keep telling myself it's the dampness in the air responsible for the discomfort and not the cartilage degeneration my physician insists I'm suffering." He extended a hand with the fisherman's ring facing upward.

Stendardi had been briefed to kiss the ring and not shake the hand in deference to the pontiff's reverence. After straightening, he looked directly into the pope's radiant blue eyes and knew immediately that the information contained in his folder was true.

"Thank you for granting me an audience, Holiness," said Stendardi.

"What is the nature of your business?" asked the pontiff. "I believe you indicated to Cardinal Pollini that it was of a personal nature. I hope you're not here to sue me, Mr. Stendardi." The pope had a warm, gentle laugh and Stendardi began to like him.

"Of course not, Your Holiness, but what I have to say is rather confidential," Stendardi said, glancing at the pope's secretary.

The pope dismissed Cardinal Pollini with a quick flicker of his blue eyes. "Please sit, Mr. Stendardi."

"We thank you for the sympathetic and understanding attitude you have toward the Jews."

"You are Jewish, Mr. Stendardi?"

"Yes. Does that make a difference?"

"Not at all; we are all children of the same God."

"It took great courage endorsing the belief of your predecessor that the Jews are blameless for the death of Jesus."

Pope John Pietro I looked uneasily at Stendardi and fiddled nervously with the beads of his rosary. He glanced down at the partially open drawer of his desk to make sure the ivory-handled gun lying harmlessly on a square of velvet was still there. The weapon had been placed there at the insistence of the cardinal as a precaution against the possibility of some religious fanatic with a grudge against the pontiff accidentally being granted an audience without being thoroughly investigated.

Stan Miller

He prayed silently that this was not one of those moments!

"But that is not the reason for my visit," announced Stendardi.

The pope closed the drawer and leaned back in his chair, feeling somewhat relieved. "Then pray, tell me the reason," he said calmly.

Stendardi shifted uneasily in his seat. It was a delicate matter he was presenting to the pope and he did not know what kind of reaction to expect from the holy man. "You have heard about 'Kristallnacht'?" asked Stendardi.

"Night of Broken Glass?" replied the pope, perking up at the strange question. "Yes, unfortunately I know about that dreadful time." He wondered what that event had to do with him; he was only a young boy at the time.

"Yes," said Stendardi, pensively. "The shattered store windows of Jewish owned businesses turned the streets into shiny rivers of glass. The pogrom in Nazi Germany took place on the ninth of November, 1938. On a single night, ninety-two Jews were murdered and thirty thousand arrested and deported to concentration camps. The discussion between Reinhard Heydrich, Joseph Goebbels, and Herman Goering in the aftermath of that event made it abundantly clear what the Nazi hierarchy wanted—the extermination of the Jews." Stendardi paused to wipe his brow with a folded handkerchief. "But I digress."

"The world's darkest hour," murmured the pope.

"It was common practice among Jewish parents who feared that fate," continued Stendardi, "to farm out their children to Christian families who were compassionate enough to take them into their own households and raise these Jewish children as their own. Most of the Jewish parents were rounded up and sent to the death camps, where they perished. The main objective was to save the lives of their children, even if it meant that they would be brought up in a different faith, never knowing their true heritage."

"Sad times, indeed, but many children were spared in this way," said the pope.

"After the war," continued Stendardi, "some children were traced by their parents who had survived the catastrophe and were then re-united with their families. Most, however, remained assimilated in the German society, although, thank God, still possessing their Jewish souls." Stendardi bit his lip; he did not wish to insult the pope through the discourtesy of a

The Papal Secret

disparaging remark against another religion.

"Why are you telling me all this, Mr. Stendardi?"

"It will become apparent in a moment, Your Holiness," said Stendardi. "One such Jewish child, a small boy, was in his parents' jewellery store the day preceding *Kristallnacht*, when a woman from a wealthy German family entered through the front door. She was looking for a diamond ring and knew the Grossmans, the owners of the store, well enough to trust their honesty. She saw three rings she liked and was looking at them closely in order to arrive at a choice, when a commotion outside drew their attention to the window." Stendardi continued to relate the story of the event. He had to pause to wipe the tears from his eyes when he reached the part where the young boy was shot. "Can you imagine that, Your Holiness, asking a mother to choose which child should live and which one should die?"

"What happened next?" the pope asked. He could feel his throat tightening in sympathy.

Stendardi continued with the story of how they had placed a golden cross around their son's neck before Mrs. Klinsman left the shop with the boy.

The pope had turned ashen. His hand involuntary went up to his throat and he fingered the chain under his robe.

"I urge you to examine your cross more closely, Your Holiness," said Stendardi softly.

With shaking hands, Bandini removed the crucifix from under his shirt. He picked up his reading glasses from the pouch on his desk and slowly put them on. He held the cross in his hand and looked straight into the eyes of the lawyer as if waiting for the devil to pronounce a curse. Then, slowly, he lowered his eyes to the object in his hand. He turned it over and examined the back of the cross. The *chai* was where the lawyer had said it would be—at the base of the golden cross.

The cross fell from the pope's hand and clattered onto the wooden desk.

Chapter 2

Portofino – August

When the sun rose over the rooftop of the ancient battlements of Castello Brown, it seemed to pause momentarily to greet the quaint little fishing village of Portofino with a generous dose of summer warmth. The gentle breeze blowing across the Golfo Marconi carried with it an unusual chill for that time of the year, but the day promised to be bright and sunny. As the sun oozed through the entrance of the harbour, the town suddenly began to fill with early risers, and the aroma of espresso from the coffee bars in the town square permeated the air. The white topsides of moored fishing boats shone in bold relief against the backdrop of dark green pines running up the mountainside.

It was time for the shutters of the shops to swing open, and through their old-fashioned portals, a multitude of Italian designer names could be seen in strange juxtaposition with the architecture of old buildings that hadn't changed in centuries.

The sheer face of the coast makes it possible for large boats to ride anchor close to shore. Two medium-sized pleasure yachts were moored at the quay-side at the end of the row of buildings on the south side of the harbour. On the foredeck of the smaller vessel, the *marinai*, the boatman, began his morning chores. He was dressed in a dark blue t-shirt and long white trousers rolled up to his knees to prevent them from getting wet as he mopped the deck. A party of six passengers was boarding in two days' time for a five-day cruise along the Italian Riviera, and the captain was making sure that the wealthy Italian banker from Milan who had chartered the *Bella Mare* would find no fault with the ship's cleanliness and comfort.

He looked up at the deck of the bigger vessel moored next to his and envied the large crew who were gathering on the poop-deck for their morning briefing. His own boat berthed six in three comfortable suites, and had three smaller cabins for the crew: his own, one for a cook-cum–chambermaid, and another for the multi-task deck hand, both of whom were due to arrive the next day.

"*Buon giorno*, Michael," the captain of the bigger vessel yelled in greeting. "If you would only offer decent wages perhaps you'd attract a crew!"

"The feeble wages you offer is the reason you employ a trawler crew to mess up your pleasure boat," retorted Michael, followed by loud jeering from the men on the other deck. "When do you set sail?"

"This evening."

"Good, then I'll have all the young maidens in Portofino to myself."

"Even the old ones don't look at you anymore, my friend."

"We'll see about that." He turned back to his work. Michael had bought the yacht four years previously, and had relocated from London to Santa Margherita Ligure, a short distance south along the coast from Portofino. He had a small apartment there, but was happiest during the summer months when he lived mostly on the boat. He had closed his law practice in London shortly after his wife's death and sold the mansion for less than he should have, according to his agent, but he wanted to get away from the city and all its memories as soon as he could. His friends, critics really, labelled him crazy for giving up such a successful law career in the prime of his life, and blamed the decision on the influence of depression resulting from his wife's untimely demise. They told each other that, after a healthy recovery period, he would soon come to his senses and return to a proper job.

The yacht had become his life and the sea his refuge. He thought he would tire of it after a few years but never did. His only responsibility was the yacht and his only concern was with the weather. There was no shortage of charter, and business found him without even having to tout for it.

He wiped away a trickle of sweat running down his brow before it could run into his eyes and irritate them. It was then that he noticed a stain on the deck and knelt down to examine it. He dipped a cloth in the bucket of water and rubbed furiously at the blemish until it disappeared. Suddenly a shadow drifted across his body, diffusing the strong sunlight.

He raised his eyes and saw a pair of red sandals planted firmly on the deck in front of him. He stood up quickly and looked at the woman. She was wearing a gauzy, soft, white dress. It clung and highlighted every curve of her body. Her full breasts, wide hips, and slender, shapely legs, plainly outlined through the fabric of her dress against the sun shining directly behind her, held his immediate attention. She was stunningly beautiful, and her sharp features were framed by black hair hanging down to just below her shoulders. Her nose was narrow and a little too long to be perfect, but it didn't detract from her loveliness.

The woman sensed that it was the transparency of her dress which had rendered the deck hand mute. "When you're finished ogling, perhaps you will tell the captain I wish to speak to him," she said.

"Who shall I say it is?"

"Just take me to him."

Michael held the door open and gestured for her to enter the deck lounge. "Wait here, please," he told her. He descended some steps to the sleeping quarters and, when he got to his cabin, he quickly changed into clean white pants and a shirt to match, and perched his braided captain's cap at a slight angle on his head. A quick glance in the mirror reflected the grey hair of his sideburns beneath the brim of his hat and he made a mental note to have them dyed at his next visit to the hairdresser. He loosened the top button of his shirt and was ready to face the woman who had appeared on his deck like an angel from heaven.

When he reappeared in the deck lounge, he couldn't be sure if her lips parted in a grimace of surprise or annoyance.

"Captain Michael Frost at your service, *signora*," he said with a casual salute.

"You could have introduced yourself in the first place," she said, "instead of letting me make a fool of myself thinking you were nothing more than a deck hand."

"Ah, it is the modesty of my nature," he replied. "How may I help you?"

"I am Isabella Rochi. My husband has chartered your boat."

"Forgive me for not knowing you, Signora Rochi, but you are two days early."

"I came to ensure the itinerary has been followed correctly," she said. "We are entertaining important guests and I want to make sure that nothing can possibly go wrong."

"The vessel is ship-shape and I have navigated these waters for many years. What could possibly go wrong, signora? Your beauty will repel any possible mishap."

"Using charm on me, captain, is a waste of effort," said Isabella without smiling. "We have hired you only to do your job."

"But of course."

"Can you show me to my cabin?"

"But, signora, it is not yet ready for occupation," said Michael in alarm. "The linen and toiletries are only arriving tomorrow morning. Sleeping on board tonight is impossible."

"Then what do you suggest?" she asked. "I am here and not going to sit on the wharf until your boat is ready."

"There is a quaint hotel on the square," he said. "I will arrange a room for you. You should first absorb the atmosphere of Portofino before sailing away. There is a unique charm about this place which you should spend some time seeing."

"Very well," she said abruptly. "Thank you."

He dialled a number on his mobile phone and after a heated argument which lasted nearly five minutes, he snapped the phone shut and smiled. "It is settled then," he said. "Come, I will take you there. It's only across the square." He picked up her two cases and walked down the companion ladder. She followed obediently. He never saw the trace of a faint smile forming on her lips as he led the way. He had threatened the manager of the hotel with dire consequences if he didn't find a room for her and she wondered what poor patron had been forced to find alternative accommodation.

She was walking a couple of paces behind him. He had a strange elegance of posture for a sailor. He walked tall and had a good physique for a middle-aged man. He was ruggedly handsome, but there was something about him she just couldn't make out. He seemed a little out of place in his role as captain. His pants were tailored perfectly, and his polo shirt hinted an aristocratic taste. He looked more the boardroom executive than a sailor. Finding out more about him would at least pass the time until the others arrived.

"You speak Italian quite fluently for an Englishman," she said.

"I've been here nearly four years and have a flair for languages." he replied. "As a matter of fact, I speak French and German as well."

"Aren't you a little over-qualified for a mariner, Mr. Frost?"

"Please call me Michael." He ignored her question.

Stan Miller

"I'd rather stick with Captain or Mr. Frost, whichever you prefer," she replied. "If we're on a first-name basis when my husband arrives, he'll suspect there's something between us."

"Why is it that beautiful women are regarded as licentious?"

"Perhaps it's because they are the most vulnerable—to the advances of flirtatious men, that is. A constant irritation, I might add." She paused to carefully consider her next words. "Sometimes an impulsive indiscretion allows resistance to slip through the net, and they succumb."

He smiled at her use of third person plural, plainly indicating that she was not one of them. "You certainly would qualify as the catch of the day," he said.

She ignored his remark but smiled inwardly at his feeble attempt at Latino flattery.

They crossed the busy piazza in silence and had to wind their way between the sidewalk tables of a bistro which had spread itself across the approach to the hotel. A floral canopy over a doorway identified the entrance.

They entered and went directly to the front desk. The concierge, a bald man with a neatly trimmed moustache, greeted Michael with a scowl before turning to Isabella and welcoming her with a broad smile.

"I'm afraid I only have a side room, signora," he apologized. "The reservation was such short notice, and the season has already begun." He frowned at Michael again. "It has a grand view of the mountain and is less noisy than the rooms overlooking the square."

"Nice try, Luigi," said Michael. "You make it sound like the side room is a first choice."

"I'm sure it will be suitable," said Isabella, putting an end to the squabble.

The boutique hotel had its own gracious character and style; luxury combined with the romance and history of eighteenth century architecture. The floral wallpaper and subdued lighting softened the ambience to suggest that this was an establishment of quiet refuge.

"I have to return to the *Bella Mare*, Mrs. Rochi," said Michael, now that she was comfortably ensconced in her side room. Since the loss of his wife, this was the first woman he had met who caused his pulse to race, and he looked for an excuse to be with her again. "Portofino is not a setting to be wasted on an early night," he heard himself say. "Permit me to take you to dinner this evening—as captain and host, of course."

"Thank you," she accepted gracefully.

* * *

Isabella was quite looking forward to dinner with the captain. His role as 'chaperone,' as he euphemistically called it, would not tarnish the sanctity of her marriage. After all, she had been sent ahead by her husband to prepare the vacation and he hardly expected her to wander around on her own. What better companion than the man entrusted with their well being during the voyage. Her conscience cleared, she turned her attention to her wardrobe.

She wasn't dressing particularly for him—she always liked to be chic—but something in the way she chose her underwear went beyond overt elegance. She selected a pair of black bikini panties and a lacy half-bra to wear under her black, sleeveless dress. When she slithered into her dress, she felt comfortable that the hemline fell to a respectable, if somewhat tantalizing, length a little above her knees. The low neck-line revealed a wisp of lace and a prominent cleavage: Isabella Rochi had come to town and wasn't going to go unnoticed!

Michael Frost was aroused the moment he saw her. She descended the stairs with such stateliness that he almost bowed. Instead, he took her arm. "You look lovely, Mrs. Rochi," he said. "I will be the envy of every man on the Riviera di Levante."

"And a dead one if any of my husband's people sees us together."

He let go her arm and ushered her through the door. As they walked, he told her something about the place. "The origin of the name Portofino stems from the Roman 'Portus Delphini—Port of the Dolphin.' They say dolphins used to leap from wave to wave in the alcove, but another theory is that it was named because of the dolphin-shaped peninsula that forms the harbour. Would you like to walk up to the Church of Saint George? There's a magnificent view of the town from there."

They walked up the steeply sloped path shaded by purple bougainvillea and Michael threw caution to the wind by taking hold of her arm again. Her shoes were not meant for stone paving and he didn't want her to stumble and sprain an ankle. In fact, she did falter moments later and fell against him. He could feel the softness of her breast as it pressed against the back of his hand.

"Sorry," she said, and quickly restored a respectable distance between them.

When they reached the top of the hill, they stopped in the small piazza in front of the tiny stone church. The cliff on the one side dropped straight down to the Mediterranean; the other side overlooked the town.

"It is a lovely setting," said Isabella, "but I fail to see any resemblance between a jumping dolphin and the shape of the peninsula."

"You require imagination and a keen sense of romanticism to do so," said Michael. "That's why Italian artists are the best in the world."

She smiled and her face brightened. "You are quite perceptive for an Englishman."

"Do you think the English are unromantic?"

"On the surface, yes—stiff upper lip, as they say."

"James Bond is an English gentleman and the most romantic spy in the world."

"Fiction, Michael," she said his name. "That doesn't count in our debate."

"I wish I could prove it to you some other way." Straight away he regretted saying it.

"It's a little chilly up here, captain. Perhaps we should go back down."

By the time they got back to the piazza, the sun was setting behind the vineyards of Camogi. The shops were still busy and visitors strolled along the quayside taking pictures of the boats, window shopping, or making plans for dinner. Waitresses darted back and forth carrying platters of food for patrons already seated at tables under umbrellas.

"I have reserved a nice table on the patio," announced Michael. "We can take in the ambience of the village while we eat—unless you're still feeling cold; we can change it for one inside?"

"No, Michael," she said softly, touching his arm. "This table is perfect."

The trattoria was full and the steady hum of voices filled the air with vitality. They started the meal with a plate of lasagna al pesto, covered with a sauce of herbs, cheese, olive oil, and crushed nuts. The main course which followed was the house speciality, king prawns on a bed of steaming rice. He watched her as she tore the flesh from the shell with her teeth and dared to lean across the table to wipe away a trickle of juice that was running down her chin. She did not pull away, but smiled in appreciation. Finally, there was a mountain of empty crustaceans piled on their side plates, and they leaned back, satisfied.

He touched her hand which was resting on the table. "Coffee?" he asked.

Neither of them saw a man standing in the doorway taking pictures of them.

Chapter 3

Milan – August

Giorgio Rochi leaned back in the chair and looked out the window. He could see the tops of the steeples of the Duomo and a thousand figurines appearing like fairies suspended in a clear blue sky. His office in central Milan was on the eighth floor of the Centrale Investimento Banca building and two floors below the penthouse office where Carlo Pistoni, the bank's chief executive officer, had enthroned himself.

The bank's shares had fallen to a record low recently because of some unsatisfactory foreign investments, and responsibility had to be attributed to somebody; the 'buck' had finally come to rest on top of Rochi's cluttered desk.

Rochi had learned three weeks earlier that his performance was being investigated for the poor returns that some investments had generated, when his friend, Franco Martini, the only ally he had on the Executive Committee, burst into his office with the bad news.

"Giorgio," he said breathlessly. "I have learned from one of my reliable sources that the board is considering your retrenchment."

"Franco, I'm fully aware that your 'sources,' as you so euphemistically call them, are nothing more than a string of secretarial concubines!"

"You'd be surprised what you learn from women during post-orgasm conversation," replied Franco proudly. "And may I remind you that it is the secretaries who type out the minutes of all meetings."

"Fair enough," smiled Rochi. "What exactly did you hear?"

"That they're apportioning the blame onto you for the bank's poor performance."

"And the king on his throne upstairs is blameless, I suppose?"

"He's the one who put your name forward."

"*Bastardo!*" exclaimed Rochi. "He's afraid that his arse will be removed from that chair if he doesn't find a fall guy." He stood up. "How long do we have before a decision is reached?"

"We?"

"Don't fool yourself, Franco, into thinking that you won't fall with me."

"Nonsense!"

"I suggest you use your cock wisely next time and find out for sure."

A day later, Franco returned in a state of agitation. "Giorgio, you were right," he moaned. "Even my sources are beginning to drop me like a piece of shit!" He flopped in a chair and buried his head in his hands. "We will receive a handsome severance package, won't we?" he asked looking up.

"Only enough to keep you in condoms for a year, and then what? Our reputations will be ruined. We'll never find another job in banking."

"My wife will kill me. We've been looking at a nice little villa in Como."

"I don't suppose they'll do anything until the trustees' meeting in three weeks' time." Rochi considered his words. "In the meantime, I'm working on a plan, if you're interested."

"What kind of plan?" Franco asked eagerly.

"A plan which carries a degree of risk."

"What—life threatening?"

"No—life imprisonment!"

* * *

That had been three weeks ago. Rochi turned from the window. The scheme had taken ten days to plan and a week to execute. He opened his briefcase and removed a laptop. He placed it on his desk and while it was booting up, he went over to the door of his office and turned the key. It would not do for anyone to barge in while he was busy.

He opened the email which had arrived on his private address earlier that morning. He hadn't wanted it on the bank's computer because the information could be damaging to him if the contents fell into the wrong hands; he knew that even deleted information would remain somewhere in the hard drive and forensics were capable of extracting it. He plugged the laptop into a printer that had no memory and printed out the seven pages he required. He made an additional copy and folded each set into an envelope, which he tucked into his inside jacket pocket. He deleted the email and returned the laptop to its case. Then he unlocked the door and went back to his desk to dial Franco's number.

"Everything's in place," he said softly.

"How long before they discover the money's missing?" Franco asked when he arrived.

"It will take months of investigative effort. By then we'll be long gone and they'll start blaming each other."

"It's not what I heard," Franco asked in a worried tone.

"Still at it, are you? What did you hear?" Rochi was not worried. The three percent he had siphoned off each account in the pension fund the bank invested for its clients had been transferred into various bank accounts he had set up around the world. He was confident that the deficit would remain unnoticed for a while. He had only skimmed from the accounts of middle-aged investors that wouldn't be maturing for quite a long time.

"No one suspects anything yet," said Franco, "but something in the system has caught the attention of Dr. Milo Umbretti."

"That prick," replied Rochi. "We have nothing to fear from that accountant."

"He's not just an accountant," Franco warned. "He's the bank's forensic auditor."

"What's he looking into?" Rochi asked.

"I don't know."

Rochi raised an eyebrow.

"Giorgio, I'm not intimate with every woman in the building!" Franco admitted. "God knows I've tried."

"You're on speaking terms with him. Why don't you ask him?"

"An enquiry of any sort will serve only to arouse his suspicion," answered Franco, "and we don't want to direct the focus of his attention in our direction."

"Invite him to join us on a five-day cruise along the west coast."

"Cruise? What cruise?"

"We'll take a cruise along the Italian Riviera—all expenses paid," suggested Rochi. "That should appeal to his parsimonious nature, the stingy bastard. We will then be able to soften him up and extract the information from him."

"What if he declines?"

"Tell him I wish to discuss with him security issues in one of our programs. Tell him it will be a kind of working holiday in secure surroundings. If, in fact, he is on to something, it's far better misleading him with the impression that we're allies rather than perpetrators."

"Good idea."

"Is he married?"

"No."

"Does he have a girlfriend?"

"Not that I'm aware of—the man's in love with his computer."

"No matter," said Rochi. "I'll supply the mistress. It will also give you the rare opportunity to fuck your wife for a change."

Franco ignored the remark. "You do realize this could open up a can of worms."

"Maybe, but my worms are poisonous!"

Chapter 4

Portofino – August

The next morning, Isabella informed Michael that her husband and guests had been delayed and would only be arriving the following morning. He welcomed the free time to drive into Santa Margherita to buy extra provisions.

"I'd like to accompany you," she said, dumping her cases on the bed. Her cabin was ready and she had checked out of the hotel.

"I'd be delighted," Michael said truthfully. "My car is parked at the top end of Via Roma on the other side of the chain which seals off the town from traffic."

"I don't mind the walk."

As beautiful a spectacle as it was, she didn't enjoy travelling on the cliff-hanging road into Santa Margherita. How the cars negotiating the sharp bends didn't knock each other into the sea below was a miracle of driving skills the locals possessed. She did not appreciate the scenic view of the sea breaking against the rocks at the bottom of the cliff, as she had her eyes tightly shut most of the time and only opened them properly when they arrived at their destination. She released the tight grip she had on the arm rests which allowed the blood to flow back into her knuckles and restore feeling again.

He bought the supplies and they spent the rest of the morning walking up and down the promenade looking into shop windows or just sitting on a bench enjoying the sunshine. They had lunch on the sun-deck of a seafood restaurant in the harbour and watched the fishing boats off-loading their catch of the day.

"You have an apartment here, don't you?" Isabella asked while they were walking back to the car.

"Yes; it's where I live when I'm not at sea."

"A perfect world you've made for yourself."

"A perfect world is living at home with a family," he said sadly, "but I'm happy."

"Are you really?" she asked. "I sense something is missing in your idyllic lifestyle—a woman, perhaps?"

"Perhaps," he answered. She spoke the truth. The memory of his wife was getting distant, but it was still there and he wasn't convinced that finding love again wouldn't betray her memory. For that reason, he had never allowed any woman close enough to get his affection—until now with the woman next to him. A married woman!

"Where is your apartment?" she asked.

"At the top of the ridge near the railway station," he answered.

"May I see it?"

"Of course, but it's quite small—not what you're used to, I'm afraid, but the view is spectacular."

Isabella liked the apartment. It may have been small but it was quaint, furnished like a bachelor's—functional without much ornamentation. Michael opened the door leading out onto the balcony. The smell of the sea mixed with the scent of flowers from the gardens below filled the air with fragrance. She leaned against the wrought iron balustrade and admired the view.

He stood behind her and felt her hair tickle his face as it swirled in the breeze. He encircled her waist with his arms and felt her lean back toward him. He could feel her tremble slightly as she wrestled with her resistance. He raised his hand over her stomach until he touched the firm bulge of her breast. She wasn't wearing a bra under her cotton blouse and he could feel her hardened nipples pushing against the fabric. On impulse, he tried to undo the top button of her blouse. At first she did not resist, but suddenly she pushed his hand away.

"No, Michael," she breathed into his ear. "I want to, but I cannot confront my husband tomorrow morning with the guilt of an adulteress."

"I understand."

They didn't see a man standing in the shadows of a tree in the street below. He had the pictures he wanted, so he replaced the camera in its pouch and moved off down the road.

Chapter 5

Portofino – August

It was not until ten-thirty in the morning that Isabella's husband and his four guests arrived on board the boat. Michael was busy in the control room preparing for the voyage when they trooped up the companion ladder. He watched from the window as Isabella embraced her husband and greeted the others with much excitement. He descended the ladder to meet his passengers.

Michael didn't like Giorgio Rochi from the moment he shook the man's hand and looked into his cold, dark eyes. He wasn't sure if his dislike of Rochi was due to the ruthless intensity of the man's stare as they locked eyes with each other, or a simple case of jealousy that he was married to the woman he was beginning to fall in love with. He turned away to speak to the others and looked briefly at Isabella and saw her quickly lower her eyes.

Rochi noticed his wife's self conscious response as the captain glanced in her direction and decided to keep a watchful eye on both of them to see if he could detect any suspicious signs of intimacy between them. They had spent two days together and he began to regret the delay in his arrival. However, he had more pressing things on his mind and dismissed his intuition as paranoia.

The party consisted of Franco and his wife Katherine, who seemed to be a little indifferent to her husband's attentiveness, Milo Umbretti and a blond woman named Carla, and, of course, Isabella and Giorgio—the hosts. They were shown to their cabins by Mario and Claudia, the only two crew members for this voyage.

"I suppose," grumbled Katherine, "Isabella has already chosen the nicest suite?" The complaint was met with an icy stare from her husband.

"They are all nice, Mrs. Martini," Claudia assured her. "I

guarantee you won't be disappointed with whichever one you get."

Catherine yelped in delight when she saw the plush décor of her cabin. "Thank you; this will do nicely," and she flopped on the bed to test its comfort.

Dr. Umbretti looked around his cabin and seemed somewhat shocked that it contained only one double bed. Carla pushed past him and did a pirouette to show her delight.

"A little bit of bedroom sport won't hurt you, Milo," she chanted. His face flushed and turned red. He remained standing at the door as if entering the cabin would be committing a cardinal sin.

Rochi observed Milo's reluctance and sighed, realizing it was going to be harder than he thought to soften the little bastard.

When Michael joined them below, he gave his usual warning. "Please bear in mind that the walls are only wood panelling and are not completely sound proof." He left them to decipher the implication. He knew from experience that the sea air and the gentle motion of the boat over the swells had an aphrodisiac effect on passengers and their moans of ecstasy often permeated the thin walls to advertise the couple's salaciousness. He also knew from experience that the warning was seldom heeded. "I'll leave you to settle in," added Michael. "We'll be under way in an hour. I recommend that you gather on the aft deck for drinks and a light lunch and enjoy the spectacle of departure."

They all arrived promptly on the aft deck an hour later. Drinks had been prepared for them by Claudia, who was lovely enough to have attracted the attention of Franco, behind his wife's back. Michael kept a discreet distance and allowed the passengers to chat frivolously about the forthcoming voyage. The weedy looking man, introduced as Dr. Umbretti, was the focal point of attention, and Michael guessed that it was he whom Rochi wished to impress.

Michael left them to settle in, and went outside to the upper deck and wheelhouse. He had to screw up his eyes to block out the fierce glare of the sun. It was a lovely day with only a few fluffy tufts of cumulus cloud breaking the blue canopy of sky above. Sunny weather had been forecast for the next few days and he was confident that he and his two crew members would cope adequately in the perfect conditions.

Claudia emerged from the galley to assist Mario on deck. They stole an intimate look at each other, which Michael was

Stan Miller

quick to notice, before taking up their pre-sailing positions. Mario, a tall, good-looking youngster in his mid-twenties, rushed down the companion ladder and began loosening the guide ropes. In spite of having no previous sailing experience, Michael had hired him because of his enthusiasm to learn and his energetic application to whatever he was given to do, and he needed someone to do the work of two men. It also hadn't taken Mario long to form a romantic bond with Claudia, so the two of them worked harmoniously as a team to provide efficient service and create a favourable reputation for the *Bella Mare* as a most sought-after boat to charter.

It looks as though I'm going to be the only celibate one on board, Michael thought to himself. "Prepare to cast off!" he called to Mario, who was waiting on the quayside. He watched the youngster untie the ropes and dash up the companion ladder. He rolled it in and stored it in place along the railing. Then he looked at Michael, gave the thumbs-up sign, and smiled boyishly.

Michael shifted into reverse throttle and slowly eased the boat away from the wharf. Claudia had positioned herself at the stern to get a clear view of the harbour entrance, and by a series of signals, guided Michael safely past the fishing boats moored in shallow water a few metres off the little pebble beach. Suddenly the door to the bridge burst open and Isabella stepped inside.

"I've come to watch you work," she smiled. "I hope it is permitted?"

Usually Michael kept passengers away from the bridge until the boat was safely out of the harbour, but Isabella wasn't just an ordinary passenger. He had developed strong feelings for her and even though her arrival caused a slight loss of concentration, he still managed to manoeuvre the boat successfully through the narrow harbour mouth.

"Isn't it a bit risky being here?" asked Michael. "I mean, your husband may get the wrong impression."

"His jealousy is driven by pride, not the risk of losing love," replied Isabella. "I'm really nothing more than a presentable prop for him to put on display at his side when negotiating business deals." She looked at Michael self-consciously. "And as long as I'm there in bed beside him whenever he has the urge to reach out for me, he feels he has a good marriage."

"And you?"

"Ah, me . . ." she said sadly. "Who am I to complain? I live a very comfortable life."

"The idea is to live a very loving life," said Michael.

Isabella turned away. He had spoken the truth and it brought a tear to her eye which she did not want him to see.

At slow throttle, Michael helmed the *Bella Mare* around in a 180-degree turn until the prow was pointing toward open water, and as soon as the boat reached the broader channel, he opened the throttle to three-quarter setting and set course to pass the breakwater buoy on the seaward side. Soon they were in the deep water channel, and the boat ploughed gracefully through the mild swells to settle into a gentle rocking motion. He intended sailing south along the western coast of Italy, keeping land in sight at all times on the port horizon. They would be making several stops before heading back via the island of Sardinia. Their first port of call would be Marina di Pisa near Livorna. There, he would take them on an overland excursion to Pisa and Florence. The vessel was equipped with the latest electronic positioning equipment, including satellite navigational bearings, but as they were not venturing far out to sea, most of them would remain inactive. He would only need to set the electronic path of the Loran in a mode to control the steering of the autopilot. That would allow him time to mingle with the passengers while Mario kept watch on the bridge. With only a crew of three, it was going to be difficult to give all six passengers enough attention for them to feel fussed over. Sun bathing and copulation, Michael hoped, would keep them busy enough. He adjusted the channel settings of the single side-band radio so he could monitor Coast Guard information and the proximity of other ships, and turned his attention back to Isabella, who had taken a seat by the port window.

He was familiar with beautiful women. His wife had been a finalist at the Cambridge Beauty Pageant and probably would have gone on to win it had her father not died suddenly. As a favour to a friend, he had driven her back to London to attend the funeral and had hung around waiting for the week's mourning period to end so that he could drive her back to the university they both attended. They had formed a close relationship during that week, with sorrow being the grout which bonded them together—she needed consolation and he gave it willingly. They had married in their final year and were good together until . . . He snapped out of melancholy and looked at Isabella.

She was provocatively dressed in a t-shirt and a short

skirt, which was not unusual on a cruise like this. He had seen many semi-nude women on previous voyages because passengers on such an intimate boat discarded whatever inhibitions they had and regarded the crew as fixtures and fittings with no eyes. He couldn't help appreciating Isabella's beauty—her nipples were showing prominently through the thin fabric of her top and her skirt barely covered her slender thighs.

"I thought I'd lost you for a moment," she said.

"Just making sure I hadn't forgotten anything," he lied. "I wouldn't want this cruise to end up on the rocks."

The door opened and Mario entered the wheelhouse. He looked at Isabella appraisingly and turned to Michael. "I'll keep watch, skipper," he said cheerfully. "Claudia says lunch is ready and expects you would want to dine with the passengers during our first meal at sea." He made no attempt to mask the direction of his stare as Isabella uncrossed her legs and stood up.

Michael left the wheelhouse a few minutes after Isabella. He was not looking to create suspicion and was waiting for Isabella to take a seat next to her husband before he made his appearance. This was the part he hated the most—making polite small talk with people he didn't know and would probably never see again. Only the presence of Isabella made it pleasurable this time.

Claudia had decided to impress the guests with cold lobster and avocado salad. She had succeeded in procuring the biggest crustaceans on the northwest coast of Italy, and they proudly lay on their plates daring the diners to finish them all. The meal was eaten in gluttonous silence. Only the sound of cracking shells rose above the waves lapping against the side of the boat.

Finally, Giorgio Rochi pushed away his empty plate and turned to Michael. "You studied at Cambridge, I'm told." It sounded more like a statement of fact than a question.

Michael looked at Isabella, who kept her eyes lowered. Then he addressed Rochi. "Yes. I haven't always lived the ideal life like this one."

"You read law?"

"I practiced for nearly two decades before arriving at the conclusion that there was more to life than standing in front of a judge and using the full extent of my rhetoric to persuade a jury that my client, probably as guilty as sin, was innocent."

"The whole essence of advocacy," said Rochi, "is to triumph against all odds. What a satisfying challenge it must be winning a case that everyone is convinced should be lost."

"Defending murderers and returning them to the streets began to destroy my soul," said Michael. "I got out before the devil could grab it entirely."

"Sensible decision," said Katherine Martini. "And a brave one, I may add—giving up a reputable profession for the life of a sailor."

"A good life, and I have enough money to satisfy my needs."

"You can never have enough money," said Rochi. "What do you say, Dr. Umbretti?"

Milo Umbretti looked up for the first time. He had been studying his meal as though every empty shell had to be accounted for. "There is no disgrace in having lots of money—as long as it was acquired honestly," he said at last.

"Spoken like a true accountant," said Rochi. "Pity it's always someone else's fortune you have to count."

"I'm not an accountant," answered Umbretti quietly and without emotion. "I search for irregularities in companies' transactions."

"How impressive," said Rochi sarcastically.

"There is a plunge pool situated on the foredeck," intervened Michael. "I suggest you relax there this afternoon while it is still hot. This evening, we will be berthing at Marina di Pisa, where you will have the opportunity to visit the quaint harbour shops before dinner at the best restaurant in town. All part of the package, I assure you." Michael stood up. "In the morning, we will visit Florence. Now, if you will excuse me, I have to set course for our destination."

* * *

At seven the next morning, with the *Bella Mare* safely secured in her berth, and Mario and Claudia happily staying behind to watch over her, the six passengers, led by Michael, boarded the bus to Florence. A day was not really enough time in Tuscany, but most of them had been to Florence before, and one could never tire of the place. Michael wanted them to at least visit Michelangelo's statue of *David*, so he took them directly to the Gallery of the Academy of Florence to view the giant sculpture carved out of a single piece of Carrara marble some eighteen feet high.

"Isn't it magnificent?" said Michael. "The large size of the *David* seems to suggest an imposing yet restrained majesty," continued Michael. "The artist is showing the confident pose of a man capable of winning any confrontation. In reality, *David* was a mere boy when he slew Goliath."

From the gallery, they went to browse the shops on the Ponte Vechio, while Michael secured a table at a nearby trattoria. They still had a busy afternoon ahead of them.

Chapter 6

West Coast of Italy – August

Michael was used to the gentle humming of the boat's generator, but some other noise woke him suddenly. He leaned over and looked at the time on the luminous dial of the bedside clock —quarter to one in the morning. He remained absolutely still, waiting for the sound again. He heard footsteps on the deck above him; someone was moving about outside.

He slipped on a pair of shorts and left his cabin, closing the door quietly behind him. His quarters were situated at the end of the passageway near the steps so he didn't have to pass any of the other cabins. His bare feet made no noise as he stepped onto the deck outside. A few street lamps twinkled on shore but they weren't bright enough to spoil the splendour of a starlit sky, which gave off only enough light to distinguish shapes and forms without detail.

Creeping slowly along the upper deck and keeping his back against the wall as he edged forward, he moved toward where he had last heard the sound. There was nobody in sight but he was certain the footsteps he had heard were moving toward the prow. Despite the fact that he had spent a lot of time on board the *Bella Mare*, what was usually familiar to him took on an eeriness that unnerved him. The faint light threw shadows that took on a foreboding appearance wherever he looked.

When he came to the top of the steps descending to the prow deck, he stopped. The sound of muffled voices drifted upward. Michael moved forward toward the railing and peered over the edge. Two ghostly figures were huddled against the bulwark. They were talking softly, and by the tone of their voices, their conversation was argumentative. One he recognised as Martini, but the other figure was facing the opposite direction. It was not his intention to eavesdrop, but something prevented him from leaving.

"Now is the perfect opportunity." The muffled voice drifted

into Michael's auditory range.

"To do it now would defeat the whole purpose of the cruise," whispered Martini loudly.

"We have to make certain."

"Certain of what? With him out of the way, we're in the clear."

"We must stick to the original plan," insisted Martini. "Timing is everything—and the time will be when we dock at Santa Margherita."

"That's where the captain lives?"

"Exactly!"

Michael hurried back to his cabin. He lay on his bunk staring into darkness. He went over the conversation again in his mind trying to decipher some meaning. What were they preparing to do and why was his name mentioned? Who was the other man? Was it Rochi or a stranger who had come aboard for the encounter? The voyage had suddenly taken on a sinister twist and they were due back in Santa Margherita in only three days. Perhaps it was time enough for him to uncover their plot before something dreadful happened. He had entered the realm of thought, another sleepless night.

Chapter 7

Pisa – August

The old city of Pisa lies on both banks of the River Arno. Its main attraction, the famous bell tower, built entirely of marble, is a fine example of Romanesque architecture. The tower, the cathedral, and the baptistery form one of the most famous building groups in the world, the most well-known being the Leaning Tower of Pisa. Built in 1174, the ground beneath the campanile started to sink after the first three stories were built. The tower has increased its lean to nearly sixteen feet out of line, and contrary to what the passengers of the *Bella Mare* thought, it was in no immediate danger of toppling.

"I'm not going up there!" exclaimed Katherine Martini.

"It's only a hundred and seventy-nine feet fall," said Michael. "Actually, it is well reinforced to make it absolutely safe to climb the three hundred steps to the top. The view of the surrounding countryside is well worth the risk."

"I'll wait for you on the ground, if you don't mind," persisted Katherine.

"Captain?"

Michael turned around to see what Franco Martini wanted.

"Be a good fellow and show my wife the cathedral while we visit the top of the tower. I'm sure you've seen the view on numerous occasions."

"Sure," replied Michael. He had done the climb hundreds of times, but with Isabella nearby, this would have been the best. Nevertheless, he had little choice but to agree. "We'll meet at this spot in forty-five minutes."

Michael led Katherine through the columns at the entrance of the cathedral. She was genuinely intrigued by the architecture. "Look at the splendour," she said excitedly. "Such beauty. The artists of the age took the world to the brink of perfection."

"Indeed they did," agreed Michael, wondering if she knew anything about her husband's business. They walked along the centre aisle. "Tell me, where does Dr. Umbretti fit in with Mr. Rochi and your husband? He hardly seems the type of person they would befriend."

"He's a bit of a nerd, actually, and no friend. He's involved in investigating some sort of irregularity in the company."

"Nothing too serious, I hope?" Michael fished.

"I'm not really sure. Serious enough to call in the best forensic auditor in Milan. It's something to do with a leakage of funds from some trust accounts."

"Did Mr. Rochi hire him?"

"Oh, no! The board of shareholders did."

"So Mr. Rochi and your husband are not above suspicion?"

"Captain!" Katherine looked shocked. "How can you insinuate such a thing?"

"Why was he invited on this cruise, then?"

"I was wondering the same thing myself. I suppose they're consulting with each other during the voyage. No interruptions, I guess." She walked away toward the altar. "I'm not involved in my husband's business affairs. Maybe you should ask him yourself, not that it's any of your business, I might add." She walked away from him to examine a figurine standing on a ledge in a narrow recess.

Michael decided to back off. He had stirred the pot sufficiently for her to report their conversation to her husband, and it would be interesting to see what kind of reaction it caused.

* * *

The *Bella Mare* was well out to sea by ten o'clock in the morning. Michael set course for Sardinia and activated the auto-pilot. He left Mario in the wheelhouse to keep an eye on things and went on deck to enjoy the fresh air. He leaned over the railing and stared down into the water. A school of common dolphins were playfully leaping in and out of the water trying to match the speed of the boat. They were black with prominent grey and brown stripes on their sides, and Michael wondered why he rarely saw the grey bottlenose variety in these waters. Soon, the school tired of the company of the boat and veered away sharply, leaping and bounding over the swells until they became small, dancing specks on the horizon.

Michael turned to look at the women sunning themselves at the small swimming pool situated on the rear deck. Carla was just about to get into the pool when Rochi appeared. He grabbed her arm and pulled her behind the balusters. Isabella and Katherine were reclining on their sun beds and facing the other way so they did not see Carla disappear. Michael was standing too far away to overhear anything, so he moved back into the shade of the deck cover and waited to see if anything untoward happened.

"Let go of my arm—you're hurting me," cried Carla, pulling away from Rochi.

"We're halfway through the voyage and you've found out nothing!" said Rochi tersely.

"Milo doesn't confide in me," she moaned.

"A good fuck disarms the most resilient of men," said Rochi. "I didn't bring you along just to tan your tits!"

"He hasn't touched me yet," complained Carla.

Rochi laughed mockingly. "Well, shove your tits in his face and arouse the little shit. Most men lower their guard and babble after a good screw. I want to know if he suspects anyone—and who it is."

"He's in his cabin now—says it's too hot on deck." Carla smiled seductively. "Perhaps I can entice him away from his bloody computer."

"Do it now," ordered Rochi. "I want to know what he's discovered and I want the password to get into his laptop."

* * *

When Carla entered the cabin, Umbretti was sitting at the small table below the porthole, peering at the computer screen. He was so engrossed in what he was doing that he didn't hear her enter. Only when she laid her hands on his shoulders and began massaging them gently did he look up and smile at her.

"Why aren't you lying at the pool?" he asked.

"Because I'd rather be with you right now," she said sweetly. She glanced at the computer and saw columns of figures filling the screen. He noticed the direction of her stare and quickly snapped shut the laptop lid.

"You work too hard, my dear," she whispered in his ear and ran her hands down his chest.

"What are you doing?" he asked, pushing her hands away.

"What do you think I'm doing?" she said, and swivelled the chair so that he was facing her. She reached behind her back and loosened her bikini top. She removed it and let it fall to the floor. She remained standing close to him so that her large breasts were almost brushing against his nose. Umbretti stared at them wide-eyed. Most men would have groped at them immediately, but he only stared with squint eyes at her cleavage.

Fuck, I'm going to have to rape him, she thought. She took hold of his hands and placed them firmly on her breasts. *Squeeze them, you idiot*, she wanted to tell him.

Suddenly, and totally out of character, he moved his hands away and took her right nipple in his mouth.

At last; the man's alive, she thought, and reached down into his lap to see how far his arousal had developed.

"My, my, we are ready," she breathed in his ear. She led him to the bed and when he offered no resistance, she unbuckled his belt and undressed him. Removing the bottom of her bikini, she straddled him like a jockey on his mount, and guided him into a gentle canter. She smiled to herself, not because she was enjoying the encounter, but because the first part of her mission was about to be accomplished.

Afterward, as she lay next to him with her head resting on his chest, she looked up into his eyes. "What is so pressing that you spoil the enjoyment of the cruise with work?" she asked, faking genuine concern for his well-being.

"I have to complete my investigation and file the report the moment we get back," he answered, unsuspecting. "My schedule doesn't leave much time for fun."

"I think you're wonderful. I mean, not only your integrity as an accountant, but also as a lover. The company is lucky to have you to help them uncover whatever it is, and I'm lucky to have you between my legs."

Umbretti coughed shyly. He was already beginning to feel uncomfortable lying naked next to a woman. He was forty-three years old and had only been with a woman once, and that had been a disaster; he had ejaculated all over her while they were changing positions. Work was his gratification; no embarrassment there. Sex was for men like Rochi and the captain. "My job is pretty boring, really," he confessed at last.

"I don't find you boring." She reached down for him, safe in the knowledge that he wouldn't be ready to perform again.

"Thank you," he said.

"I am so interested in what you do," she said, coming straight to the point. If she could get what Rochi wanted from him, she wouldn't have to do this again.

"It's highly confidential," he said.

"Milo, after allowing you inside me, I think we've been intimate enough not to keep secrets from each other."

"Very well," he stammered, "but this must remain between the two of us."

"Of course, silly," she lied. "I wouldn't want to jeopardize a promising relationship."

"A large amount of the bank's money has been inappropriately diverted to a mystery account," he said, adopting the formal tone of business that he was more comfortable with. "It is my task to identify the culprit so that legal action can be taken against him and the money returned to the company."

"Do you know who it is?" she asked, trying to sound like an excited little girl listening to her father reading the last page of a bedtime story.

Milo Umbretti remained silent. He stared upward, as if approval to divulge was going to flash across the ceiling. "Yes," he answered finally. "Someone close," was all he was prepared to say.

* * *

"The bloody nerd's on to us!" moaned Rochi later that afternoon when he was alone with Martini on the aft deck. He wasn't taking any chances that they could be overheard. He spoke as if he were throwing his words into the wind and letting them blow away like a child's balloon.

"How could he possibly have traced the bogus accounts to you?" asked Martini, showing concern.

"It's bad enough he found them at all!"

"What are you going to do?"

"Get into his laptop and delete the fucking evidence!"

"You won't get close to it," said Martini. "He even shits with it on his lap. Why don't you just toss it overboard, if you get the chance?"

"He keeps it chained to his desk like a wild dog."

"He's probably got the information backed up on a USB memory stick, anyway. You'll need to find that, too."

"First I've got to see the evidence," said Rochi. "If it's

damning, then we'll have no more than a couple of days to leave the country after we get back." He leaned over the rail and spat into the sea. "Carla has to find a way of getting me Umbretti's password."

* * *

Carla did find a way, and it was easier than she expected. Of course, she had to endure another romp on the bed. He was getting better at it, she had to admit, but his fetish for oral sex was not something she enjoyed. After their final encounter of the night, she was lying on the bed feigning sleep. He rose quietly from the bed so as not to disturb her. *At least he's a considerate little bastard*, she thought.

He returned to the bed and sat crossed-legged, facing her. He placed the computer on his lap and opened the lid. Behind him was the dressing table mirror. Behind her, above the headboard of the bed was another mirror hanging on the wall.

Suddenly, she sat up. "Milo," she said, "you're not working again?"

When he nodded, she turned and knelt on the bed facing the mirror on the wall and positioned herself so that she could see the screen of his laptop. She began combing her hair while watching him closely. When he keyed in the password, she saw the numbers reflected in both mirrors appearing so that she could read them. Her memory was not good, so she slid off the bed and smiled at him.

"Let me freshen up," she announced, rising from the bed and going into the bathroom. She wanted to write down the numerals before she forgot them. Hurriedly, she jotted down the password on a piece of toilet paper with her lipstick.

* * *

"Excellent!" cried Rochi, delighted with the scrap of toilet paper she handed him. "That's my girl; I knew you could do it." He pulled a five-hundred Euro note from his pocket and gave it to her. "Spoil yourself at our next port of call."

When they anchored in Cagliari, their only port of call in Sardinia, Rochi feigned a severe migraine and excused himself from the overland excursion. He complained bitterly to Isabella for having to miss the tour and even made an effort to come out on deck, where he collapsed in pain.

"Go right back to bed and lie down," insisted Isabella. "You

The Papal Secret

are in no condition to travel."

"I'm fine," he protested, trying to make the complaint seem genuine. "I'd hate to miss the visit to the Bonaria Basilica and not see the Porticoes of Via Roma."

"You'll have time to see all that later this afternoon when you're feeling better," insisted Isabella.

"You're right, as usual, my love," he capitulated in triumph. "I think I'll spend the morning in bed." With head bowed, he descended the steps to his cabin. He watched the party disappear down the Via Roma from his cabin porthole and, without any further delay, rushed straight to Umbretti's cabin. The laptop computer was attached by chain to an eye-hole in the bulkhead to prevent it from being removed.

He lifted the top and waited for the computer to boot up like an expectant father about to see his first child. Then he keyed in the password and began scrolling through the programme.

"Jesus, how am I going to decipher all this?" he asked himself. "So much to comprehend. Projections, cash-flow analyses, comparable transaction analyses." He clicked on the latter. He scrolled down the list of entries looking for something that might have caught Umbretti's eye to make him suspicious. A review of the company's acquisitions over the last six months was nothing to be concerned with; company expenditure would be the auditor's focal point.

Using a computerized programme named Surveillance System, specially designed to identify irregular transactions, Umbretti's investigation led directly to the company's Retirement Annuity Trust Fund. Rochi was amazed at how deeply Umbretti had delved, and it was there where he had discovered the source of the financial leakage. He had taken some of the portfolios that were due to mature in ten years' time, and did a calculation to see what their present worth would be if they were maturing now. He had found a shortfall in each and every one! From there, Umbretti had done a trace to see where the money had gone.

Rochi recognised some of the intermediate accounts he had used to set up his system. Umbretti had managed to trace some of them to one of his destination accounts. A simple phone call and the auditor would be able to establish the registered owner of the bogus company. That alone would incriminate him in fraudulent dealings. The balance of the money Umbretti had failed to find. If there was to be any chance of enjoying his wealth, the auditor had to be stopped before he released his findings, which would undoubtedly lead to his arrest. The anticipated time, although a little premature, had finally arrived for him to make his get-away to Australia, where the rest of his money was lying in wait.

Rochi closed the programme and was about to turn off the computer when he noticed an icon on the desktop labelled "Vatican." He looked at his watch; he had been occupied for nearly an hour, and as he didn't expect the others to return for another couple of hours, he felt he had the luxury of time to be more inquisitive. He double-clicked on the icon.

A copy of a letter sent to a cardinal in the Vatican caught his attention. It was addressed to a Cardinal Albertini, and it was about the transfer of some funds to the cardinal's account. That alone didn't bother Rochi, but when he saw the amount of the transfer, he froze in his seat. It was the exact amount of money from one of his secret accounts, the one Umbretti had uncovered. The headache Rochi had feigned earlier that morning suddenly developed into a very real one. He felt incensed that the money he had stolen had now been stolen from him! If it wasn't such a large amount, he might have laughed at the irony.

He opened the drawer in the desk hoping to find a spare memory stick so that he could download a copy of the letter, but there wasn't one. He wrote down the name of the cardinal and the details of the account into which his money had been transferred, and, on impulse, also noted that it was the same cardinal who had booked the boat for a planned "Vatican Cruise." Any information could be useful in the future. He switched off the computer, looked around the cabin to make sure he hadn't disturbed anything, and went on deck to get some fresh air. He needed to think of a plan quickly; the cruise would be ending the next afternoon and he would have to confront Umbretti before they docked. It now seemed that there was little danger of the auditor reporting Rochi's dishonesty to the group in view of his own involvement in the fraud, and there was a chance they could come to a mutual arrangement to ensure each other's silence.

As he looked out over the blue sea and the coastline that stretched out on either side of him, his mind was elsewhere, and the charm and beauty of the Costa Smeralda—the Emerald Coast—was lost on him. He was trying to figure out what the Vatican had to do with all of this.

Chapter 8

The Vatican – May

Pope John Pietro I remained seated in his chair long after Stendardi had gone. He was so drained by the shock of the lawyer's revelation that he could not have risen to his feet even if he wanted to. He glanced down at the crucifix lying on the surface of his desk as if it were an ornament of the devil waiting to scorch his hand if he touched it. If there was any truth in what the lawyer had said, it would herald the end of his papacy.

With an unsteady hand, he pressed the button on the intercom. "Angelo, would you cancel my appointments for the rest of the morning, then please come in."

"Are you ill, Holiness?" asked Pollini, who was waiting in the outer office.

"Worse than that."

A few minutes later, the door opened and Pollini entered. He was dismayed at how pale the Holy Father looked. "You seem tired, Pietro," he said tenderly. They had been friends since they had studied together at the *Istituto di Sacerdote*—Institute of Priests—and had formed a trustworthy bond of fellowship which allowed them to dispense with formality whenever they were alone together.

The pope trusted Pollini implicitly, and he was the only human being on earth in whom he fully confided. God controlled his heart and conscience, but Pollini controlled his sanity, for without his friend's compassionate ear, he would have gone mad long ago. The papacy was a lonely seat, and knowledge of this latest development, falling into the wrong hands, would make the seat a dangerous one, as well. His rivals would crucify him just on the possibility that what he had been told was true.

The cardinal saw the cross lying on the desk; it was Pietro Bandini's most treasured possession, a family heirloom which the pope never removed from around his neck. A sense of

Stan Miller

foreboding overcame him. "Pietro, is anything the matter?"

"I just had the strangest of visits," said Bandini.

"Mr. Stendardi? Yes, he was fully cleared."

"A Jew, Angelo; did you know that?"

"Yes," replied Pollini. "It is Vatican policy not to discriminate."

Bandini smiled for the first time since the visit. "You are preaching tolerance to me, a champion of the oppressed?" He rose uneasily, steadying himself against the desk. Pietro Bandini was one of the youngest popes elected to the papacy. His tenure had been easy these past five years, but now his sympathetic attitude toward other races and creeds, admired by non-Catholics the world over, had come to destroy him. He felt his seventy-four years resting heavily on his shoulders. "Let's walk."

"Where are we going?"

"To my private chapel," said Bandini. "It's close to my bedroom, where I'll need to rest after our little talk. We can speak safely there."

"With all due respect, Holy Father," said Pollini, reverting to the required formality, "this is the Vatican. We can speak freely anywhere within these walls."

"Angelo, my friend, your goodness sees no wickedness in those around you. Even the righteous are sometimes swayed by ambition. It would be naive to think that this papacy has no enemies among us." The pope leaned conspiratorially close to Pollini. "What I have to tell you must remain strictly between us. No one else can know. My ecclesiastical standing could be compromised."

Cardinal Pollini could not remember, in all their years of friendship, ever having seen Pietro Bandini as sombre as he was this morning. He was aware of the pope's German background, but he was only a small child during the war, so there could be no scandal of Nazi affiliations in his history to tarnish his reputation. "There is nothing you can do to harm your reputation in the Holy See," he comforted his friend.

"Ever heard of *Kristallnacht*?" asked the pope.

Pollini turned to look at him with a puzzled expression on his face.

"Let me explain. I warn you, Angelo, it is a strange and harrowing story."

Pollini listened in astonished silence as the pope related the content of Stendardi's revelation. They walked slowly together, stopping every now and then to look each other in the eye. They passed through the corridors of the papal apartments and continued until they arrived at the little chapel. The pope knelt before the altar and crossed himself while examining his emotions for any indication of doubt in his piety. Could he detect a different soul trying to reach into his subconscious mind?

He stood up wearily and turned to the cardinal. "We must first establish if this Jew is telling the truth," he said.

"It is not for you to prove his claim false; it is for him to prove it is true." Pollini spoke for the first time since hearing the story.

"How do you explain the emblem on the cross I've been wearing ever since I can remember? How does Stendardi know of it if what he said were not true?"

"It proves nothing. Anyone could have given it to you when you were a child."

"I have a sentimental attachment to it; I can't explain why," Bandini confessed, leaning a heavy hand on his friend's shoulder. "No, it was not given to me by just anyone—I can feel it."

Pollini looked directly into Bandini's blue eyes and shivered uneasily before recovering his composure. Everyone knew the colour of the pope's eyes. It would not be difficult for Stendardi to concoct a story around that fact. "Let us not assume anything," he said finally. "A rumour of this kind could bring the papacy into ridicule."

"And if it is true?"

The cardinal remained silent and crossed himself repeatedly, as if trying to ward off any evil thoughts. True or not, a real danger existed from within the Vatican itself should the slightest fragment of rumour reach the wrong ears. The pope's detractors would seize any scrap of information to discredit the incumbent occupier of the throne of Saint Peter to further their own greedy ambitions, especially, he thought sourly, Cardinal Vittorio Albertini.

"Wherever the truth lies, we must not utter a word of this to anyone," said Pollini. "We cannot allow the papacy to be brought into disrepute by an alleged claim."

"We may not be able to conceal it," replied the pope, sadly. "Stendardi may have other plans."

"Silence has a price," said the cardinal. "Whatever it is, we will pay."

The pope sat down on the bench in front of the altar. "Do you remember when we administered last rites to my dear mother before her passing, God rest her soul?" said Bandini tearfully, recalling fond memories of her. "How she fondled so affectionately the cross hanging around my neck when I leaned over to kiss her—this very cross?"

"Yes, she was a good Catholic woman acknowledging the sign of Christ in her dying moments."

"You make it sound so innocuous, my friend."

"Wasn't it?"

"She whispered something in my ear before she died. Now it's beginning to make sense."

"What did she tell you, Holiness?" asked the cardinal apprehensively.

"She told me to always remember my mothers."

"The plural must have been a slip of the tongue during her state of incoherency."

"I thought so, too, until now. I also remember her being lucid enough to tell me my greatness would not be in the priesthood."

"With all due respect to a great woman of blessed memory, I think she may have erred in that prophesy, Holy Father," said Cardinal Pollini, knowing that such a remark would not spoil their strong bond of friendship.

"Her prophesy may not as yet have come to pass," said the pope, rising. "But I agree. It may be wise to remain silent for the time being."

* * *

Cardinal Vittorio Albertini paused to inhale the sweet aroma from the small rose garden positioned in the midst of all the greenery. There was no need to stoop and place his nose in the flower's proximity to enjoy the strong scent the bud had to offer because there was a slight breeze from the east blowing in his direction, carrying with it the full fragrance of all the flowers. Albertini had not entered the Vatican garden with the sole intention of enjoying its beauty, but to meet with Fabio Mento, a senior officer in the Pontifical Swiss Guard. He was born a Swiss Catholic and fulfilled the special agreement between the Holy See and Switzerland that membership be restricted to Swiss male citizens.

The Papal Secret

Cardinal Albertini had cultivated many contacts within and outside the walls of the Vatican and, like anything else, even the ecclesiastical order had its rotten politics. He had been convincingly beaten in the last papal election and had not adjusted to defeat amiably. To make matters worse, the present pontiff was a little younger than he was and would probably outlive Albertini's own ambition to succeed to the Throne of Saint Peter. *Of course,* smiled Albertini, *anything could happen to change the status quo.*

Fabio was already waiting for him at the Fontana della Barchetta—their designated meeting place. Albertini wasn't concerned if anyone saw the two of them together, because as senior representative of the Papal Commission for Vatican City State, he had carte blanche to meet with whomever he wished. The outdoor meeting place was purely so that their conversation would not be overheard.

"The garden is looking lovely, is it not?" said the cardinal, as if the meeting were a routine inspection of the facilities.

Fabio looked at him expectantly. Their private meetings usually resulted in a task for him to perform, accompanied by an envelope filled with Euros. Fabio's appointment to the Swiss Guard had been due entirely to Cardinal Albertini's intervention. Certain indiscretions in his past were not conducive to Vatican appointment, but Albertini had suppressed those nefarious deeds from Mento's CV in order to turn him into his own henchman, so that he would perform special tasks for him under threat of exposing his false tenure in the Vatican. Fabio was not stupid; foolish perhaps, but not stupid. He was fully aware that his primary function in the Vatican was to be Albertini's puppet. But the job was interesting and the pay extremely good.

"This is a private matter between you and me, Fabio," said Albertini. "Not a word to anyone—not even your family, if you have any. Do you understand?"

"Clearly, Your Eminence; have I ever failed you?"

"Do you see the fisherman's ring on my finger?"

"No, but you can't blame me for that. I had no control over the voting."

"With the right information," sighed the cardinal, "things may have turned out differently, but, as the saying goes, 'Someone becomes wise by watching what happens to him when he isn't.' Perhaps what I asked you to do was beyond your capability?"

"Your Eminence . . ." Fabio began to protest but was cut short by the cardinal's raised hand.

"His Holiness had a visitor this morning," said the cardinal.

"The pope?" uttered Fabio in surprise. He lifted the envelope he had been given. "This doesn't feel thick enough for a task of that magnitude."

"My concern is not with the pope," said Cardinal Albertini. "Not yet, anyway. A Jew was granted audience with the Holy Father recently, which seems to have disturbed him. I want to know who the man is and the reason for his visit."

"Does this man have a name?"

"It is written on a piece of paper in the envelope. Don't lose it in your haste to count the money," warned Albertini.

"Please don't confuse my need with greed," replied Fabio.

Cardinal Vittorio Albertini smiled and the men parted.

Chapter 9

Cagliari – August

The first thing Dr. Umbretti did on his return from the excursion was to go to his cabin and switch on his computer. He was expecting an email giving him his next instruction. As the computer was booting up, the Intrusion Alarm Indicator blinked orange, warning him that someone had switched on the machine in his absence. He was not unduly worried, only irritated that his computer had been touched, but when the indicator started flashing red, showing "deep intrusion," he began to panic.

"Impossible!" he said aloud. "I'm the only one who knows the password." Yet the system had been breached and the programme accessed. He noted the entry had been granted access at the first attempt, so whoever it was must have been in possession of the password. He noted the time the programme had been breached. Only Rochi had remained on board during that time frame, and he was convinced that he was behind this invasion of his privacy. If so, what had he learned? Certainly he would have found the transfer of the funds out of his own secret account. Would he have noted the name of the recipient in the double scam? Rochi couldn't go to the police, and neither could he; the checkmate was reciprocal! There was still time to take action.

He had to inform the cardinal immediately. He typed out a message and hoped for a quick response. It came five minutes later: "Get rid of the problem."

* * *

Rochi joined the others for lunch on the upper deck, telling them he was feeling much better and fit enough for a brief spell of sightseeing. His primary objective of going ashore was to find a public phone from which he could make some phone

Stan Miller

calls verifying the transfer of his money to a Cardinal Vittorio Albertini in the Vatican. Maybe there was still time to abort the transfer if it was not already too late. His eyes were still bloodshot, and he was still feeling like shit—but that wasn't caused by his migraine. He also sensed Umbretti staring at him unnaturally, but maybe he was just being over-reactive.

He wolfed down his meal and pushed his chair away from the table. "Even the sun has to set on such a beautiful place," he said. "I'd better get going if I am to see everything you did."

"I'll come with you," said Isabella. "I don't mind seeing it all again."

"No, no . . . it will be quicker if I go alone." He grabbed his camera and dashed down the companion ladder.

The Via Roma was indeed as grand as they had told him. The avenue stretched all along the waterfront, flanked on one side by the sea and several yacht clubs, and stately buildings on the opposite side. He glanced briefly at them in his haste to find the post office and a telephone. He stopped a fisherman laying out his net on the sidewalk.

"*Bon giorno, signore,*" said Rochi. "I need a phone—where's the post office?"

The fisherman gave Rochi a disinterested glance and raised a bony finger. "Up there," he said, and turned his attention back to his net.

Rochi continued walking in the direction of *up there* until he saw the post office building. There were three public telephones against the wall to the right of the entrance, each one separated by an opaque Perspex divider. The phone on the right was being used by an elderly gentleman, so he chose the phone on the left, leaving the vacant one between them. It didn't really matter if a stranger overheard part of his conversation, but his guilty conscience made him instinctively furtive.

He dialled the private number of his contact at the bank, inserted the required coinage when somebody answered and announced himself. "Tony, is that you?"

"Si."

"Giorgio here," he said in a low tone. "Listen, somebody's been tampering with my account."

"Which one?" Tony asked.

"You know which one—the second one I established."

"Hold on."

Rochi waited. A strong wind had come up off the bay. He

The Papal Secret

watched disinterestedly as a young woman approached the post office. She was wrestling to keep her skirt from billowing up to her waist. She was trying valiantly to protect her modesty in the strong breeze, but her flared skirt was swinging dangerously from side to side, revealing too much of her long legs and shapely thighs. She gave Rochi a nasty stare as she walked past him, as if it was his fault her dress would not stay in place.

Tony was on the line again. "The funds were transferred to another account," he said.

"On whose authority?"

"Giorgio, the request came from you."

"I gave no such instruction!" The sharpness in his voice became more noticeable.

"The pin-number was correct and all the internet transferring procedures were done properly. If it wasn't you, then someone has breached your security."

"Can the transaction be reversed?" asked Rochi.

"Afraid not, Giorgio; the funds have already been transferred and your account closed as per your original instruction—same as the previous one."

Rochi replaced the receiver and leaned his head on the wall.

"Are you okay, sir?" asked a young girl trying to be helpful.

"Fuck off!" he answered and walked away. He didn't see the girl burst into tears—his mind was focussing on how to kill Umbretti.

* * *

The *Bella Mare* left her moorings that afternoon at five o'clock. Michael steered her safely out of the harbour and set course for the Italian mainland. They were due in at Santa Margherita at first light the following morning. He had noticed earlier that Rochi had returned from his brief excursion in a state of agitation which he tried unsuccessfully to mask. The others didn't seem to notice anything unusual about his mannerism because champagne was flowing freely and they were all in a joyous mood. Even Isabella, the closest to him, seemed unaware that anything was wrong with her husband. Not surprisingly, as the focus of her attention was on Michael standing in the wheelhouse one deck above where they were sitting.

Michael had arranged for the dinner table to be set on the foredeck so that, once safely out to sea and while the light was still good enough to see what was ahead of them, he could set the controls to automatic pilot and join them for the evening meal. After dark, and throughout the night, he and Mario would take shifts on the bridge in front of the radar screen.

He couldn't help noticing how lovely Isabella looked—her olive-tanned skin, enhanced by the white sleeveless dress she was wearing, exuded natural sensuality. They were all seated now: Michael at the head of the table, Isabella to his left, with Rochi beside her. Rochi seemed oblivious to how beautiful his wife looked; he was watching Umbretti with hatred in his eyes.

Michael recognised a reciprocal glare in Umbretti's stare. The ice-cold glances which he kept giving Rochi belied the timidity of his nature presented to all of them during the voyage. Only Carla's flirtatious attention softened his countenance. Michael was thankful that the end of the voyage was near so that the two of them could leave before an outbreak of trouble drew him into the conflict. He still remembered the threat he had overheard a few nights ago: "With him out of the way, we're in the clear," he recalled the unknown speaker saying. "The time will be when we dock in Santa Margherita, where the captain lives." Why was he mentioned? Were they plotting against him? He looked at Martini carefully, but the man was so engrossed with his food that he showed no sign of nervous anticipation that something sinister was about to happen.

* * *

It was around four in the morning, during the last night-shift on the bridge, that Michael heard a rustling of fabric. The only light in the wheelhouse was coming from the red glow of the radar screen and the dull emergency light above his head, but he saw her quite distinctly standing just inside the door.

Isabella was wearing a short silk gown held closed by a sash loosely tied into a bow. She reached down and untied it, allowing her gown to part. She was naked underneath and, even in the dimness of the room, Michael could make out the fullness of her breasts and the dark triangle between her legs. He looked at her in surprise when she allowed her wrap to fall to the floor. She slowly approached him, her eyes on his face. She put her arms around his neck and kissed him.

"Make love to me, Michael," she breathed into his ear. "I cannot leave in the morning without having felt you inside me."

"Your husband . . ."

"Shh." She put a finger to his lips. "He took a sleeping tablet; he will not wake up until morning."

"Are you sure you want to do this?" he asked, feeling his heart thumping in his chest.

"He's cheated on me many times," she answered, "and you are the only one who has ever entered my heart so completely."

"I have the same feelings, too," he said, hoping the reciprocal cliché did not sound insincere.

"Take off your clothes before I tear them off you," she smiled teasingly.

He undressed quickly and placed his clothes on the floor for them to lie on. A cursory glance at the radar screen showed that there was nothing ahead, so he devoted his complete attention to the lovely creature beneath him. She lay on her back, and opened her thighs to him and pulled him down upon her. He entered her easily and he heard her moan. The excitement of their coupling was intense, fuelled by their desire for each other which had been building up for several days. He kissed her breasts and ran his tongue over her hard nipples and felt her shudder beneath him. Their love-making went on and on and, for the first time since his wife had died, her memory did not intrude into his ecstasy.

Satisfied and being content just being with each other, they lay together, sated and happy beyond contentment. The love he felt for Isabella was cathartic for his guilt feelings of betraying the memory of his dead wife with another woman.

The *Bella Mare* continued to plough her way unguided toward the distant coastline of Italy and the town of Santa Margherita. Isabella returned quietly to her cabin before the break of dawn.

Chapter 10

Rome – May

Cardinal Angelo Pollini looked at himself in the mirror. He very rarely wore a suit and tie except for when he had private business to take care of in the city. He was a handsome man and looked quite debonair in civilian garb, with his thick, grey hair giving him the appearance of a successful businessman. He brushed a bit of dust from his jacket collar—he only possessed one suit and had not worn it for a long time—and straightened his tie. He threw a robe over his clothes to conceal them and made his way to the car park, where his car was stored under a canopy to keep it cool. He wanted his departure past the guards to seem routine, so as not to arouse suspicion should anyone query his whereabouts. He sometimes ventured into the heart of Rome as a representative of the pope and the Vatican whenever his presence was required at functions or arbitrating clerical altercations.

He signed out at the gate, observing normal protocol, and joined the traffic along the Vittorio Vaneto. He had to make one brief stop to deliver an official document to the local archdiocese before his unscheduled detour to the offices of Tony Stendardi, attorney at law.

Arriving there half an hour later, Cardinal Pollini, having disposed of his robe and not looking like the cleric he was, entered the building. He paused briefly to glance behind him before disappearing through the revolving door, not that he thought he was being followed, but more from the instinctive behaviour of a man doing something out of the ordinary. He announced himself at the reception desk and was told to pin on his identification badge before proceeding upstairs. So it wasn't just Vatican paranoia about security, he thought to himself. He took the elevator up to the third floor and tapped on the frosted window of the lawyer's office.

Stendardi was sitting behind a huge desk lost in the

The Papal Secret

spaciousness of the room. Like the desks in most law firms, this one was littered with several stacks of files needing attention, and Pollini had to look twice to find the lawyer seated behind them.

Stendardi rose. "I'm so pleased you decided to come," he said, stretching out a hand in greeting.

Pollini took it limply. He still felt uneasy about the visit and had only agreed to meet with the lawyer to try to get to the bottom of the horrid affair and appease the pope's concern.

"You will find the proof you seek quite remarkable," Stendardi said, wiping his spectacles and re-seating them on his nose. He picked up a yellow folder sitting on top of the pile and opened it.

Pollini smiled cynically. The lawyer seemed to have had no doubt that he would, in fact, turn up for the appointment and had the file ready for his arrival.

"First, Cardinal Pollini, how is the Holy Father?" the lawyer asked.

"He is in good health, thank you very much, Mr. Stendardi, but let's dispense with formality and get down to business," said Pollini.

"Very well," continued Stendardi. "Let us begin with the premise that the pope is my client's son."

"Certainly not!" said Pollini, showing signs of annoyance. "That still has to be established."

Stendardi pushed the file across the desk and leaned back in his chair, waiting expectantly for the cardinal's wrath to explode. He did not have long to wait.

"How dare you!" bellowed Pollini, rising in anger. "Testing the pope's DNA without his consent is highly illegal. As a lawyer, you should know that!"

"That I do," replied Stendardi. "It's certainly inadmissible as evidence in a court of law."

"Exactly."

"But as we do not wish this matter to become public knowledge, your objection is over-ruled."

"By what means were you able to establish his Holiness's DNA?"

"No one is to blame and no one has betrayed the privacy of Pope John Pietro I," explained Stendardi. "Please sit, Your Eminence."

Cardinal Pollini lowered himself back into the chair and felt for the rosary he usually wore around his neck.

"We acquired samples of the pope's hair when it was cut in his hotel suite during his visit to Como. We managed to retrieve some off-cuts before disposal." Stendardi reached for the file and opened it. "We already had our suspicion two months ago."

"Why now? Why the revelation now? What precipitated your enquiry, or is this a case of common blackmail? Is it money your client wants?"

"My client is a very wealthy man," replied Stendardi. "No, it's not blackmail. It is a matter of compassion."

"Compassion? I don't understand."

"Yes. It's the wish of a dying father to see his son."

Pollini stared out the window for several seconds, with eyes that did not see. He was trying to comprehend what he had just been told. Compassion toward others was the very essence of his faith and a request of such magnitude could not be ignored. If the pope was indeed the dying man's son, it would be an enormous sin to ignore the request. If the whole thing was false, and the dying man believed it to be true, it would be a great blessing to grant the man his last wish so that he could die in peace. The truth would be established in heaven. Maybe it had already been established on earth, thought Pollini. The pope wouldn't have been told if the DNA match hadn't been conclusive.

Stendardi interrupted Pollini's thoughts. "Would it help if you met the man?" he asked.

"What's his name?"

"Samuel Grossman."

"Very well; send for Mr. Grossman."

"I cannot do that," said Stendardi. "Mr. Grossman is a man of ninety-six. He's too infirm to travel. You must go to him."

"It would be best," said Pollini, "if I heard the story from his own lips."

"We can leave right away."

"Where is he?"

"In Israel."

Pollini laughed nervously. "You expect me to travel to Israel?"

"There is a private jet waiting for you not far from Rome. Everything has been cleared with the authorities, both here and in Israel. With a bit of luck, you'll be home before morning."

"A private jet?"

"Yes. As I said, Mr. Grossman is a very wealthy man."

"Will you be accompanying me?"

"Of course," smiled Stendardi. "I wouldn't leave you in the hands of strangers."

* * *

Fabio Mento shifted uneasily in the car seat. He had been watching the entrance of the building Cardinal Pollini had gone into for over two hours now. The cardinal, although dressed in civilian clothing just like everyone else going in and out of the building, had a distinguished presence about him and would not have gone unnoticed. And besides, his car was still parked under the tree where he had left it. Something was wrong. He decided to phone Cardinal Albertini on whose instruction he was working.

"Vittorio," he whispered in the mobile phone as though it were a loudspeaker, "Pollini hasn't come out yet."

"Are you sure you didn't miss him leaving the building?" asked Albertini.

"Positive. His car is still here."

"Go up to the lawyer's office and make sure." Cardinal Vittorio replaced the phone on its cradle and closed his eyes. Was he chasing shadows? Was something going on that he wasn't supposed to know or was he merely exaggerating the gravity of his suspicions? It was imperative that he find out anything he could use in his favour against the pope. He leaned back and waited for Mento's call. When it came, he didn't like what he heard.

"What do you mean they've gone?" he asked in despair.

"Just that; the office is locked and no one's there."

"Find out what they're up to."

"How, Eminence?"

"How do you think?" said Vittorio gruffly. "Break into his office; lawyers record everything."

* * *

If the circumstances of Cardinal Pollini's visit to Israel were different, he might have enjoyed the adventure. The cabin

Stan Miller

of the aircraft was spacious and comfortable—not what he was used to—and the food excellent. He tried relaxing by lowering the back of the seat into a comfortable position, but his discomfort was not physical; the stress was coming from his mind and another cushion wasn't going to help. He was afraid that his visit with Mr. Grossman was going to have disastrous consequences.

He sipped his lemonade and glanced out the window. He saw Italy slipping away under the wing and the great expanse of the Mediterranean Sea filling his vista. The neutrality of the sea was a little comforting—while remaining over it he had nothing to worry about, but the closer the aircraft got to the shoreline of Israel, the more intense his concern became.

He turned to Stendardi, who was sitting next to him. "Tell me about Mr. Grossman," he said. "It may help to open my mind to whatever I have to face when I meet him."

"Quite a man, actually," Stendardi began his dissertation. "He achieved a great deal of good for his country and humanity in the years since the war. A generous philanthropist, considering he left Auschwitz a broken man of skin and bones."

"What happened?"

"He had nothing, of course, when he stepped off the boat," continued Stendardi. "He was sent to a kibbutz in Northern Galilee to rehabilitate and contribute to the settlement's prosperity. They hoped he would adjust quickly by giving him something tangible to do. When Israel gained independence in May 1948, Samuel Grossman relished going into the Israeli army. He wanted to know what it felt like to be able to fight back; he didn't care who the enemy was so long as they hated Jews."

"How did he become so wealthy?" asked Pollini.

"Mrs. Klinsman, the pope's foster mother, did a very brave thing."

"Really?"

"After the Nazis had arrested the Grossmans and deported them to the concentration camp, Mrs. Klinsman broke into the jewellery store and stole all the diamonds before the Nazis ransacked the place. Quite a fortune in diamonds, I might add."

"I suppose she used the money to give her adopted son a good education?" the cardinal speculated glibly.

"Actually, she hid the diamonds away and vowed to return them to Mr. Grossman after the war, if he was lucky enough to survive the death camps."

The Papal Secret

"And did she?"

"When she eventually found out that he was still alive and living in Israel, she returned them to him through an anonymous courier."

"She made no attempt to see him?" asked Pollini, mystified.

"No," replied Stendardi. "She was prepared to return the jewels, but not his son."

Cardinal Pollini remained thoughtful for a while. The woman had displayed such a magnanimous spirit in returning the man's wealth but, at the same time, showed such a cruel and deceitful nature by retaining something far more valuable than money—his only child!

"Surely, he must have known that Mrs. Klinsman had sent the stones?"

"Naturally," replied the lawyer. "The first thing he did was try to find her. He wanted his son back and to thank her."

The discourse was interrupted by the flight attendant placing a tray of refreshment in front of each of them.

When she was gone, Stendardi continued, "Mrs. Klinsman's husband never survived the war. She resettled in Rome when the war ended, and fell in love with an Italian doctor whom she married. She disappeared from the system with her change of name. The public records in Germany were in such disarray after the war that Grossman was unable to track her down. Her motive for marrying so quickly, I suppose."

Cardinal Pollini pondered what he had just been told. The story was beginning to sound feasible. A cold chill fell over him. If the Holy Father was indeed the boy in the story, the smoke above the Vatican would never be white again, thought Pollini cynically. His purpose in Israel was to ascertain whether there was any truth to the claim and, if so, to negotiate silence. He looked out the window and saw the coastline of Israel ahead. He somehow wished for the journey to never end. "How did you manage to find her?" asked Pollini.

"We didn't," replied Stendardi.

"So how did you learn about her?"

"By reverse tactics," said Stendardi.

"I don't understand."

"Let me explain," began Stendardi. "It is like starting with the answer and working back to the question."

"Now I am really confused," admitted Pollini

"God works in miraculous ways, Your Eminence," continued

Stendardi. "It was the pope himself who started Grossman on this quest."

"Impossible!" said Pollini, raising his voice. "The pope knew nothing of this."

"Do you remember the papal visit to Auschwitz four months ago? He was the guest of honour at a memorial service for the six million Jews who perished in the holocaust."

"Yes."

"Of course you do," smiled Stendardi. "You stood beside him when he bent down to place the wreath on the unknown grave. The photograph appeared in *Time* magazine."

"Yes, I saw it."

"What you didn't see was the cross the pope wears under his robe hanging free as he leaned forward. Mr. Grossman might be an old man but he still has an excellent memory. He recognised the cross as the one given to his son by his wife that day in the jewellery store before they were arrested by the Nazis and deported to the death camp. We had the photograph magnified many times. The Jewish symbol of *life* was easily recognisable, and, of course, the pope's beautiful blue eyes. That's the one thing Mr. Grossman always remembered about his son—those blue eyes."

An announcement from the flight deck told them that they were about to land.

"We also ran a check on the pope's late mother," continued Stendardi, buckling his seat belt. "Everything seemed to fit into place. That's when we decided on a DNA comparison, just to be sure."

"The final proof?

"Conclusively."

Chapter 11

Santa Margherita – August

The *Bella Mare* slipped unseen into the little harbour of Santa Margherita in the pre-dawn darkness of Thursday morning. Michael guided the boat into its mooring place as easily as parking a car in an empty lot. The slight touch of the boat against the mooring tyres hanging against the side of the wharf was so soft that none of the passengers on board so much as stirred in their sleep. He walked down the companion ladder, tied the boat to the securing posts, and went through the main gate onto the esplanade running along the waterfront. The street was still deserted and there was very little chance of a coffee bar being open so early in the morning. He thought of his friend Gino, who ran a bakery not too far down the road from the harbour.

Gino was an early riser—not by choice, but through the necessity of baking bread and rolls for the many bistros lining the seaside street that had to receive their consignments before the doors opened for business. Gino was renowned for his coffee made from beans specially imported from South America, and Michael had a sudden yearning for some of the hot brew. Gino often boasted that he had been weaned on coffee instead of mother's milk and his percolator standing on his kitchen table was never switched off. Michael began walking in that direction.

The front entrance to Gino's Bakery was still locked, so Michael went round to the back and entered through the kitchen door. Gino was where he always was at quarter to five in the morning—bent over his baking trays singing his favourite song *Santa Lucia Luntana*, in a voice that caused anyone who heard him to hate that rendition of it. He looked up at Michael and stopped singing. "Ah, *buon giorno, amico*; is it me or the coffee you have come for?" he asked, smiling.

"I'm here to do the townsfolk a favour by stopping your dreadful singing," replied Michael, moving toward the percolator.

Stan Miller

"The coffee, I knew it," Gino said, throwing his hands in the air. "And, tell me, what do you know about good music?"

"Enough to know when it's badly performed."

"Pour me a cup, Michael," said Gino. "God knows, I've earned it." The sound of someone coming down the stairs made him pause. "*Uno momento*," he said. He went over to the door. "Get the first load into the truck!" he yelled. Turning back to Michael, he lowered his voice. "That son of mine, he'd sleep until midday if I let him. If the deliveries are late, there'll be discontentment, and it's not wise to make bad friends in a small town."

They drank coffee and talked gossip—what people do best when everybody knows each other's business.

"Did you find a first mate for your latest voyage?" asked Gino, swinging the topic of conversation.

"I already have a first mate, Gino."

"I'm not referring to Mario," Gino said scornfully. "I'm talking about companionship, Michael. It's not good to live alone. It's time you found a good woman and settled down."

"Actually, there is someone," said Michael, finding it easy to confide in the older man.

"Bravo! When do I meet her?"

"She's a married woman, Gino."

"*Merda*," moaned Gino. He reached for a bottle of grappa and poured a hefty tot into Michael's coffee. "It helps uncomplicate things," he explained. "Drink up. You're an Englishman," he added. "Why follow the Italian way?"

"Love follows its own course," replied Michael.

"Is the feeling mutual?" asked Gino.

"I think so."

"Good. Then you're halfway to a solution."

"Oh?"

"Yes. She can divorce him, or is she Catholic?"

"He's a wealthy banker, a powerful man, and he is Catholic; he'll never let her go."

"Then walk away, Michael, before someone gets hurt, and that someone will probably be you." They sat in silence for a while before Gino pushed his chair back and stood up. "Back to work, I'm afraid, before my son takes verbal revenge on his father."

The idyllic life of Michael Frost came to a sudden end the

The Papal Secret

moment he answered the mobile phone ringing in his pocket. He wasn't sure, he would later recall, whether it was the frantic tone of Mario's voice or the words that he uttered that set the alarm bells ringing inside his head.

"You'd better get back to the boat right away," Mario said, breathlessly.

"Are the passengers awake already?" Michael asked, hoping that was the reason for the call but knowing it wasn't.

"Something terrible has happened."

"I'm on my way." Michael gulped down the rest of his coffee and said goodbye to Gino.

"Trouble in paradise, Michael?" he asked.

"What paradise?" Michael wanted to know. "It ends when you're weaned off your mother's breast," he added, and rushed outside.

The passengers and crew were gathered on deck when Michael came up the companion ladder. "Where's Rochi?" he asked. Four of the passengers were huddled together at the bottom of the steps. Mario and Claudia had distanced themselves from the others, as if wanting nothing to do with what was going on. Carla's eyes were red from crying. Isabella was standing against the railing looking out to sea. Her face was expressionless, and when she turned to face Michael, he saw that her normally sparkling eyes were like glass orbs staring sightlessly into space. No one uttered a word.

"Will someone tell me what's going on?" Michael asked, fearing the worst.

"You'd better take a look in your cabin for yourself," Mario said.

"My cabin?" Michael wasted no time asking any more questions. When he reached his cabin, he pushed open the door tentatively and peered inside. For a brief period, he just stood in the doorway and stared. He went rigid when he saw the body of Giorgio Rochi lying twisted on his bed. There was blood everywhere from stab wounds to his chest. The killer had left the knife protruding from Rochi's chest with the final thrust of the weapon. It looked like an ordinary kitchen carving knife found in most homes, but he knew at once that it came from the set standing on the side table in the ship's scullery. Instinctively, he leaned forward to feel for a pulse in Rochi's neck. There was none.

"Careful of the blood on the floor," warned Mario.

"Have you notified the police yet?"

"No, captain," replied Mario, "I was waiting for you."

Michael dialled the number of the local police department on his mobile phone. "Inspector Conti, please," he told the girl on the phone. He had met the inspector on several occasions—not officially up to now, but through acquaintances who knew him. It was only a small town and the police chief thought he owned it. From the first impression of the man, he didn't like him and thought him to be a supercilious little prick. The inspector had a reputation of regarding everyone with suspicion until they satisfied his curiosity. "A big ego in a small town," Michael had surmised.

"Ah, inspector," Michael said into the telephone when he heard the policeman's voice. "It's Michael Frost here. I'm afraid there's been a murder aboard my yacht. Yes, you had better get over here right away. Pier four."

Inspector Alberto Conti arrived with his team twenty minutes later. The usual bunch of lawmen, Michael thought, his side-kick, Sergeant Thomas, probably shortened from Tomassini, a forensic expert, and the medical examiner.

"Had to get the medical examiner out of bed," he said by way of apology. "Where's the corpse?"

"In my cabin."

The inspector raised an eyebrow. "Anything you want to tell me before we proceed?"

"No. I wasn't even on board at the time," answered Michael.

"Oh, and what time was that?"

"When the body was found. We docked at four thirty a.m. and I decided to go to Gino's Bakery for coffee. It's the only place in town open at that time of the morning."

"So in your expert opinion, the murder took place after four thirty?"

Michael looked at him and shrugged. "I was on the bridge since midnight and went straight ashore on arrival."

"You never returned to your cabin to freshen up first?"

"No; I didn't want to disturb the passengers."

"Perhaps you should have."

"Then perhaps I might have been the second victim," Michael said cynically.

Inspector Conti entered the cabin, with the medical examiner following closely behind. They put on gloves and examined the body more closely.

"It looks as if he's been dead for several hours," the doctor said as he steadied the camera in his hands and snapped off several shots. "The body feels cold already. I'll be able to give you an accurate time-frame after the PM."

"Wait for me on deck," Inspector Conti said to Michael. "And please inform the passengers and crew that no one is to leave the ship, including you, captain. I want statements from everyone, starting with the victim's wife."

Isabella Rochi was relatively calm in spite of the fact that her husband had just been murdered. The inspector began with routine questions that seemed trivial. It was a technique he used to put suspects at ease. He found her complacency quite strange under the circumstances; he would have expected a tear or two. Usually, in cases like this, it took all of his compassion to break through the hysteria of the surviving spouse. This woman, he noted in his little book, answered his questions as if she were being interviewed for a job.

"What kind of marriage did you have?" The inspector decided to change the tempo of his interrogation.

"I beg your pardon."

"Were you happily married, Mrs. Rochi?" He couldn't help admiring her beauty; she was an exquisite looking woman even with makeup from the night before. Strange that she would have gone to sleep without removing her makeup first, thought the inspector, especially a sophisticated woman such as she was. He lowered his eyes from her cleavage to her fingers which were fidgeting with her wedding ring—the only sign she displayed of any nervousness.

"Of course we were," Isabella said, looking him straight in the eye. "Why do you ask?"

"Forgive me for being so forthright, Mrs. Rochi," the inspector continued, "but I'm only doing my job."

"Of course you are, inspector."

"Word is you were having marital problems."

"Hearsay," she replied, without trying to conceal the annoyance in her voice. "Who told you that? It's nothing but inadmissible gossip."

"We're not in a court of law, Mrs. Rochi. I can explore any rumour or delve into the personal lives of anyone associated with the victim if it helps me reach a successful conclusion to my investigation." He leaned back in the chair and put his hands behind his head. He believed that the stance gave an impression of confidence that might lure the respondent into thinking that he possessed some secret knowledge that could

Stan Miller

be incriminating. "You do want your husband's killer brought to justice, don't you?"

"Indeed I do."

"Good. When did you last see your husband alive?"

"I came to bed late, around midnight, I guess. He was already asleep. Too much wine, I suppose." She was fidgeting with her rings again.

"Where were you?"

"I was out on deck enjoying the sound of the sea and the fresh air."

"Was anyone with you?" asked Conti, examining his finger nails. "A witness would be of great help to you."

"No; I was alone."

"Come, come, Mrs. Rochi; this is a small boat. Surely someone can corroborate your claim."

"You'll have to direct that question to the others," Isabella replied in a steady voice. "I never saw anyone."

"Fair enough," conceded the inspector. "So he was asleep and very much alive when you went to bed?"

"Yes."

"And when you woke up this morning, he wasn't there?"

"I was woken by Mario with the terrible news."

"Thank you, Mrs. Rochi. That will be all for now," the inspector said. "Let me offer my condolences on your tragic loss." He took her hand and felt it was a little sweaty. "We'll get to the bottom of this, I assure you."

The last person the inspector called in was Michael. "You say that you were in the wheelhouse from midnight until you docked this morning," he asked.

"That's correct, inspector. We are only a crew of three, and Mario and I take alternative shifts. Claudia has no sailing experience."

"Did you see anyone on deck during that time?"

"No. The passengers celebrated the end of the cruise last night with a bit too much to drink. They retired at ten o'clock."

"So early?"

"A boat cruise is a very romantic experience," Michael said. "You should try it some time, inspector. Women tend to be very amorous and responsive."

Without warning, Conti changed the direction of the

questioning. "You didn't perhaps see Mrs. Rochi out on deck around midnight, by any chance? It must have been very frustrating being the only person on board without a companion. I mean, with everyone at it and you sitting alone in the wheelhouse."

"I won't dignify that remark with a response."

"You should," the inspector said, pushing a folder across the table in front of Michael.

Michael reached for it and opened the cover. When he saw the top photograph, he felt the sweat beginning to trickle down the back of his neck. "Where did you get these?" he asked.

"I found them in Rochi's briefcase," the inspector replied. "It seems the cuckold was him and he knew it."

Michael examined the photographs again. Two of them were of him and Isabella holding hands in a restaurant—not all that incriminating—but the third was the spy-photographer's coup de grace. It showed Michael and Isabella standing against the balcony rail of his apartment. He had his arms around her waist with one hand over her blouse just beneath her breasts. A very suggestive pose, Michael feared. He looked up at the inspector.

"Do I need a lawyer?" he asked.

"I would think so."

"These photographs suggest that he had motive to kill me, not the other way round. I didn't kill him."

"Then you have nothing to worry about. But somebody does."

*　*　*

"You have reached the office of Tony Stendardi. Please leave your message after the tone."

"Tony!" Michael yelled. "If you're there, pick up the goddamn phone!"

"Michael, is that you?" Stendardi responded. "I thought I recognised your cordial tone of voice. To what do I owe the honour?"

"I'm in trouble. There's been a murder on my boat and I'm the prime suspect."

"Good Lord!" Stendardi exclaimed. "What have you done?"

"Thanks for the show of confidence. I've done nothing."

"I believe you, Michael. I don't suppose they'll let you come to Milan?"

"I'm a suspect, for God's sake. You know very well they'll never let me leave the district."

"Have they charged you with anything?"

"No, not yet."

"Then don't say anything. I'll be there first thing in the morning."

* * *

After a day and night of rain and cloud, the sun came out with the arrival of Tony Stendardi, attorney at law. Unfortunately, thought Michael, metaphorically speaking it did nothing to brighten the bleakness of his predicament. The boat had been impounded as a crime scene, so Michael had moved back into his apartment on the hill while the others had booked into a hotel. On Stendardi's advice and from his own experience as a lawyer, Michael had convinced Isabella that they should remain apart during the police enquiry. There was no point in making the inspector even more suspicious of them.

Stendardi sat at the dining room table sipping from a can of Coke. He had commandeered the table as his war office and had covered every square centimetre of it with files and notes.

"Where are we going to eat?" Michael asked, feeling like an outsider in his own home.

"If we don't come up with a strategy pretty soon, you'll be dining on bread and water in a prison cell," Stendardi replied, as if fobbing off an irritating child. "So you overheard Mr. Martini and an unseen collaborator discussing something that was going to happen at the end of the voyage? If the other man was Umbretti, and you can't be sure, then we have a good chance of introducing doubt into the scenario. If it was Rochi, then we're fucked."

"Rochi is our silent witness," Michael suggested. "We have to delve into his past to see who might have wanted him dead—and it can only be one of five people."

"Are you including his wife?"

"As much as I hate to, there's no other choice." Michael was a retired lawyer and he couldn't let sentiment cloud his judgement. "We'll try and eliminate her as a suspect first."

"The inspector has his own agenda," warned Stendardi

"Maybe, but he's starting with me first."

"I'll speak to him and see where we stand. In the meantime, I'll make a few phone calls and get some background on the victim."

"What do you want me to do?"

"Go to the hotel and speak to the passengers. Try to gain their confidence and see what you can find out, and . . . Michael," Stendardi gave him a stern look, "try not to pose for any more pictures with Isabella!"

Chapter 12

Jerusalem – May

Cardinal Pollini had never been to Jerusalem before; in fact, he had never visited the Holy Land in all his years with the church. Tony Stendardi had the good sense to allow the cardinal some free time to explore the hub of Jerusalem, the Old City. He had arranged for someone to show him some of the Christian places of interest, making it quite clear to the guide that only two and a half hours had been allotted for the excursion, after which time, old man Grossman would have completed his afternoon rest and would be strong enough to meet the pope's representative.

Pollini began his tour with the Church of the Holy Sepulchre, also known as the Church of Resurrection. The cardinal marvelled over the Byzantine architecture of the basilica and could have spent the entire day in the church but for a gentle nudge from the guide to remind him that time was of the essence. He made the traditional walk along the Via Dolorosa, the route taken by Jesus from the Judgement Court to the place of his execution and burial. Tablets set in the walls denoted the Fourteen Stations of the Cross.

The brief tour was soon over and he prepared himself for his meeting with Mr. Grossman, the actual reason for his presence in Jerusalem. He did not relish what he might hear from the lips of the old man.

When Cardinal Pollini arrived back at the Sheraton Hotel where he had been booked in for the day, Stendardi was already waiting for him in the foyer. "I trust you had a memorable afternoon?" Stendardi enquired, rising from the chair near the door.

"Indeed I did," Pollini replied, clutching the packet of souvenirs he had purchased so selectively.

"I suggest you go up to your room and freshen up. It's almost time for our meeting with Mr. Grossman."

The Papal Secret

"I shan't be long; it was only a mild exertion," he said before disappearing into the second lift from the left.

Fifteen minutes later he emerged from the same lift looking a little less weary.

"Come, Your Eminence," Stendardi said. "Our transport is waiting for our departure." A black limousine with tinted windows was parked in the driveway outside the front entrance of the hotel. The back door was open, beckoning them inside. "It's only a short journey," added Stendardi when they were comfortably ensconced in the plush leather seats of the vehicle. "The apartment building is just down the road near the Dan Hotel, overlooking the Jaffa Gate to the old city."

When they arrived, they took the lift to the top floor. "Mr. Grossman is too frail to go out much," explained Stendardi, "so he takes his delight in sitting by the window and enjoying the panoramic view of the old city."

Pollini was too engrossed in his own thoughts to comment. He was anticipating what he might be asked and his possible response.

Mr. Grossman's home was surprisingly modern for a nonagenarian. The carpets were light and the furniture designed for comfort rather than style. Paintings of scenes from the old city adorned the walls and it was evident from the Jewish ornamentation that filled the room that Mr. Grossman was a religious man.

They found him reclining in his favourite armchair by the window. In spite of the warm weather, a blanket was draped over his legs. The view, as Stendardi had mentioned, was indeed a spectacular vista of Biblical architecture. The Citadel of Jerusalem, popularly known as David's Tower, could be seen to the right, while the golden roof of the Dome of the Rock shone in the distance. Pollini guessed that the focus of the old man's attention was always directed somewhere below the Dome to a spot unseen from his window, the holiest place on earth for the Jewish people—the Western Wall. Pollini's eyes were first drawn to the window before a conscious effort allowed him to lower his gaze to the man sitting in the chair.

Grossman was staring at him through narrowed eyelids, as if trying to get the cardinal into focus. His face was badly wrinkled but his head of thick white hair and his deep blue eyes suggested to Pollini that the old man must have been quite handsome in his younger day; he still had an air of nobility.

Stan Miller

He approached the man cautiously. "Mr. Grossman," he said by way of introduction, "I'm Cardinal Pollini."

"I know who you are," answered Grossman in a coarse voice. "I sent for you." He nodded to a chair opposite him. "How is my son?"

The question caught Pollini by surprise; he had not yet accepted the possibility that this man was the pope's father. He sank into the chair like an already defeated interlocutor. "Your son?" he stammered.

"I have experienced just about everything life can throw at a man during my ninety or so years in this world, so I consider myself a wise man. You are an educated theologian, so let's not waste time fencing with each other. Is my son in good health?"

"Yes," Pollini surrendered. "He is quite well and happily enthroned on the seat of Saint Peter. His only distress is the anxiety you have caused him."

The old man smiled. "Spare a thought for my own distress having spent the past seventy years as a survivor of the holocaust and without my son."

"Is it not too late to make amends?" Pollini asked. "Your son is the most powerful cleric in the world. Would you want to destroy all that he has worked for, all that he represents, so that you may spend your last days with him?"

"It is not my intention to expose him," Grossman said, wiping away a tearful eye. "It is up to his conscience and Jewish soul to decide what's best. All I want is to hold him in my arms once more and tell him that I love him before I die."

Chapter 13

Santa Margherita – August

Michael had one stop to make before complying with Stendardi's instruction to go to the hotel and meet with the passengers. He drove over to the northern side of town where the line of shops ended and the road began to wind its precarious way along the side of the mountain to Portofino. The house he was looking for was in a side street at the end of the commercial district. He had to pass the harbour, where he could see his yacht guarded by two policemen standing at the bottom of the gangplank. He wanted more than ever to be free of the quagmire in which he had found himself and continue with his idyllic lifestyle, sailing the Mediterranean with paying tourists with the weather his only concern.

To be the prime suspect in a murder case was ridiculous, but certain ill-judged actions had contributed to the authorities focussing their attention on him. When he thought of Isabella, he had no regrets – only that he hadn't been discreet enough. Stendardi was an excellent investigative lawyer and should uncover something to exonerate him.

He stopped outside an old double-storied house with a steeply pitched roof. Although it rarely snowed in this region, it gave the house an appealing character that made it stand out among its neighbours. He knew from previous visits that the home doubled as a place of residence and a business. It was conducive for the owner to use the ground floor as a holiday booking agency while being close to her family upstairs.

A middle-aged woman who spoke English with a slight French accent welcomed him at the door. She was dressed in a navy slack suit with a white blouse underneath giving the outfit some contrast. They had met in London some years ago while he was still a practicing lawyer and she the chief executive of a travel agency. Years later, when they discovered that they had both relocated to the same seaside town in Italy, they resumed their friendship and business relationship. She secured his various charters for him.

"Michael," she said sadly. "What have you gotten yourself into?"

"Hi, Cheryl," he said. "Absolutely nothing. I'm a victim of circumstances."

"Well, your circumstances are bad for business. Come inside; I've just made some espresso." She ushered him into the dining room which doubled as her office. "You've already had a few cancellations."

"Probably just as well. They won't let me back on the boat until I'm cleared of suspicion."

"It had better be quick. You have a charter in three weeks," she said, turning the pages of an A-4 diary.

"No problem."

"The bank doesn't think so. You still have an outstanding loan on the yacht and they are a little concerned. If you're not back at the helm in ten days, they may institute proceedings to repossess."

"Most of the debt is paid off," Michael said adamantly. "They can't take my boat away."

"They can and they will," Cheryl said emphatically. "There's a chance you'll spend the next twenty years in jail if you can't prove your innocence!" Her countenance changed and she softened her approach. "Look, Michael, the bank is giving you some time to clear your name. They must like you very much."

"Who has hired the boat for the next voyage?"

"A very strange commission, this one," she mused.

"Do you have the client's name?"

"Yes. The Vatican!"

* * *

Michael found Franco Martini sitting alone in the hotel bar. It was as good a place to start as any. "Need company?" he asked.

"Be my guest." Turning to the barman, he said. "Bring another Peroni."

Michael sat on the stool next to Martini. "What's your opinion of all of this?"

"I shouldn't even be talking to you," Martini said, looking

into the bottom of his glass. "You're the prime suspect."

"We're all suspects, Franco," Michael said, switching to first names now that the cruise was over. "If they establish the time of death to be while we were still out at sea, the killer could very well be you."

"You'll have a hard time proving that."

"Not me, Franco, Inspector Conti, and he's a resourceful man. If there's anything unusual about any of us, he'll find it." Michael lifted the glass of beer and took a mouthful. Wiping the froth from his lips, he looked closely at Martini. "I overheard you and someone—either Rochi or Umbretti—talking on deck late the other night. I could only see you. I heard you saying that 'timing was everything—and the time will be when we dock at Santa Margherita.' What did you mean by that?"

"I don't recall saying anything like that." He turned to look into his glass.

"And the fact that I live here," Michael continued, "seems to have had some significance."

"Are you calling me a liar?"

"If I'm not lying, then you are."

"You'll have a hard time making the inspector believe that story."

"I don't have to," Michael said, draining the rest of his glass. "I just need to plant the seeds of doubt. You can be sure the inspector will follow it through." He got up and left the bar.

It was a little harder getting Umbretti to see him. "I'm busy," he told Michael over the hotel phone. "A visit is very inopportune right now."

"Okay," Michael said, dispassionately. "No problem." He decided to take a chance. "I was just wandering about the conversation I overheard between you and Martini that night on deck. Franco just confirmed it. What did he tell me you said? Oh, yes, that 'timing was everything and with him out the way, we're in the clear?' What did you mean by that?"

"You'd better come up."

Umbretti still looked shaken when he opened the door. He offered Michael the only chair in the room and sat opposite him on the edge of the bed. The laptop was closed, but a brush of the hand as Michael sat down revealed to him that it was still warm.

"Always busy, aren't you," Michael asked.

"What did you say over the phone?"

"That you and Franco are up to no good and that maybe Franco is beginning to have a conscience about it."

"It's nothing but bullshit."

"I overheard it and it wouldn't be hard for the inspector and me to make a case against you and your friend."

"He's not my friend."

"Your co-conspirator, then. Listen, Umbretti," Michael drew closer. "Rochi's killer has to be one of us and I didn't do it. If you had waited until we docked, your defence would have been that anyone could have come aboard and murdered him. But you and Franco were too impatient."

"The inspector is convinced it's you, Captain Frost," Umbretti smiled, having gained some of his composure. "The photographs, remember?"

"I wasn't aware he showed them to you."

Umbretti remained silent and looked away. Perhaps he had said too much already. "I think you should leave," he said.

"Rochi was up to something," Michael threw a curve ball hoping to see an element of truth reflecting in Umbretti's eyes. There was a slight reaction of shock which was quickly masked, but Michael didn't miss it. He was trained to pick up body language in witnesses he cross-examined. The technique was the tool of a good lawyer. "When the inspector finds out what it is, we may have a real motive for Rochi's murder. Have a pleasant day."

There was no point in talking to Katherine Martini or Carla; they would only babble about the inconvenience of being detained against their will. The inspector could deal with them. Michael wanted to be alone with Isabella. He hesitated before pressing her doorbell. He remembered Stendardi's warning, yet the desire to hold her in his arms again was more compelling. He wondered if her reaction to him would be the same as it had been prior to her husband's murder. Only one way to find out. He pressed the buzzer.

* * *

Inspector Conti sat at his desk reviewing the evidence detailed in the case file. Most of the input into the dossier came from his own notes, so he was familiar with all aspects of the case. At face value it seemed to be an open and shut case. The killer was one of eight people on board the yacht, if he included the captain and crew, and all he had to do was

The Papal Secret

find the person with the greatest motive to be rid of the Milanese banker. There was always motive in every murder case—he just had to find it. Once narrowed down to fit the most likely suspect, he would wear the culprit down by continuously being in his or her face. Under pressure, most people made mistakes; then he would pounce.

Sergeant Bruno sat opposite him. Unlike Conti himself, Bruno was a big man, and if it hadn't been for a severe shoulder injury a few years back, he might well have made it into the Italian rugby side and done the department proud. As it was, he was still a popular figure in the town and doors opened to him more readily than they would have if Conti had rung the bell. The inspector was happy to have such an assistant on his team, even if the man would eventually take his job!

"You know, sergeant," Conti said, looking up from the case file, "I don't think the captain did it."

"That's a sudden change of heart," Bruno replied. "A few minutes ago Frost was the prime suspect."

"Yes, the evidence, the photographs, certainly seems to suggest him being the most likely culprit."

"I hear a rebuttal coming."

"My doubt stems from these photographs," Conti announced.

"What about them?" Bruno looked puzzled and a little sheepish in having missed something that his superior had spotted.

"The fact that they exist at all." Conti spread them out on the table in front of him.

"Care to explain, inspector?"

"They were taken before the cruise. Someone was already preparing to incriminate Frost."

"Maybe it was Isabella Rochi they were trying to trap," Bruno said, trying to redeem his astuteness. "Perhaps the deceased already suspected his wife's infidelity."

"With someone she had not yet met?" Conti continued the debate. "How would Rochi know his wife would be attracted to Frost, let alone conspire to betray him?"

"Maybe she's done it before, and certainly he was proved right on this occasion."

"Something to look into," Conti said, and then changed the direction of discussion. "Photographs are a perfect surface to capture fingerprints."

"So?"

"There aren't any," Conti looked at Bruno. "Don't you think it strange that there are no fingerprints on any of them? Had they been taken at Giorgio Rochi's behest, there would be no reason to wipe them clean. It looks as if he never even saw them."

"But they were found in his briefcase."

"They could have been planted by someone; the killer, perhaps?" Conti wondered.

"That rules out Frost and the victim's wife. They wouldn't plant evidence against themselves."

"Precisely," Conti agreed. "Of course, we cannot rule out the obvious, but, for the time being, we can focus our enquiries in a different direction."

"Martini and Umbretti?"

"Exactly." Conti nodded. "However, it has come to my attention that Frost and his lawyer are doing a little snooping of their own. I don't want them to stop if they think we're turning our attention away from Frost." Conti smiled. "A cat among the pigeons might scatter one of them into our gun-sight."

"It has to be one of those aboard the yacht," Bruno said, holding up the coroner's report. "Time of death was while they were still out at sea."

"Even with only eight possible suspects, it is easier to hypothesise who it might be than prove it conclusively. This is still a difficult case, and if we don't make an arrest soon, we'll have to let them all go, and you can bet your last Euro they'll disappear into seclusion." In most of his other cases, it was conceivable that the victim had been in the wrong place at the wrong time. But in this case, a boat at sea offered no alternative suspects other than those on board during the cruise. A simple case? It would be if he could find the suspect with the strongest motive.

"Roll up your sleeves," he told Bruno. "It's time to start digging."

* * *

Isabella opened the door. She was wearing the hotel's towelling gown. Her wet hair hanging over her shoulders indicated that she had just stepped out of the shower. Michael marvelled at how lovely she looked even without makeup. He could smell the fresh fragrance of the bath soap on her, and the only sign that something was wrong was the tiredness in her eyes.

"I'm glad you came," she said, falling into his arms.

"How are you feeling?" he asked.

"Fine, I suppose; better, now that you are here."

"The police have intimate photographs of us," Michael told her.

"Yes, I know," she replied, closing the door behind him. "I saw them. I had no idea my husband suspected me of being unfaithful."

"You are a desirable woman," Michael said. "You can't blame him for being jealous."

"He had his mistresses," she said. "I suppose he was checking to see if I had any lovers."

"Don't take this the wrong way," Michael said cautiously, "but did you?"

"Fuck you, Michael!" she said sternly. "Besides you, it's none of your business!"

"I'm sorry, but the inspector will be asking you the same question."

"On hindsight, Giorgio sent me ahead with the intention of testing me." She lowered her face into her hands. "It seems I failed."

"Our relationship has nothing to do with his murder."

"No? How can you be so sure?"

"I think that whoever took these pictures was trying to blackmail him."

"Nonsense," she said, looking up at him. "I'm the one who should have been blackmailed, not him."

"Perhaps he found out, and when confronting the blackmailer, a scuffle broke out and he was stabbed."

"Leave that conjecture for the police."

"They've already decided it was me."

"That's preposterous!" she replied. "We are all under suspicion. Sometimes they start with the least likely suspect to throw the others off guard."

"I hope you're right," replied Michael, relenting as he grasped the intent of her words. "However, the police are famous for making saints look like killers."

"How are you going to prove your innocence?"

"Thank heavens we still live in a civilised society. It's for the state to prove guilt. In the meantime, my lawyer and I are already working to clear my name."

"Perhaps I can help," she offered.

"Any information will be valuable," Michael said, brushing his hand through her damp hair.

"I don't trust Umbretti. He gives me the creeps, and Martini and my husband were up to no good. I think they were siphoning funds from the bank."

"Jesus, Isabella!" Michael exclaimed. "That's a hell of an explosive accusation to make."

"Giorgio deposited a large sum of money into my account. He told me he'd explain later."

"And did he?"

"No. He was murdered before he could tell me."

"How much did he put into your account?"

"Half a million Euros."

"If the inspector finds out, he'll regard that as a strong motive for murder."

"What possible motive is that?" she asked. "I already had the money before he was murdered. What is wrong with a husband giving his wife a gift?"

"Nothing, I suppose," admitted Michael. "Just be careful."

"Why?" she said, seductively. "The curtains are closed." She guided his hand beneath the gown and pressed it to her breast. "We've come this far," she added, slipping out of her robe. "Why stop now?"

Chapter 14

Rome – May

Pope John Pietro I was the absolute ruler of Vatican City, having full executive, legislative, and judicial power, heading all branches of the government. Since he devoted most of his time to spiritual and ecclesiastical matters, he had to delegate most of his temporal authority to other officials. The state's foreign relations are entrusted to the Holy See's Secretariat of State and to his principal subordinate, the president of the Pontifical Commission for Vatican City State, Cardinal Gianni Luca. It was to him that Cardinal Pollini was directing his carefully prepared recommendation.

"A window of opportunity has presented itself for His Holiness to make his long desired visit to Jerusalem," he began. "The President of the United States is going on an official visit to Israel next month and the Prime Minister of Israel has indicated that he would welcome a simultaneous visit from the head of the Vatican."

Gianni Luca, who sometimes found these meetings boring, and fully expected this one to be no different, suddenly perked up from his slouch in the chair at the head of the table. He was a tall man, and by straightening his back, he appeared to be in the process of rising. A few of the eight members of the Council of Cardinals sitting around the table shuffled their chairs in an attempt to stand in deference to the senior cardinal, but were signalled to remain seated by an irritable wave of the chairman's hand.

"Next month?" he said indignantly in his deep baritone voice that made the paintings on the wall begin to shake. "It takes months, if not years of planning for the pontiff to visit a foreign land."

"Indeed," continued Cardinal Albertini, eagerly taking up the cudgel against Pollini. "May I ask the General Secretary why the sudden haste?"

Under normal circumstances, Pollini would have agreed with the council's objection to sanction the pope's visit to Israel at such short notice, but these were not normal circumstances. Grossman's words were still vibrating inside his head. "All I want to do is hold him in my arms once more and tell him that I love him before I die."

The pope had also been moved by those words and had instructed Pollini to make the arrangements for the trip. "I have to win over the council first," Pollini had said.

"They are no match for your intellect," the pope had encouraged him. "Persuade them. Create any subterfuge to justify the journey. I must see Grossman."

Like a gift from God, the justification had fallen into his hands—the Middle East Peace Conference, which the American president would be attending.

The subterfuge with which he had to cloak the proposal sat uneasily on his conscience, and was pacified only by the pope's insistence that he make the trip. Pollini cleared his throat before resuming the debate. He realised that if he could allay the concern of the council about security measures for the pope's visit, he could win them over.

"Stringent security measures are already in place for the visit of the president of the United States. The CIA and the Israeli Security Service have already agreed that our own security team can piggy-back, so to speak, on their arrangements, so long as the pope's arrival coincides with the arrival of the president. The two leaders will travel together in the same convoy during their two-day visit to the Holy Land." Pollini paused, and felt satisfied that he had won over the approval of most of the council members by noting the slight nodding of heads as he was speaking. It would save a great deal of the Vatican's money through the joint venture, and he knew that would appeal to most of the cardinals sitting around the table.

Now for the coup de grace, he thought. "The Holy Father himself has sanctioned the visit and humbly requests the council to do the same." Pollini resumed his seat and listened to the silence.

The cardinals were in no hurry to make up their minds. Each was considering the ramifications of the decision. To vote against the proposal might irk the Holy Father and have far reaching repercussions concerning future appointments. Voting in favour of such a hasty itinerary, however, could place the pope's safety in jeopardy.

The first voice of support came from an unexpected source, which made Pollini stiffen in surprise.

"I think it would be prudent to seize this opportunity we have been presented with so magnanimously by the Americans," Cardinal Albertini said in a steady voice. "The security arrangements as illustrated by Cardinal Pollini seem more than adequate," he smiled before adding, "and at minimal cost to the Vatican Bank. I vote in favour of the proposal." Cardinal Albertini sat down in satisfaction. He wasn't really worried about the Holy Father's safety. If the pope wished to risk a hasty demise, then so be it. His own ambition to ascend to the throne of Saint Peter disarmed him of any concern.

As they were leaving the chamber at the conclusion of the meeting which had voted in favour of the pope's visit to Israel, Albertini laid a restraining hand on Pollini's shoulder. "A word, if I may," he breathed heavily into Pollini's ear. Pollini paused at the top of the stairs. When they were alone, Albertini continued. "You were missed at prayers last night. In fact, you weren't seen at all the entire day."

"I had business in Rome which took longer than anticipated," replied Pollini, uneasily.

"What business?" Albertini asked bluntly.

"A matter presented itself for my attention which has nothing to do with you, Vittorio."

"Come, come, Angelo," Albertini said, continuing with the informality. "There are no secrets within these holy walls, and I am one of the Holy Trio, after all."

"There are many secrets in this place. One, for example, is your desire to be the next pope."

"Isn't that the dream of us all?" he began descending the steps, "to serve the flock?"

"My reason for going into Rome was a private family matter," Pollini said, keeping up with him.

"Oh?"

"It would do you no harm showing some humility in admitting that humans occupy the Vatican, not ethereal beings. Most of us have families on the outside who sometimes need our assistance."

"If there is anything I can do to help, please ask," Albertini said in a melodic voice filled with insincere charm.

Pollini nodded. "Thank you for your support in there," he added.

Stan Miller

"My pleasure," Albertini replied. "I hope you know what you're doing." He watched Pollini exit a side door leading into the Cortile di San Damaso. "Because I certainly intend finding out the real reason for His Holiness's visit," he added quietly to himself.

Chapter 15

Santa Margherita – August

Dr. Milo Umbretti removed the memory stick from the side of his laptop, and satisfied that all the information was safely stored in it, deleted the programme from the computer and closed the lid. He was beginning to feel claustrophobic cooped up in the hotel room all day, and his thoughts turned to Carla in the room down the passage. She had awakened in him desires and feelings that he thought were long dormant. Just the thought of her gave him a pleasurable urge, so he smoothed his hair in a vain attempt to look suave, and left the room.

Carla was surprised to see him standing in the passage when she opened the door. He brushed past her and entered the room without invitation. She noticed he was perspiring profusely and his breathing came in gasps. At first she thought him to be ill until he pressed his hand on her breast and tried to kiss her. She rolled her eyes in exasperation when he wasn't looking and wondered if her obligation to service him still applied now that Giorgio Rochi was dead.

What the hell, she thought, *anything to pass the time.* She slipped out of her dress and waited for him to join her on the bed.

* * *

Cardinal Albertini went into the garden and sat on the bench he usually used whenever he wanted to make a discreet phone call. He was surrounded by low shrubs which offered no concealment for an eavesdropper. He withdrew a cell phone from his pocket and dialled a number.

"Umbretti," he said, "can you talk?"

Umbretti looked down at the top of Carla's head bobbing up and down on his naked stomach and cursed the cardinal for his ill-timed phone call. "Yes, but make it quick, Your Grace," he said, keeping Carla's head in place with his hand.

"I read the news about Rochi," Albertini said. "Was it necessary?"

"Yes, he found out."

"What about the money?"

"Safe."

"You're absolutely sure the transfer went through?"

"Of course."

"And the other matter?"

"In place . . . as planned . . . waiting for your signal." Umbretti was breathing more heavily now and wanted desperately to end the call so he could enjoy the full extent of his ecstasy.

"Umbretti, are you alright?"

"Yes . . . perfectly . . . got to go." He snapped the phone shut just in time for an unrestrained groan of delight.

* * *

Cardinal Albertini looked up to heaven and sighed. He dialled another number and, while waiting for the call to go through, looked around once more to ensure he was still alone.

"I have another assignment for you," he said. "How soon can you despatch a courier to Santa Margherita?"

Chapter 16

Israel – June

The Vatican jet landed at Ben Gurion Airport half an hour before Air Force One. It allowed the Prime Minister of Israel and his entourage sufficient time to welcome Pope John Pietro I properly, while eagerly awaiting the president's arrival. When the United States aircraft landed and disgorged its VIP guests, they were formally welcomed and, together with the papal party, whisked off to the Renaissance Hotel in Jerusalem situated just off Ruppin Street.

Tony Stendardi had arrived the day before and had booked into the nearby Park Plaza Hotel. Cardinal Pollini, still dressed in his clerical suit and Roman collar, was browsing in the hotel gift shop when Stendardi found him. Pollini followed the lawyer into the coffee shop where they settled at a secluded table in the corner.

"It's best we schedule the meeting at night," Stendardi said in a conspiratorial voice.

"It will have to be tonight, then," replied Pollini. "The Holy Father can retire early with the excuse of being tired after his journey. No one will think it unusual. How will we get him out of the hotel without anyone noticing?"

"The lifts go directly into the underground parking basement. I have a suit of clothes and a hat in this bag," Stendardi said, patting the overnight case lying at his feet. "His Holiness will have to go incognito."

"I can't allow him to go unescorted," Pollini cautioned.

"No one else must know where he is going. I have arranged for a Mossad agent to drive us in an unmarked car to the home of Mr. Grossman. His Holiness will be back in his bed in a couple of hours."

Being a man of the cloth all his adult life, Cardinal Pollini was not comfortable with having to sneak around like a spy and, to make the situation even worse, he had to do it with one of the most recognisable figures on earth—the Holy Father himself. An action, no doubt, which would have resulted in his excommunication or a death sentence just a century ago. What made it possible was the pope's complicity in the whole affair, and the help of the Israeli secret service.

Using the full extent of his persuasive powers and a nod from the pope, the papal guards allowed the two priests to descend alone in the lift to the third floor on the pretence of a meeting with the American president in his suite. Pollini pushed the button for the third floor and allowed the lift to stop there for a moment in case the guards were watching for the number to light up above the lift door. He hoped they would not become suspicious and raise the alarm when the lift continued with its decent into the parking basement.

Agent Zev Levy and Tony Stendardi were waiting for them when the lift door opened.

"Your Holiness," Agent Levy said, "you must remove your robe now. I will leave it in the boot of the car until your return."

Pollini helped the pope remove his vestment and reveal his secular attire beneath. The Israeli beckoned to them.

"Please hurry," he coaxed. "The longer we take, the greater the risk of being seen." He indicated the front seat. "It's best you sit up front, Your Grace. They'll be more interested in who is sitting in the back." He didn't bother explaining who the "they" were supposed to be.

The limousine was made to stop at the exit boom, where a police officer examined Levy's documents. He looked briefly at the two passengers and waved Levy through.

Peak hour in Jerusalem never seems to end, and it was with difficulty that Agent Levy squeezed into the flow of traffic. He was being extra careful, because an accident now would cause complications, least of which would be the loss of his job.

The pope was not one prone to exercise, and the excitement of being spirited away in secrecy and the anticipation of what was to come when he finally met Samuel Grossman had worn him out. He tried closing his eyes to the throng of humanity flashing past the window on either side of the car, but in the solitude of darkness inside his mind, he was confronted with the prospect of dealing with Grossman's revelation, so he opened them again. Crowds were impersonal; he could cope with watching them more easily than speculating on an outcome that might not happen.

The Papal Secret

Agent Levy waited for the light to turn green and stepped on the gas, moving the vehicle into the far lane so that he could turn right into Keren Hayesod Street and proceed directly to the building where Samuel Grossman lived near the Bloomfield Garden.

He eased the vehicle into the parking space designated for him and switched off the ignition. Another agent was quick to open the front passenger door and help Bandini out of the car. He clasped the pope lightly on the arm to steady him so that he wouldn't stumble over the paving blocks and guided him into the building. Cardinal Pollini and Stendardi followed closely behind them.

No one spoke as they rode the lift to the seventh floor. Bandini and Pollini exchanged glances that questioned the wisdom of what they were doing. The pope was looking up at the light pausing on number seven when the door suddenly opened.

"We're here," the Mossad agent announced.

In normal circumstances, Bandini was a man of infinite confidence and mild temperament and did not panic easily. He was usually in full control of his emotions and could handle the most severe dilemma with calm aplomb. Now, for the first time in his life, he felt unsure of himself and uneasy with the situation that confronted him. Even while waiting for the vote to be counted to announce his succession to the papacy, he had remained calm. He knew that his appointment ultimately was in the hands of God and whatever the outcome was due to Divine Providence. Perhaps it was the same in this case.

He wasn't prepared for the initial shock of seeing Samuel Grossman. The old man was lying in bed propped up by a mountain of cushions. His blue eyes were blazing with intensity as they focussed solely on Bandini as he approached the bed. In those seconds of realization, Bandini was immobilized by the feeling of affection for the stranger in the bed. He felt an unnerving connection to the man. He moved his hand toward Grossman's hand lying uncovered on top of the blanket, and touched it.

The old man took hold of Bandini's hand and squeezed it affectionately. An immediate bond between the two of them was sealed by a single touch.

"Bless you, my son, you came," Grossman breathed heavily. "I have been waiting nearly seventy years for this moment. It's what kept me alive."

"It was my wish to see you, too, Father," replied Bandini.

A tear appeared in Grossman's eye and trickled down his cheek into the corner of his smile. "I have never stopped loving you, even when I wasn't sure if you survived the Nazi persecution."

"You saved my life by sacrificing me to another faith," replied the pope. "Life dealt us both a heavy blow."

"No, my son. God decreed it. He had a different plan for you. The Sages teach us that nothing happens by chance."

Bandini smiled. "Like He sent Moses to grow up in the house of Pharaoh?"

It was Grossman's turn to smile. "Pharaoh had his own gods. You and I worship the same one and only true God, albeit from different perspectives. If what you teach is tolerance, compassion, and morality, then our faith is the same." Grossman sighed. "Enough theologising, I did not bring you here to convert you back to Judaism; the world is too fragile in its religious conviction to cope with such an announcement."

"Then why did you bring me here?"

"To hold you in my arms again and to beg your forgiveness for what I did."

"My forgiveness? For what?" Bandini asked in surprise.

"For my lack of faith."

"I don't understand."

"They were dark days in Germany in 1936 when you were born," explained Grossman. "Jews were disappearing without a trace and Hitler's doctrine of anti-Semitism was no secret. It was part of his master plan to rid Germany of us. That's why Gertrude and I committed the sin by not having faith in God."

"Gertrude?"

"Your mother, may God rest her soul."

"And what was the sin you blame yourself for?"

"In order to protect your life, we broke our covenant with God." Tears were flowing down Grossman's cheek without restraint. Bandini removed a silk handkerchief from his pocket and wiped them away. "We chose not to circumcise you so the Nazis would never find out that you were Jewish. Your blue eyes looked so Aryan we knew we could deceive them when the time came."

"In the same way as Yocheved placed her son Moses in a basket of reeds by the side of the Nile River?" commented Bandini. "To deceive Pharaoh so that Moses would survive?"

"You know our history?"

The Papal Secret

"I studied Chumash for a better insight into the Lord's teachings."

"That is good."

"You don't need my forgiveness, Father. You deserve my gratitude," Bandini said. "If you are looking for forgiveness, you must seek it from God."

"Indeed," the old man replied with a twinkle in his eye, "that I will be doing shortly, in person." He reached for the top button of Bandini's shirt and loosened it. With a shaking hand, he groped for the cross that his wife had placed around their son's neck when they sent him away with Mrs. Klinsman. When he touched it, he leaned forward to see it. The years came flooding back, a time so long ago when his two-year-old son used to sit on his lap and hug him before that dreadful day. The man in front of him was now also old and not a little boy anymore, but the desire to hug him again was overwhelming. He opened his arms and drew Bandini into them. The two men remained locked in familial embrace for a long time.

Cardinal Pollini could not prevent his own eyes from watering, and said a silent prayer praising God for this happy reunion of father and son. Stendardi wiped away his tears and was thankful his efforts had brought this about.

"God bless you, my son," Grossman whispered before releasing Bandini. "I am ready to join Gertrude and face my maker a happy man. May the Lord guide you wisely in however you decide to serve mankind."

Pope John Pietro I kissed his father on the lips. "God bless you, too, my son," he said, turning away to weep.

Chapter 17

Santa Margherita – August

The man who stepped off the train at the station had never been to Santa Margherita before. He was not a sentimental person and saw the world through cold, calculating eyes that were focussed on two things only: carrying out the job he had been given and staying alive. He had no interest in scenery, no matter how beautiful the vista was. The town, nestling on the slopes of the mountain and spreading serenely toward the water's edge, held no attraction for him. His only interest was the address written on the piece of paper he was holding, and the name on it. Splendour was not part of his world.

It was a hot and humid day, but Hendrik Vlok was unmindful of the discomfort. He kept his jacket on to hide the bulge of the Luger tucked safely in the holster under his arm. He had trained his body to be immune to the influence of temperature, whether cold or hot, no matter what clothing he wore. He allowed nothing to distract him from his task. Even the sight of a young girl in a mini-skirt showing too much leg elicited absolutely no reaction from him.

He hailed a cab and sat in silence during the short journey down the twisting road that wound its way from the station to the foreshore. The taxi pulled up in front of a new, modern hotel juxtaposed against the old architecture of the surrounding houses. With an abrupt nod of the head, he paid the driver and manoeuvred through the revolving doors.

It took only a cursory glance to memorize the layout of the foyer. Before any assignment, he planned his escape route first. He would never proceed to the next phase of a job until he was satisfied he could make a safe getaway, even in total darkness. The door marked *Emergency Exit* to the left of the lifts was his first objective and he strolled purposefully through the foyer toward the door. A man who seemed to know where he was going rarely attracted attention. Without hesitation, he opened the door and entered the stairwell. Before

The Papal Secret

the door closed, he glanced over his shoulder to see if anyone was following him. No one had paid him any attention.

The lighting in the corridor was bright; the primary function was to provide enough illumination to escape safely in an emergency. An arrow on the wall pointing down the stairs indicated the way out, so Hendrik descended the eight steps to the fire escape exit door and stopped in front of it. It was probably triggered with an alarm siren if opened for no reason, so he refrained from touching it. Suffice to see that in compliance with safety regulations, the door could easily be opened from the inside by pushing down on the horizontal bar across it.

"Can I help you?" a voice came from the top of the stairs.

Hendrik looked up and saw a hotel porter in his blue uniform staring down at him. He unbuttoned his jacket in case he had to draw his gun quickly and smiled for the first time that day. "I'm a little lost," he said. "Where's the lavatory?"

"It's one flight up, sir, not down," the porter corrected him.

"Sorry," Hendrik said. "Instinctively it's easier going down steps than up them."

"I know what you mean, sir. Stairs are a killer if you're unfit." The porter turned and went back into the foyer.

Hendrik made use of the toilet in case he was being watched, and went back out into the street. He already knew the room number so he didn't need to speak to anyone at the front desk who might later identify him. The porter was the only glitch so far. He still had a few hours to wait before dark and decided to find a suitable restaurant and order an early dinner. It was not until the waiter placed a plate of veal marsala in front of him that he realized how hungry he was. He had eaten nothing all day and would need energy to get through the night. He refrained from ordering wine and settled for a Coca Cola, instead, to keep his head clear for the job he had to do. During the meal, he kept a watchful eye on the door and other patrons. He needn't have bothered. Only one man knew that he was there and the reason for his presence in Santa Margherita.

* * *

"Tea?"

"I think I need something a little stronger than that."

"There must be liquor somewhere in this suite," Isabella

Stan Miller

said, moving to a cabinet next to the TV set. She opened the door and withdrew a miniature bottle of whiskey. "You're in luck," she said.

Michael filled a glass and held it in an outstretched arm toward Isabella in silent offering.

"No, thank you," she declined politely. "Apart from wine, I don't touch alcohol."

"I need it to steady my nerves and clear my head."

"Since when does booze clear your head?"

"Since nothing else does," he replied, downing the tot. He had a lot on his mind, in particular the murder rap hanging over his head. "I didn't do it, you know."

"I never thought for one moment that you had," she replied, exonerating him from her suspicion. She came across the room and kissed him on the lips. "The inspector is allowing me to go home tomorrow."

"Are you going?"

"There is no reason for me to stay here," she said, "unless . . ."

"Of course, I want you to," he answered her unfinished question. "I was hoping there is more to our relationship than a fling on a boat."

She smiled at the florid description of their affair. "You know there is," she replied.

"You can stay with me until . . ." He stopped himself from placing a time limit on their intimacy.

"Until?" she persisted.

"Forever, I was hoping."

"We'll see," she said coyly. "The inspector will be very intrigued if I move in with you so soon after my husband's murder."

"It may convince him that I'm innocent if he sees that the wife of the victim thinks so."

"Or he may interpret it as a sign of my complicity in the murder. He'll realize that my husband and I were not in love with each other. That's motive enough for murder."

"Someone on board had a bigger motive and I intend finding out who it is."

"How do you propose doing that?"

"My lawyer is already working on it," he told her, "and don't forget; I was once a very successful investigative lawyer myself when I had my own practice."

"I have an idea where we can start," she said, suddenly remembering something. She opened her handbag, rummaged through the contents, and withdrew a narrow plastic object that looked like a cigarette lighter. "I found this lying on the floor of your cabin when they called me in to see Giorgio's body. It was partly concealed so the police didn't see it." She handed it to him.

"A USB flash drive? You didn't tell the police about it?"

"No. Should I have?"

"Yes; concealing evidence is a crime, my dear, but I'm glad you didn't. It may contain information that we need to see first."

"There's no computer here."

"I have one at home."

She picked up her handbag. "I'm ready; let's go."

Michael assumed they were all under police surveillance, so it wouldn't be long before the inspector contacted him to find out what was going on. In the meantime, he was hoping that something on the memory stick would shed more light on the case.

Ten minutes later, he was sitting at his desk in his apartment staring at the computer screen. Isabella leaned over his shoulder trying to decipher the file contained in the flash drive. Michael could smell the scent of her perfume and the fragrance of her body and it took all his concentration to focus on the figures scrolling down in front of him.

"It looks like a list of accounts," Isabella observed.

"There appears to have been a hostile entry into the file," Michael pointed out. "It took three attempts before the correct password was accepted."

"What does that mean?"

"It means that whoever gained access to the program was not the primary user."

"So, if my husband was up to something cagey, someone found out about it?"

"It looks as if he was paying himself an advisory fee of half a percent on all pension fund investments with the bank over the last five years. Just look at the list."

"Is that allowed?"

"Absolutely not, but he has camouflaged it to look like legitimate expenses relating to policy management."

"I don't think I understand," Isabella frowned.

"Neither do I," admitted Michael, "but only an expert looking specifically for fraudulent rake-offs would discover the scam."

"You mean an expert like Umbretti?" Isabella suggested.

"That's what I was thinking. He was called in by the bank's chief executive to investigate suspected irregularities, so I learned from Katherine Martini."

"Then surely if Umbretti found out the truth, he would have been the victim instead of my husband?"

"At first glance, that would be my conclusion, too," Michael said, "but if you look at these sets of figures, it's evident that all the money in your husband's various accounts has been transferred to other recipients."

"Whose?"

"Half was redirected into someone's private account, presumably Umbretti's, and the rest went into an account at the *Istituto per le Opere di Religione*!"

"The Vatican Bank."

"Strange, isn't it?" Michael observed. "Your husband must have found out what Umbretti had done, downloaded the file, and confronted him with it. Of course, he couldn't go to the police because of his embezzlement in the first place, so perhaps he was trying to salvage some of his funds by making some sort of deal with Umbretti. Maybe, he even threatened to expose him at the risk of them both going down."

"What are you going to do now?"

"Give this memory stick to Inspector Conti so he can arrest the real culprit so that I can get on with my simple life."

The phone on his desk rang obnoxiously. It startled both of them. Michael pressed the answer button. "Yes?"

"Captain Frost?"

"Yes."

"It's Inspector Conti."

"What can I do for you, inspector?"

"Someone has broken into your boat. Perhaps you should go there and see what was taken."

"I thought your men were guarding it," Michael said when he arrived at the harbour. "Crime scene, remember?"

"Sorry, but it happened. Someone will be reprimanded," the inspector assured him.

Michael ignored the apology. "I hope you'll release the boat and allow me back on it. I can't rely on you people to protect it."

"Sure; there's nothing more to examine."

Michael turned to Isabella. "It seems as if Umbretti has been looking for the memory stick," he whispered. "We'd better be careful from now on. One person has already been killed for it."

* * *

Dr. Milo Umbretti was moping in his hotel room. He had unsuccessfully searched the *Bella Mare* for Rochi's computer evidence against him. Only Rochi could have used the missing flash drive he had stored in the drawer in his cabin. He knew that had the police found the USB flash drive he would have been arrested for Rochi's murder by now. He had not found it on the boat so surmised that either Captain Frost or Rochi's wife had found it. Either way, he had to get it back at any cost.

He had swum out to the boat from the beach, approaching the vessel from the direction of the sea. The police sentry standing on the wharf at the bottom of the companion ladder had not seen him climb on board and disappear into the cabin area. A thorough search of Rochi's cabin revealed nothing. Luckily, nothing had been touched in the captain's cabin and everything was exactly as it was at the time of the murder. If the memory stick that Rochi had threatened him with was still there, he hoped to find it; he had not!

Now, he was pacing the hotel room with grave concern. Sooner or later, whoever possessed the memory stick would find out what was on it and they all would be fucked. What worried him most was his impulsive foolishness in informing Albertini. He should have tried getting it back first before alerting the cardinal. God knows what he might decide to do.

* * *

Michael stared at the mess in his cabin. Drawers had been emptied and anything that could be moved was strewn all over the floor.

"What was he looking for, captain?" Inspector Conti asked.

"How should I know?"

"Don't be ridiculous," the inspector said, raising his eyebrows.

"We searched everywhere ourselves. What have you got that the killer came back for?"

"I'm pleased to hear that I'm not the primary suspect anymore," Michael replied.

"I never said that," the inspector said smoothly. "Please answer my question."

Michael had hidden the memory stick in his apartment and had not yet decided on a course of action. He had already made up his mind to hand it over to Conti but wanted a little time to think things over first. Did the money Rochi deposited in Isabella's account reflect anywhere? He didn't want her to be dragged into the financial enquiry that would result from Umbretti's murder trial. First, he wanted to examine the file again to make sure her money wasn't implicated.

"Find that answer, and you'll have your murderer."

"Don't get sarcastic with me, Mr. Frost," the inspector snarled. "You can have your boat back, captain, but don't think of sailing into the sunset just yet."

* * *

Hendrik Vlok paid for his meal and went outside into the twilight. He patted the gun under his arm to reassure himself that he was ready for the night's work. By a stroke of luck, although he didn't know it at the time, Dr. Umbretti had done him a huge favour. When he arrived at Michael's apartment building, he was relieved to find the flat unoccupied. He was unaware that Frost had been summoned to the boat, so he set about picking the lock. After a few seconds, the latch clicked open and he went inside, making sure to lock the door behind him.

The interior of the apartment was extremely neat, like a home that was hardly used, and it made his search easier—no rummaging through rubbish to find the memory stick. "Don't break in if he's there and don't touch anything. Just find that flash drive, and proceed with your contract," was the essence of the instruction he had been given.

Hendrik Vlok began his search of the apartment at the computer desk. The drawers contained the usual household stationary. He pushed aside the assortment of pens, pencils, and erasers in the top drawer and saw nothing else lying there. The middle drawer contained computer paper, so he went directly to the last one. Not suspecting to what length someone might go to get the memory stick, the captain had not bothered to conceal it very well. He had dropped it into a tray filled with paper clips.

Vlok switched on the computer and inserted the stick. He had no password to get into the program and only wanted to see the name beneath the icon. He checked it against the name written on the piece of paper he withdrew from his pocket and smiled. "Easier than I thought," he said to himself. He switched off the computer and left the apartment as quietly as he'd gained access.

The next phase of the operation would be much more difficult. *You cross the line of no return with murder*, he told himself, but he had done it many times before and regarded the deed as just a job he was very good at. His victims were usually only faces on photographs given to him by clients, so he could dispatch them without emotion. Crimes of passion, on the other hand, were difficult to get away with. Involvement with the victim created a conscience, no matter how slight, and that caused hesitation during the act, and loss of nerve resulted in mistakes. One needed a clear head to succeed and a sense of detachment from the victim that wouldn't arouse any moral sensibilities.

He arrived at the hotel at exactly nine o'clock, just as it was getting dark. At this time of the year, coastal hotels had a high occupancy rate, so there were quite a few people milling about in the foyer. The two desk clerks who were attending to an elderly couple having problems with room service never noticed Vlok as he made his way to the lifts. He walked slowly across the foyer, timing his gait to coincide with the arrival of the first lift. He kept his handkerchief over his nose as if wiping a cold to avoid being later identified on the security cameras. He quickly stepped into the lift and, instead of pressing the sixth floor button, he punched the fifth floor button. It would be safer going the remaining flight via the stairwell. The last thing he wanted was to confront someone who would later remember him exiting the elevator on the floor which was soon to become a crime scene.

* * *

Dr. Umbretti, in his agitated state, suddenly had the urge. He left his suite and walked down the passage to Carla's room.

"What now, Milo?" she asked, showing signs of hostility

when she saw him standing there. She hoped he wasn't horny again and had just come to get something he had left behind after their previous session.

"I need you," he said sheepishly.

"It's going to cost you this time, Milo. I'm not doing it again for nothing."

"Okay, okay; whatever you want."

"I've just done my makeup," she said gruffly. "This time, stick it where it's supposed to go!"

* * *

Hendrik Vlok opened the stairwell door on the sixth floor and peered out. The corridor was deserted and the success of slipping into the room unseen was now in the realm of chance. He very rarely relied on luck, but sometimes there was no other choice. He was acutely aware that someone could suddenly come out of any of the seven rooms on that floor. There was no need hesitating any longer; perfect timing was out of his control. He proceeded down the corridor and stopped in front of the door marked Suite 613. After quickly looking around to make sure he was still alone, he inserted his skeleton key into the lock, and after a few turns of the instrument, heard the latch click open.

He opened the door and slipped inside like a slither of paper. Leaning with his back against the now closed door, he listened for any sound that might reveal the presence of the occupant. There was none. He edged into the hallway and peered into the living room. It was empty. He proceeded down the passage to the bedroom. The carpet was thick and soft and his footsteps made no noise. The room was dark, but there was enough light filtering through the lace curtains from the street below to allow him to see that the bed was still made. He looked around and saw an easy chair in the corner of the room opposite the window. It was the darkest section of the room and would be a good place to wait for the occupant's return. Then he noticed a door leading out onto the veranda. He opened it and stepped out of the air conditioned room into the warm night air. Perfect. From out there, he could watch anyone moving about in the bedroom and pounce at the most opportune moment.

He checked to see if the silencer was properly attached to

The Papal Secret

the barrel of his gun and settled down on a metal chair to wait the arrival of his victim.

* * *

Dr. Milo Umbretti reached the destination of his pleasure in a convulsive shiver. At first, Carla thought his heart had given in and she would be saddled with the inconvenience of a dead body in her room. Then she saw a broad grin appear on his face and couldn't help feeling a little disappointed that the effort she had put into her sexual performance had not proved lethal. She never wanted to go through this ritual again with this insignificant pervert. She couldn't wait to get back to Milan again where she could choose her own sexual clients.

"Thank you, Carla; that was lovely," he said, pulling up his underpants. "Sorry about the makeup."

"Fuck off, Milo. I'm going down to the bar—alone," she told him, pushing him out of the room while he was still buttoning up his shirt.

Milo Umbretti stumbled down the corridor toward his room a happy and well satisfied man. Tomorrow, he would show Carla proof of his wealth and ask her to marry him. He had diverted a sizable portion of Rochi's money into his own account and he was sure that the staggering amount would impress Carla into accepting his marriage proposal. He would sleep soundly tonight.

He entered his suite noisily. The scent of Carla clung heavily to his body and he was tempted to go to bed without showering so that he would be reminded of her until sleep took away the happy memory. But Umbretti had a fetish for his own cleanliness, probably the primary reason why he abused hers, so he went straight into the bathroom and switched on the hot water tap. While he was waiting for the water to heat up, he stepped out onto the veranda to get some fresh air.

That was when it hit him. At first he didn't know where the blow came from. He staggered back, half stunned, against the wall. When his eyes cleared, he saw a man standing in front of him with a gun levelled at his chest.

"What do you want?" he stammered.

"Nothing personal, Dr. Umbretti," Vlok said, without emotion. "Will you please step back inside?" The last thing he wanted was for some observer looking out the window of a nearby apartment building see him kill Umbretti. "You fucked up," he continued. "You shouldn't have left this thing lying around after you killed Rochi." He held up the memory stick he had retrieved from Frost's apartment. "The information could send you away for life, not to mention the trail of money, which you were supposed to conceal, leading all the way to the Vatican. Very careless of you. The chief is not at all happy."

"I can explain," Umbretti babbled frantically.

"It's too late for excuses," hissed Vlok. "The information on this stick could ruin a lot of important people." Vlok was blessed with a fearless disposition, but it was a trait that could also be compromised by complacency. He expected this assassination to be easy and was not ready for Umbretti's uncharacteristic response.

As Umbretti staggered back into the room, his hand brushed against a marble figurine standing on a pedestal next to the open curtain. He was not street wise, but his instinctive desire for survival made him react quickly. His hand tightened around the head of the statue and, as it was partially hidden by the curtain, Vlok didn't see what was coming.

Umbretti lashed out with a backhand stroke and connected a heavy blow against Vlok's right temple. It was not severe enough to drop him, but the blow forced him backward against the parapet. Off balance, he squeezed off a shot, which went straight into the ceiling above Umbretti's head.

Before Vlok could back away from the railing, Umbretti charged at him, shoving him firmly in the chest. Vlok reeled backward against the railing and his momentum caused him to lose balance. He groped furiously for support, but the weight of his muscular body carried him over the edge. Moments later, the body of Hendrik Vlok landed on the sidewalk outside the entrance of the hotel six floors below, accompanied by several screams from people walking past.

Umbretti had one saving grace; he was not prone to panic. He had the analytical mind of his profession which saved him from rushing around aimlessly and making mistakes. He stood at the veranda door wondering what to do next. First, he resisted the impulse to look over the parapet to see where his assailant had landed, in case anyone was looking up and saw him. Not one for making the same mistake twice, he looked around to see where the memory stick had fallen as his assailant groped for a handhold before he fell. He found it lying against the wall in the far corner of the veranda. He retrieved it and tucked it safely in his pocket. If he returned it to the chief, he wouldn't be punished. Next, he realized he had

The Papal Secret

to get out of the suite as fast as possible and go somewhere to establish an alibi. He was certain the police would search every room, including his—no, especially his—to find proof of his involvement. He tidied up as best as possible, remembering to switch off the tap in the shower, and went down to the basement garage by way of the stairwell.

He found a side exit and went into the street. He could hear a commotion of frantic voices coming from around the corner, so he hurried off in the opposite direction. He decided to go to the nearest coffee bar where witnesses, when asked, would corroborate his story that he was having coffee at the Bistro on the Bay when the incident at the hotel occurred. Of course, he'd have to rely on the human trait that people were not always sure, when questioned, of the exact time of the thing they were trying to recall.

He found a table near the window and sat down unobtrusively, hoping that no one had seen him arrive. He heard police sirens in the distance and decided it was time to be noticed. He beckoned to a waitress standing at the counter.

"I think I'm ready to order now," he said, as if he'd been deliberating for some time over what he wanted to have. "I'd like a café latte and a toasted cheese sandwich, and it must be with mozzarella." He pointed to the window. "What's going on out there?"

"Probably another break-in," the young waitress said. "It's happening all too often these days. You work hard all day long, then some fucking creep takes all your money from you." She held a hand to her mouth when she realised what she had said. "Sorry, sir, but the increase in crime is starting to piss me off!"

"I totally agree with you, miss . . ." he leaned forward to read her name tag, "Gabriella. My name is Milo."

"I'll get your order now, sir . . . er . . . Milo."

* * *

When Inspector Alberto Conti arrived at the hotel, Sergeant Bruno was already there. "What do we have here, sergeant?" he asked.

"Brains splattered all over the sidewalk, sir."

"For God's sake, Bruno, don't be so crude!"

"Take a look yourself, sir," he said, lifting the cover off the body.

Stan Miller

Inspector Conti took an audible intake of breath and turned his head.

"Told you," said Bruno.

"Yes, yes; have you established identification?"

"His driver's licence shows him to be a Mr. Hendrik Vlok."

"A Dutchman?"

"Looks like it, sir."

"Suicide?"

"I doubt it, sir. The body landed too close to the side of the building. A jumper would have landed in the middle of the road."

"Since when are you such a bloody expert?" Conti asked irritably.

"Elementary, inspector," smiled Bruno when Conti wasn't looking at him.

"Well, see how simple it is finding out whether he fell accidentally or was pushed."

"Yes, sir."

"Then you'd better find which room the deceased was in," Conti said gruffly.

"Already done that, sir. The manager says he's not a hotel resident."

Inspector Conti should have been pleased with his subordinate's initiative, but he was in a foul mood. He had been summoned to the scene at an inopportune moment. He had been in the middle of a very rare sexual encounter with his wife when he received the call. 'God only knows when she'll be in the mood again,' moaned Conti to himself. Not that she was such a great lay; whenever she got the urge, which wasn't that often, thought Conti sourly, she performed her conjugal obligation without passion. He remembered when they were first married how experimental she was in bed— enjoyed every position in the book. Now, thirty-two years later, she bordered on frigidity.

He thought how true was the old adage that if you put a bean in a bottle every time you made love during the first two years of marriage and then took one out every time thereafter, the bottle would never empty!

To compound his bad mood, Sergeant Bruno was displaying a smug attitude. "Have you discovered which room he fell from, sergeant?" he asked at last, turning his thoughts back to the current situation.

"Not yet, sir," said Sergeant Bruno, looking up, "but I'll start with the rooms in line with the trajectory of the fall."

"Next you'll want my job," mumbled Conti. "Well, don't just stand there, get on with it!" Turning to the forensic photographer, he barked. "Haven't you got enough pictures already?"

"Just a couple more, inspector," said the photographer. He found this job distasteful and was thankful he was only a part-time police reservist called out very rarely to take this kind of picture. He didn't have the stomach for it and he already had the bitter taste of bile rising into his mouth. He ran a camera shop on the main street and enjoyed developing photos of scenic beauty or lovely women, especially the half-naked ones. The way the tourists walked around in public these days was disgraceful, although, he confessed to himself, he enjoyed the voyeuristic opportunities presented to his camera lens. "Okay, inspector; all yours."

The medical examiner who had been hovering over the body like an African vulture stooped down to have a look. "He has a bruise on the side of his head," he told Conti.

"I'm not surprised. He just fell six or seven fucking floors!" replied Conti, his bad mood lingering.

"Yes, but he landed on the other side of his face."

"I want a full autopsy report by morning," Conti ordered. "We may be dealing with murder." He entered the hotel in time to see Sergeant Bruno emerging from the elevator. "What did you find, sergeant?"

"The rooms on the first two floors are unoccupied," replied Bruno, consulting his little notebook. "There's a priest on the third and an elderly woman on the fourth, too frail to even throw a cat over the balcony."

"Leave out the embellishments," Conti interrupted. "Go on."

"The guy on the fifth floor has been in the bar all evening—barman confirms it. The occupant of the room on the sixth will interest you."

"Who is it?"

"Dr. Milo Umbretti," Sergeant Bruno announced triumphantly, "one of the 'boat murder' suspects."

"Bring him to me."

"He's not in his room, sir."

"Then find him. Who's on the seventh?"

"A mother and her baby. She heard nothing, not even Vlok's

scream. Her child has been crying all night; croup, or something, she says."

"Detain Umbretti as soon as he returns. I'll be looking around in his room." In all his experience as a detective, he didn't believe in coincidences. There were usually reasons explaining similarities and a little bit of digging might well connect them. He took the lift to the sixth floor and entered Umbretti's suite with the key given to him by the concierge. Without a search warrant, he was careful not to touch anything. He could always come back later with one if he found anything incriminating.

The room was exceptionally tidy—no clothing lying about. At first he feared that Umbretti had run away, but his beloved laptop was standing on the desk. Conti was convinced that he would never have left town without it. He went out onto the veranda. The night was hot and humid and he ran his index finger under the collar of his shirt and wiped away a trickle of perspiration. Then he looked over the edge. He saw the covered body of the victim being loaded into the ambulance and shivers of vertigo overwhelmed him. What a horrible death. He moved away from the parapet. Then something caught his eye—a scratch on the top of the railing. He took a closer look and saw that the mark was freshly made; there were no signs of rust or discolouration where the black paint had been scratched off. He made a note to check with the pathologist if he found any black paint marks on the victim's belt or watch strap. If he could establish without doubt that this was the room the victim had fallen from, then he would nab Umbretti for this murder. He nearly knocked over the figurine on the coffee table as he re-entered the room and put out a hand to steady it.

He looked at the time: eleven fifteen. If Umbretti didn't return to the hotel by midnight, then he'd probably absconded—a sure sign of guilt. His mobile phone suddenly rang in his pocket.

"Inspector?" It was Bruno's voice. "Umbretti's back."

* * *

When Milo Umbretti got back to the hotel, he used the main entrance this time. There was no need to sneak around because he had already established his alibi. He was relieved to see that the body had been removed. A few inquisitive onlookers were still milling around dissecting and discussing the drama that had occurred in their little seaside town.

He looked around the foyer hoping that Inspector Conti wasn't there, and when he didn't see him, he strolled into the bar looking for Carla. He saw her sitting alone at the end of the bar counter. Her hair looked as if it needed combing, with her bangs partly covering her eyes. She sat slouched on the stool, and he noticed the strap of her sleeveless dress hanging halfway down her arm and revealing enough bosom to keep the bartender attentive to her needs. There was a half-empty whiskey bottle standing on the counter in front of her, which the barman was busy topping up. When she saw Umbretti approaching, she pushed her glass toward the bartender. "Make it a double."

"Are you drunk?" Umbretti asked, sitting on the stool next to her.

"Don't be silly," she squinted at him. "I'm still upright, aren't I?"

"Is there somewhere we can talk in private?"

"Here's fine," she stammered. "Nobody's sober enough to worry about what you're saying." She looked at the bartender. "Luigi, give us some space."

The barman moved away to speak to some other guest.

"A lot of shit has happened here tonight," she said.

"Yes, I heard."

"Where were you?"

"At the Bistro on the Bay having dinner. You heard of it?"

"Yeah; lucky you," she said, reaching for the glass.

She was clearly drunk, which worried him. He wanted her to fully understand what he was about to tell her. It would do no good if she woke up in the morning remembering nothing. "I want you to listen carefully to what I'm saying," he began. "You sure you're sober? It can't wait until morning."

"I'm fine, Milo; get on with it."

"My life is in danger," he said softly, looking around the room as if an assassin was lurking nearby.

"Don't tell me you had something to do with that poor man's death?" The glazed look in her eyes cleared as she waited expectantly for his confession.

"Not exactly," he said.

"What the fuck does that mean?" She followed the question by draining what was left in her glass. She tried signalling for a refill but he grabbed her hand.

"Enough of the stuff, Carla, I want you to concentrate." He pushed a thick envelope across the counter. "Open it."

With rubbery fingers, she struggled to tear it open. She gasped when she saw the contents. "Oh my God!" she cried out in surprise as she withdrew a wad of five hundred Euro notes and fanned them with her thumb. "There's a lot of money here, Milo. Where did you get it?"

"Never mind; they're for you," he said, covering her hands. No point in advertising to the room that she had been given a wad of cash.

"For me? Why?"

He leaned toward her and lowered his voice into a conspiratorial tone. "You're the best thing that's ever happened to me," he began. "Women never showed any interest in me before, until I met you."

"Milo, don't . . ."

"I know Rochi paid you to seduce me, but you did it with such conviction, like you really cared for me. Whether it was sincere or not doesn't matter; you made me feel good."

"I'm sorry, Milo." For once she spoke genuinely to him.

"Don't be. I am so grateful to you. I may be sad that it has come to an end, but I'm happy it happened and I want to reward you."

"You're scaring me, Milo," she said soberly. "You speak as if you're about to die."

"That man who fell came to kill me, only I pushed him first."

"That's self defence," Carla said excitedly. "If you tell the police what happened, you'll be okay."

"I can't," he said. "The police will want to know why and I dare not tell them."

You must, Milo. You can't fuck with the police. They'll eventually find out and lock you up forever."

"No, I can't." Umbretti looked around to see if anyone was in earshot. "I'm involved with some powerful and dangerous people. I have something they want." He opened his palm and showed her the memory stick.

"Give it to them and they'll leave you alone."

"The problem is what this contains is also inside my head. The information will damn a lot of important people. I'm a dangerous witness to have around."

"Are you involved with the Mafia?" She looked shocked.

"I wouldn't be surprised if this pious group of thugs had some sort of affiliation with them."

"What are you going to do?"

"I have to leave tonight, go somewhere out of their reach. The man who died tonight may have an accomplice waiting to finish the job."

He hesitated before deciding to tell her the whole story. "I have no family and you are my only friend. If anything should happen to me, I have a lot of money in a Swiss bank that will go to waste. I want you to have it. In the memory stick are two files. The one is the reason they're trying to kill me. The other is a personal file containing details of my secret bank account. On my death, my lawyer has been instructed to post a letter to you containing a photograph. There are seven well known personalities in the picture. If you take the numerical values of the first letter of each of their family names as they appear in the photo, you will have the pin number of my account. It will allow you to transfer the money out of my account into your own. Once you have successfully completed the transaction and the money is safely in your bank account, I want you to delete my file and give the memory stick to Captain Frost. He'll figure out what to do with it."

Carla sat in silence trying to comprehend what she had just heard. "I can't believe what you're telling me," she finally said. "I'm scared I'll wake up in the morning and think this story is a figment of my imagination. Maybe I have had too much to drink."

"The memory stick will prove that it was not." He pressed it into her hand. "Keep it safe and don't tell anyone. They'll come after you if they know you have it. Be careful, until you pass it on to Frost."

"What about the access password?" she asked, regaining her composure. "This thing is useless without one."

"I scratched the access code inside the cupboard door of our cabin on the yacht. I can't give it to you offhand, I'm sorry. If anything happens to me you'll have to find a way to get back onto Frost's boat."

"Where will I be able to reach you?"

"If I get through all of this, I'll contact you." Umbretti hesitated before adding. "If you then decide to join me, great; if not, I'll give you enough money so that you can find another profession. You shouldn't have to give yourself to men you don't care for." He stood up. "I must go."

"Be careful, Milo." She kissed him on the lips.

Umbretti rushed out. He figured he had a few minutes to pack his bag and get out of town quickly. As he was crossing the foyer, he bumped into Inspector Conti.

"Just the person I was looking for," the inspector said. "May I have a word with you, Dr. Umbretti?"

Umbretti looked hurriedly at his watch and nodded.

"Going anywhere?"

"To bed, inspector. I'm really exhausted."

They sat down together on a settee against the wall. "You heard about the tragic fall of one of the guests?" the inspector asked.

"Yes, a few moments ago. I just got back. Terrible business."

"Where were you this evening?"

"Having dinner at the Bistro on the Bay. Do you know it?"

"Of course I know it," Conti replied. "I've lived here all my life. Did you dine alone?"

"Afraid so."

"What time did you leave the hotel?"

"I'd say about eight-thirty."

"A man plunged to his death twenty minutes later."

"Yes, I heard the police sirens," Umbretti said, establishing his alibi. "I even asked the waitress if she knew what was happening. What was her name . . . oh yes, Gabrielle."

"What did she tell you?"

"She supposed it was another robbery."

"I see."

"You can ask her yourself," Umbretti said confidently. "I'm sure she'll remember me."

"How convenient for you," Conti muttered.

"You don't think I had anything to do with the man's death, do you?" Umbretti asked, feigning indignation. "Now, if you'll excuse me, inspector, I need my rest." He rose, and added. "I'll be happy to answer any more questions in the morning, not that I think I can be of any further assistance."

"Tomorrow, then," Conti said. He watched Umbretti walk toward the elevators. *Smug little bastard*, he thought.

* * *

Inspector Conti had barely put his head on the pillow when the phone rang. He picked it up quickly so that it wouldn't disturb his wife lying next to him.

"Yes?" he whispered.

"Alberto," the medical examiner's voice spoke into his ear. "I think you'd better get over here right away. I found several interesting things."

"What time is it?"

"Five thirty."

"You mean I've been asleep for four hours? God, it feels like four minutes. I'll be there shortly." The second interruption in one night, he thought. "At least this time I don't have to get dressed with a hard-on," he mumbled.

Santa Margherita was a small town and it did not take long to drive the short distance to the police station. He parked in his designated bay and went inside. A junior constable shoved a cup of hot coffee into his hand as he entered his office.

"Thanks, Gina," he said, as he accepted the drink gratefully. "They got you up early, too, did they?"

"No, inspector," Gina replied. "I worked night shift; going off duty in a few minutes." She ran a hand through her dishevelled black hair.

Conti saw that the top two buttons of her tunic were undone and wondered how she had spent the latter part of her shift. He took a long sip of coffee and smiled at her. "A policeman's penicillin," he said, holding up the cup. She was a pretty girl in her late twenties and if he were ten years younger, he would have tried to find out if her ambition for promotion was fuelled by promiscuous intent. He was sure his wife wouldn't care if he slept with another woman if it kept him from bothering her too often. He swallowed another mouthful of hot coffee and burned his throat. "Serves me right for such lewd thoughts," he rebuked himself.

He entered the pathologist's lab and found the medical examiner standing over a body lying on a stone slab. The doctor drew back the sheet and pointed to some scratches at the base of the corpse's spine.

"Can you see these marks here?" Dr. Mido asked.

"Yes," Conti said, looking as carefully as he could without getting too close to the body. He disliked this part of his job. It was one thing finding a dead person with a bullet hole in his chest, but a body mutilated by a pathologist's scalpel repulsed him.

"Well, I matched their position with the tears on his clothing, and guess what?"

"You found the same marks on his belt."

"Precisely. The victim's belt is studded all along its length and I found abrasions on the studs corresponding to the position of the scratches on the body."

"That proves nothing," Conti said, trying to mask his disappointment.

"Yes, but look at the traces of black paint flakes on the studs. They match the samples you took from the railing of the balcony he allegedly fell from. That confirms he fell from Dr. Umbretti's room and the fact that he toppled backward over the ledge." Dr. Mido beamed. "Not conducive to suicide, is it?"

"It's still not certain if he fell by accident or was pushed." Conti stared at the body. "The victim was very well muscled and Umbretti is too weak to overpower such a strong man. How could someone half this man's weight lure him onto a balcony and push him off it?"

"Maybe it was supposed to be the other way round," the doctor posited.

"That sounds more likely, but how the hell my suspect achieved such a Herculean feat is beyond me."

"It's evident from the bruising on the side of the victim's head that he received a heavy blow from some blunt object. Perhaps that's when he lost his balance and fell."

"The question we must ask ourselves is why this man would want to kill Dr. Umbretti," Conti said. "First, I must check out the dead man's background to find out where he comes from and whom he works for before I can determine the reason behind the killing."

"He was wearing a shoulder holster," said the medical examiner, gesturing to the body.

"No weapon was found at the scene or on the veranda." Conti scratched his head. His mouth still felt like sandpaper, in spite of the coffee, and his head ached from lack of sleep. "You'd expect metal fragments to be scattered all over the street if he had fallen while holding the gun."

"Strange," Dr. Mido said. "If the killing was an act of self defence, why did your suspect remove the weapon? Handing it over to the police would have supported a claim of self defence; he would have been cleared of a murder charge."

"There must be a damn good reason he doesn't want to get involved and I intend to find out what it is."

Chapter 18

The Vatican – August

Cardinal Vittorio Albertini looked up at the sky. It seemed strange that there were no birds flying above the garden as they usually did at this time of the morning. It was a perfectly warm, cloudless day and he began to wonder if the feathered creatures could sense the cantankerous mood he was in and gone elsewhere to feed. He wasn't even sure why he was feeling so despondent but he had a premonition that the day would not be a good one.

It was not usual for one of the senior cardinals to tend to the garden, but Albertini thought that if he watered the plants it might relax him enough to change his mood. He watched the spray of water falling delicately on the bushes and became aware of the delicious fragrance emanating all around him. There was a competent team of horticulturists who kept the Vatican gardens in pristine condition, but he felt a little more water wouldn't do the plants any harm, especially if the process soothed him back to tranquillity.

He was still convinced that some strange occurrence had affected the countenance of the pope, and he hated not being privy to the secret. Added to this was the missing flash drive, which threatened to expose his misuse of illegal funds for private gain if it fell into the wrong hands. Not that he was a materialistic man who took delight in secular possessions; on the contrary, he was using the money in a campaign to ensure that he became the next pope. He was younger than Pietro Bandini, so the opportunity would present itself eventually. He represented a group of bishops who were in favour of him succeeding Bandini when the time came, and if he could hasten that time by denouncing Bandini as dishonest, all the better. But he needed proof that the pope was not fit to hold office. Unlike his own readiness for action, he knew his supporters would never entertain any unethical practice to have the present incumbent removed; he could count on their vote but not their participation in anything untoward.

Fabio Mento arrived in the garden in a fanfare of noise; his military boots pounded the stone pathway as he made his way to where Albertini was waiting. Albertini looked down at the gendarme's footwear that had disturbed the morning's solace and shook his head.

"Perhaps you should ignore the signs in future and walk on the grass," Albertini scolded him. "It certainly would be preferable to flatten a few blades of grass than to make me suffer such a noise."

"Sorry, Your Eminence," Mento apologised. "They're Swiss Guard issue."

"What was so important that you couldn't tell me over the phone?"

"Some bad news, I'm afraid."

"Isn't it always?" Albertini waited for Mento to explain. "For God's sake, what is it?"

"Umbretti got away."

"Did your operative recover the stick?"

"No, Umbretti killed him." Mento hunched his shoulders, waiting for the tirade to explode around him.

"What?" Albertini shouted in a voice that would have carried into the papal apartments had the windows been open. "That's not possible! Did you hire a dwarf to take care of things?"

"We'll track Umbretti down. I assure you he won't get far."

"You assured me the matter would be dealt with promptly. Am I to be both cleric and field agent from now on?"

"No, of course not," Mento replied. "In any operation there's always a one percent possibility of failure."

"Am I to be impressed that you achieved it?"

Mento remained silent for a while. "It won't happen again," he finally dared to say.

"Has the lawyer been to see the pope again?" Albertini had many things on his mind.

"Only once since His Holiness's return from Israel."

"Find out what he's up to. An outsider should not have access to the pontiff's ear as often as he does. I want to know what all the secrecy is between Bandini, Pollini, and the lawyer. Something is rotten in this strange triad and I intend to purge it."

Chapter 19

Santa Margherita – August

It was a difficult walk back to Michael's apartment from the shops where Isabella had spent the morning browsing, and the incline was steep, so she decided to take the bus. She had purchased a new pair of shoes and clutched the parcel lovingly as she waited for the bus to arrive.

When it stopped for her, she climbed on, taking little notice of the middle-aged man who clambered on behind her. He slid into the seat across the aisle from her, glancing often in her direction. She was not aware of the interest he seemed to be taking in her until she raised her legs to put on the new shoes and noticed him staring at her. She gave him an annoyed look and smoothed down her skirt. She placed her old shoes in the carrying packet and looked out the window.

The town's coastal slope, raising its suburban hills a hundred metres or so above the sea, was entwined with a system of crooked streets that meandered in conjunction with the contours of the landscape. Several narrow streets lined with brick houses met the main road cautiously, as if the busy thoroughfare intruded into its sublime purpose of allowing people to mingle with each other outside their homes in relative safety. The town had a feminine feel to it, with its delicate décor of rustic houses and peasant women hanging up washing in their small gardens. A Milanese woman, Isabella was impressed by the apparent tranquillity of her surroundings and understood why Michael had given up the excitement of London for this quaint coastal town.

She was so engrossed in admiring the scenery that she almost missed her stop. She apologised to the driver as she disembarked and went straight into the apartment block. Glancing at her watch, she was pleased to see that she was ten minutes early for her rendezvous with Michael.

She felt a little perturbed when the man on the bus followed her into the building. He stood next to her while they waited for the elevator door to open. He gave her a brief smile, which appeared more wicked than endearing. His teeth were stained yellow from too many cigarettes and he seemed out of place in such a posh residential suburb.

She watched him suspiciously out of the corner of her eye as the elevator door closed and left the two of them alone in the confined space. What worried her even more was that he never selected the floor he wanted. He was standing slightly behind her and she became suddenly aware of the pungent smell of medication and turned to see what he was doing. Before she had time to react, the stranger grabbed her around the neck and pressed a white cloth to her mouth. The light began to cloud around her and her head felt stuffed and heavy. Her deadened nerves rushed toward unconsciousness but before oblivion overtook her, she recognised the smell of ether. It was strange that her last thought was that Michael would never see the new shoes she was wearing. She let go of the packet and passed out.

* * *

Michael grew increasingly worried with each minute that passed. Isabella was already half an hour late and she was not answering her cell phone. He tried calling the hotel in the event she had returned for something but was told that no one had seen her since she had checked out the day before. He ran down the stairs into the foyer, not wanting to waste precious time waiting for the elevator.

The security guard was at his desk just inside the entrance of the building. He was reading a magazine and looked up quizzically at Michael's hasty arrival. "Anything wrong, Mr. Frost?" he asked.

"Have you seen Mrs. Rochi?" Michael asked frantically.

"Yes, she went upstairs about forty minutes ago."

"Are you sure?"

"I haven't left this desk for over an hour," the guard said. "She came in and hasn't come out."

"Well, she's missing."

"Maybe she went somewhere with the man she came in with."

"What man?"

"Unsavoury-looking character. I wouldn't have let him in if

he wasn't with her."

"You sure they were together?" Michael asked.

The guard cleared his throat. This was not going well. He'd be held accountable if anything bad happened on his watch. He'd never find another job like this one once his reputation was tarnished. "They came in together; that's all I know," he said lamely.

"Why didn't you challenge him?"

"It didn't seem to bother the lady; him being there, I mean."

Michael stared at him coldly. "Can you describe the man?"

"Brown hair, dark eyes, relatively tall, firm build." The guard shrugged. He lifted his eyes to the ceiling as if an image of the intruder was scrawled on it. "Oh, yes," he remembered. "He had a large tattoo on his right forearm; an anchor with a mermaid sitting on it."

"That might help. Thanks." Michael had a phone call to make and took the elevator this time. As he stepped into the lift, he noticed a packet lying on the floor. He stooped to retrieve it and looked inside. He pulled out the pair of shoes and recognised them as the ones Isabella had put on before she left to go shopping. He had remarked about the Perspex heels being flimsy and treacherous.

"Don't be silly," she had said. "They don't design shit at these prices."

Half an hour later, Michael barged into Inspector Conti's office without knocking. "Isabella Rochi is missing," he announced.

"I thought she was staying with you." It was a small town and very little remained a secret. "How long has she been gone?"

"Over an hour."

Conti stood up. "Look, Mr. Frost, I'm a busy man. If she's not back in twenty-four hours, I'll open a missing person's docket."

"And I should sit around having tea until then?"

Conti shook his head. "She'll turn up; probably engrossed with shopping on the strip."

"Don't patronize me, inspector. She's not that irresponsible."

"Did you know that Dr. Umbretti is also missing?"

"What are you implying?"

"Nothing, really, but maybe Mrs. Rochi went off with him?"

He waited to see Michael's reaction.

"Don't be ridiculous!"

"Don't you think it strange that one of your passengers was murdered on your yacht, a stranger falls to his death from the room of another one of your passengers, and now two more have disappeared? You seem to be the fulcrum in all of this, captain. Perhaps I should arrest you now and throw away the key."

"Something strange is certainly going on," Michael admitted, "but it has nothing to do with me. Why don't you leave the comfort zone of your office and go find out what it is?"

"Are you telling me how to do my job?"

"Somebody has to."

Inspector Conti smiled. "Okay, okay; let's stop this mudslinging. We're on the same side, Mr. Frost. Can you describe this man she was with?"

"She wasn't with him," Michael corrected the detective. "Average sort of guy in his mid-forties. He had a tattoo of an anchor with a mermaid on his arm. That should help."

Conti typed the information into the computer and waited. Eventually, he looked up at Michael and shrugged. "There's nobody on record with a tattoo like that. For all you know, he may have nothing to do with Mrs. Rochi's disappearance. I'll put out an alert but I can't spare any of my men to go and search for her; not until tomorrow when it's official."

* * *

Isabella became conscious before opening her eyes. She waited, motionless, while feeling returned throughout her body. When she opened her eyes, she looked around at her strange surroundings. It was a small room with closed drapes shutting out any outside light. A small table lamp next to the bed partially illuminated the room.

She sat up with some effort, half expecting Michael to be lying next to her, but she was alone in the room. Then she remembered, and recalled the vision of that horrible man in the lift. She stood up unsteadily and looked into the mirror above the built-in dressing table. Her hair was a mess and her dress was creased. She did her best to restore some dignity to her appearance and nearly lost her balance when the room began to sway. She sat down quickly, but the motion persisted—

the room seemed to be moving. It suddenly dawned on her that she was on a boat. She rushed to the window and peered through the curtain. It was dark outside and she saw only blackness beyond the deck railing.

She tried the door and was surprised to find that it wasn't locked. She supposed her abductors knew she could not escape while at sea and didn't bother confining her to her cabin. She stepped outside and made her way to the bridge. The vessel was similar to Michael's boat, and for an instant she hoped that she would see him standing at the helm and realise that this was nothing more than a bad dream.

The man she saw standing in the wheelhouse was not Michael.

"You're awake at last," the man said. "I thought we'd killed you with an overdose of sedative."

"Who the hell are you and what am I doing here?" Isabella asked sternly, putting her hands on her hips in a show of defiance.

"You're on a little pleasure cruise," he answered sarcastically. "Until your boyfriend gives us what we want."

"Which is?"

"Don't worry your pretty little head about it. You're merely a pawn in all of this."

"Kidnapping is not a game of chess; it's a fucking criminal offence!" Isabella said firmly.

"Such foul language," he sneered. "I thought we'd captured a lady, not a slut. Perhaps we'll indulge in it while we wait."

She was about to tell him where he could stick it when she thought it advisable not to provoke him any further. "I'm hungry," she said.

"No problem," he told her. "The galley is well stocked. Go help yourself." As Isabella turned to go, he called after her. "I'm not alone on board and there are no lifeboats, so don't try anything stupid."

The first thing she looked for when she reached the galley was the cutlery; a knife might be useful at some stage if her life was threatened. All she found was a drawer of plastic knives and forks.

"You won't find any sharp knives here, if it's a weapon you're looking for," a woman's voice said from behind her.

Isabella wheeled around to see a middle-aged woman leaning against the bulkhead. Her blonde hair was thick and matted and looked as if it had not been combed in days. She wore no makeup and, although her face might have been attractive once, it had aged through neglect. Her figure, however, was slender and athletic beneath the sloppy grey tracksuit she was wearing. She gave the impression of a woman who didn't care much about her appearance.

"Who are you?" Isabella stared at her.

"Your hostess, my dear," the woman replied sarcastically. "You may call me Susan if you like but, of course, that's not my real name."

"You could get life imprisonment as an accomplice to kidnapping."

"You're not a prisoner here, Isabella," Susan said. "You are free to leave anytime you wish."

"In the middle of the ocean?"

"Ah, well," Susan sighed, "timing is everything, isn't it? Would you care for sausages and eggs?"

"Yes, please, I'm famished. How long have I been here?"

"Carlos brought you in this morning."

"Carlos?"

"Yes, your chaperone."

"You mean my abductor?"

"Call him what you will," Susan said, cracking open some eggs. "He's the hired help."

"Like Capone's trigger man?" Isabella challenged.

Susan smiled. "Make the best of it while you're here. Once we get what we want, you'll be free to go."

"Will I?"

Susan didn't answer. "Do you prefer them flipped?"

"That will be fine." She wolfed down the food and took a long drink of water from the plastic mug shoved in front of her by her captor. She dabbed her lips with a napkin and looked at Susan. "You wouldn't have some lipstick here, would you?"

Susan looked at her vacantly.

* * *

Michael didn't wait for the clock on the wall in Inspector Conti's office to pronounce the investigation on Isabella's disappearance officially open. He had to do something fast and now to find her. A good starting point was the harbour. A

The Papal Secret

man sporting a tattoo of an anchor and mermaid was probably a sailor. He went directly there from the police station.

He found a group of fisherman sitting at the end of the pier drinking hot coffee out of thermos flasks. He approached them. "Do any of you know a man with an anchor and mermaid tattooed on his arm?" he asked.

The fishermen looked at each other blankly. "Can't say we do," one of them said.

"Are there any foreign vessels in port?"

"Yeah, that one." The eldest among them jerked a bony finger in the direction of a yacht moored alongside the pier opposite to where they were sitting. The five men started jabbering to each other simultaneously and Michael couldn't understand a single word they were saying. Eventually, the old man said. "Franco here says that a fifty-footer docked yesterday and left in a hurry a few hours later."

"Did you get the name?"

"Nah! Check with the Port Authority."

Michael thanked them and went to the red brick building at the beginning of the long earthen jetty. He didn't bother knocking on the door before entering, as this was his home port and the harbour master was a friend.

"Mico," Aldo greeted Michael affectionately. "I see the police have released your boat." He had never used Michael's full name and persisted using the nickname he had given him when they had first met. "I'm glad you're off the hook."

"Like most of the fish in these waters."

"Yes," the harbour master laughed. "That's why those idiots are sitting there drinking coffee all day. I saw you talking to them, amico."

"Yes, I wanted to know the name of the boat that was docked here for a short while yesterday afternoon."

"I have it somewhere here," he said, shuffling the mess of papers scattered all over his desk. "The bastards left without paying their port fees. Ah, here it is. A yacht called the *Mermaid*. She was flying the identification flag of a mermaid sitting on an anchor. Should be easy to trace. They don't owe me much but why should they get away with it?"

"Do you know her next port of call?"

"If I did I'd be waiting there for them."

"Thanks, mate." He kissed his friend on the forehead and

rushed out. Coincidence, or not, he had to act on it. He dialled a number on his cell phone as he walked back to his car. "Mario, meet me on the boat in an hour; we're going on a little trip. I'll explain when I see you."

He returned to his apartment to pack a few things, making sure he had enough ammunition for his Smith & Wesson.

Suddenly the phone rang. "Frost speaking," he answered, hoping it was Isabella.

"Listen carefully, Mr. Frost," a man's voice said. "Do as I say and no harm will come to her."

"Who the hell is this? Where's Isabella? Harm one hair on her head and I'll cut your fucking balls out!"

"You have a data memory stick that I want in exchange for the woman," said the voice, ignoring the empty threat. "If you want to see her alive again, make sure I get it."

"How do I know she's okay? Let me speak to her."

"I'll phone back in five minutes."

* * *

Carlos came for Isabella while she was drinking her coffee and scheming how to get Susan on her side. "Come!" he barked, grabbing her by the arm.

"Where are you taking me?" asked Isabella in alarm, trying to jerk her arm away.

"To the radio room."

Isabella followed him willingly. Perhaps she could sneak back later and send out a distress signal.

"I have him back on air," said the captain as they entered the radio room.

Carlos clamped his hand over Isabella's mouth and hissed in her ear. "Just call his name, you hear? Try anything funny and you'll be thrown overboard." He released his hand.

"Michael, is that you?" she called out frantically when she heard his voice. "I'm on . . ."

Carlos clamped his hand over her mouth again cutting out any further speech. "Get the bitch out of here," Carlos barked the order to one of his men.

When she had gone, he uncovered the mouthpiece of the phone and spoke to Michael. "Put the data stick in a white envelope and drop it into the silver dustbin outside the main post office at exactly eight o'clock tomorrow morning. If my courier is detained, you'll never see your girlfriend again. Is that clear, Mr. Frost?"

"How do I know you'll honour your side of the deal?"

"You don't, but what choice do you have?" The phone line went dead.

* * *

Carla based her decision to leave out of fear that her life was in danger. If the assassin Milo had spoken about ever found out that she was the custodian of the information he wanted, he would kill her to get it. She wanted to go back home to Milan where she could disappear among the millions of people there. She would have to find another place to live if they weren't to find her. But the lure of money got the better of her. Before leaving town, she wanted to get the password that Milo had etched into the cupboard door on Michael Frost's boat. Without it, she wouldn't be able to access his personal file to find out where his money was banked.

She left the hotel and took a cab to the harbour. No one took any notice of her as she walked along the pier to where the *Bella Mare* was berthed. She was dressed in jeans and t-shirt, and wore a cap pulled down over her blonde hair, giving her the appearance of another deckhand reporting for duty. She slipped quietly on board and went below.

* * *

Michael felt panic groping about in the pit of his stomach. He had searched everywhere for the data stick, but it was gone. He remembered leaving it in the bottom drawer of his desk. Someone had removed it and it couldn't have been Isabella. Whoever abducted her would have killed her and taken it if she had it. Someone else had stolen it. He needed it in exchange for Isabella. He had to give the caller something. He inserted a blank data stick into his computer and downloaded one of his files containing some coastal charts. He re-named the file *Confidential* and inserted a security password that would keep them busy for an hour or two trying to crack it. He placed it in an envelope and went downstairs to the security guard at the entrance.

"Felici, do me a favour," he said. "On your way to work

tomorrow, drop this envelope in the silver dustbin outside the post office at exactly eight o'clock. Someone will collect it, but don't try following him. These people are dangerous and I have to follow their instructions. I'll explain when I get back."

Isabella had given the briefest of clues where she was being held. He recalled her exact words: "Michael, is that you? I'm on . . ." Was she trying to tell him that she was on a boat? It fitted with his theory.

He first stopped at Coast Guard Command to establish whether a boat had put out to sea the day before. He was told that a vessel called *Mermaid* had left suddenly during the late afternoon and the satellite transmission last showed that she was maintaining her position about fifty nautical miles off the coastline, in international waters. Probably engaged in a fishing expedition, the officer on duty assumed. So far the crew had done nothing illegal and weren't under radar surveillance any longer. He wrote down their last recorded position and handed the piece of paper to Michael.

"Are you trying to muscle in on their catch?" he wanted to know.

"Something like that," replied Michael. "Actually it's worse than that. There's a strong possibility some thugs are holding one of my passengers hostage and I intend to sneak up on them and get her back."

"Don't be stupid, Michael. If it's a kidnapping, I'll send a police launch to apprehend them."

"They're outside our territorial waters. You can't touch them."

"There's always the Navy."

"They'll kill her if anyone approaches their ship."

"Look, Michael, leave it to the experts. They won't go in with guns blazing. They'll know how to handle it."

"Let me do it my way first. If I don't succeed, I'll call in the Marines."

"A bit of advice," the duty officer said. "You'll be able to get as close as three kilometres before their surface radar picks you up. The moment you see them on your screen, log their position, back off, and stay out of range until nightfall. Go the rest of the way in a small craft like a dinghy. If you're lucky, they won't pick you up so low in the water."

Mario was waiting for him on the pier. "What's going on?" he asked. "I thought our next cruise was in two weeks."

"Something's come up," replied Michael, boarding the boat. Mario followed him dutifully. "Isabella has been abducted and I think they're holding her on a yacht somewhere off the coast," he explained. "It seems as if I have something they want in exchange for her."

"Like what?"

"It's a long story," Michael told him. "I found a data stick on the boat after Rochi's murder. I think it's got something to do with that."

"It must contain important information if they're prepared to risk life imprisonment for kidnapping to get it back."

"The trouble is I don't have it."

"Then how are you going to barter for her, skipper?"

"I've bought a little time by giving them the wrong one. We have to rescue her before they find out."

* * *

Carla was in the cabin when she thought she heard voices on deck. If the police found her on board, they might think she was trying to cover up her involvement in Rochi's murder and it would not go well for her, even if she was innocent. At best, it would delay her departure and give the killer time to find her. The urgency to find the password before she was arrested quickened her pace. She knelt down to record the numbers where Milo had told her they would be, but the password was etched into dark wood and she couldn't see the numbers clearly.

"Shit!" she said out loud, "I need a flashlight."

Suddenly she heard footsteps in the passage. For several seconds she stood staring at the door. Carla's pulse quickened as she heard someone pause on the other side of the door. She backed swiftly into the corner and waited to be discovered.

It seemed an age before the footsteps receded, and it took the sound of her own breathing to bring her out of the stupor she was in. It was only when she became aware of a low humming sound and a slight rocking of the boat that she realized the boat was moving.

"Oh fuck!" she cried. "We're under way." Her first thought was to jump overboard and swim ashore before the boat reached the harbour entrance, but she was still obsessed with getting the password. She opened the door of the cabin and peered out. The passageway was deserted, giving her safe access to the galley. She remembered there being a gas stove which Claudia had used to cook their meals, so there had to be matches somewhere, matches she could use in place of the flashlight she'd forgotten. She found them in the drawer next to the stove and was about to return to the cabin when a hand gripped her arm and wheeled her around.

"Carla!"

"Michael! What are you doing here?"

"It's my boat, remember," he said, letting go of her arm. "Why don't we start with what you're doing here?"

"I'm looking for something."

"Oh really? Would you care to explain?"

"It's a long story and I don't want to bore you."

"Try me."

"Well, alright." She had no friends outside Milan and he was probably the only one she had here, so she decided to confide in him. She related her last conversation with Milo and told him the reason why she had returned to the boat.

"You have the data stick?" he asked in surprise.

"Yes. Milo gave it to me for safe keeping. He told me someone was after him."

"Do you know what's on it?"

"No, not really," she said innocently. "He told me that there was information contained in one of the files that someone desperately wants to get his hands on, someone who's prepared to kill for it."

"So he put your life in danger?" Michael lowered his eyebrows and scowled. "Nice guy."

"That's not the reason," she said in defence of Umbretti. "There's also a personal record of some money he has stashed away, which he said I could keep if anything happened to him."

"I may need that data stick as a trade off for Isabella," he said.

"What do you mean?"

"Those people Umbretti is running away from are holding Isabella captive and will only release her in exchange for what you have."

"Copy his file onto your computer for me and you can have the damn thing." She'd be happy to get rid of it; it had already caused enough trouble.

"I've given them the wrong one to buy time, and if I can't rescue her, I may need it to barter for her life." He escorted her onto the bridge, where Mario looked at her unbelievably.

"So this is the stowaway?" he smiled. "We can't turn back now. Can you cook?"

"Of course I can," she said indignantly.

"Good; it'll save us the effort of throwing you overboard."

Carla held up her middle finger and turned to face Michael. "If you've got a flashlight, I know where the password is to open the file."

Chapter 20

Vatican – August

Pope John Pietro I lay prostrated on the cold floor in front of the altar in his private chapel. He had come to pray for divine guidance and the wisdom to solve his dilemma, and to make peace with God. But he had also come into the chapel for another reason; to mourn the death of his father.

Moments before, he had received a telephone call from Stendardi informing him that Samuel Grossman had just died in his home in Israel. What shocked him more than the death of his father was the intense sadness and pain he felt for the old man who was really only a stranger to him. His passing lay heavily on his heart and Pietro Bandini couldn't explain it; his reasoning still wouldn't accept the truth about his Jewish birth. He tried convincing himself that it was nothing more than unfortunate circumstances in a time of great terror which had spared his life. Perhaps it was to fulfil the will of God as a servant of the Catholic people. Yet, he heard himself, as though he were detached from his body, reciting the mourner's prayer in Hebrew.

He had studied Judaica as one of his subjects in the seminary when he was a young man and remembered that the mourner's *kaddish* contained no references to death; instead it sanctified and glorified the name of God. Intoning it now could do no harm.

He raised his eyes and looked at the large crucifix hanging above the altar. He felt tears trickling down his cheeks and, finally, in a moment of despair, cried out. "Forgive me, Father, for I do not know what to do!"

The pope remained prone on the floor for several more minutes before suddenly rising to his feet. It had come to him in a moment of prayer. He knew without reservation what he had to do. He left the chapel and walked back to the papal office on the same floor. Cardinal Pollini was in the antechamber, talking on the phone. He nodded toward the pope to

The Papal Secret

acknowledge the pontiff's return to his office and continued with his conversation.

Bandini went straight to his desk and sat down. Opening a drawer, he removed a folder containing Vatican stationery and removed several sheets of writing paper. He leaned back in his chair, adjusted his white skull cap, and began to write.

Fifteen minutes later, he replaced his pen in its holder and read what he had written. Satisfied with the sincerity of his confession, he folded the letter and sealed it in a white envelope. He rose from his chair with sagging shoulders and walked to the wall safe concealed behind a painting of the Madonna, given to him by an aspiring artist who was good enough to have his painting occupy such an exalted position. He placed the envelope on the lower shelf among other important documents and closed the safe. He felt secure in the knowledge that the letter would remain safe from premature disclosure, as Pollini was the only other living person who knew the safe's combination. Once back in his chair, he rested his elbows on the desk and lowered his chin onto the top of his clasped hands, and reflected on the contents of his composition.

He had recorded the entire circumstances of his Jewish birth and how the truth was finally revealed to him after nearly three-quarters of a century of concealment. He begged the Catholic people for forgiveness for deceiving them and appealed to the elders of the Church to judge him on the merits of his achievements. He had signed the document and stamped it with the papal seal. The envelope had one simple instruction: "To be opened in the event of my death."

He had appealed to the Lord for guidance, but ultimately he knew the choice of action would be his alone. Free will was a heavy burden to bear among the rightcous. At least, he thought sombrely, if he could not live in truth, he would die in truth.

Chapter 21

Ligurian Sea – Italy

Isabella tried the cabin door once again; it was still locked. The porthole behind her was sealed, so there was no way out. Even if she could leave the cabin, there was no place to go. She was trapped on a boat in the middle of the ocean. What worried her most was her uncertainty in what her captors were planning to do with her. If she was being held for ransom, she feared they would never release her alive; she had seen their faces and would be able to identify them.

Her only consolation was that Michael now knew she had been abducted, and if he had understood her brief clue, he would know she was being held on a boat somewhere off the coast of Santa Margherita. He would know what to do.

On the bridge somewhere above her, the captain was peering at the radar with some concern. An unidentified intruder had appeared on the edge of the screen.

"Carlos, take a look at this," he said, pointing to the white dot.

"What is it, another boat?"

"It's a small vessel, alright," he said, and then shrugged as the blip disappeared off the radar screen. "Nothing to worry about," he added. "It's gone."

"Keep watching. Let me know if it comes back."

Darkness had settled over the sea and visibility was no longer a factor. The radar was the only instrument protecting their position.

* * *

"Did you get a positional fix before turning out of range?" Michael asked.

"Yep, sure did," replied Mario. "I'll close in again in ten

minutes to see if they've moved."

"Good. Then we can triangulate their course and plot an intercept."

Ten minutes later, Mario reported that the other boat was still holding the same position. "What are you going to do?" he asked.

"Pay them a surprise visit," Michael said. "Remain out of range while I launch the dinghy, and stick to the plan. Only come and get me if I signal."

"I'm coming with you," Carla said from behind, and continued quickly before Michael could protest. "You'll need backup and I can cause a diversion from the dinghy if things go wrong."

Michael secured a thirty-metre rope to the prow of the inflatable so that it could trail out of sight of the *Mermaid* once he boarded her. It would also keep Carla out of his way while he attempted the rescue. He secured a flashlight to a clip on his belt to signal Mario with if he had to, and a sheath knife in the event of close combat. Finally, he seated the Smith & Wesson in its shoulder holster under his left arm and pulled his night goggles down over his eyes.

He lowered the dinghy into the water and helped Carla climb in. He followed her rapidly and started the outboard motor. He told Carla to be careful of the box of explosives secured tightly on the port side. He would use the dynamite to cause havoc during their escape. He cast off, and using the stars to navigate by, he pointed the little craft in the direction of where he hoped the *Mermaid* would still be.

A light wind had swept across the water, causing the swells to heighten. The dinghy rode high on each crest and fell sharply into the succeeding trough. Carla wished the motion would stop before the herring she had eaten a few hours earlier decided to return to the sea. The little craft rode too close to the water for her liking.

Half an hour later, Michael thought he saw something in the distance. He had to wait for the next crest to give him enough elevation to confirm the sighting. What he saw were a row of lights and the faint outline of a boat illuminated in the glow. He was thankful the crew hadn't bothered to conceal her whereabouts. But why would they? They weren't expecting anyone to come. The thought briefly crossed his mind that it might be the wrong boat, innocently sailing along and minding its own business. He dismissed it as a negative intrusion into his head; it simply had to be the *Mermaid*.

Michael continued on his present course toward the unidentified boat. He was approaching it from the stern, opposite the helmsman's line of sight. He was banking that the seaman would only be concerned with what lay ahead of him, allowing him a safe approach from behind.

The sea was not rough, but the crests seemed like mountains to the little rubber dinghy negotiating its way like a cork over them. From the top of one such crest, Michael caught sight of the boat and cut back the motor when he saw how close it was. Soon it was visible even from the depth of each trough.

He had to stand tall and reach upward to grab the railing as the dinghy drew alongside the boat. He slipped the rope attached to the dinghy around one of the uprights and tied it with a slipknot for easy release. He hoisted the kitbag containing his equipment and the explosives onto the deck and turned to wave at Carla. "Let the dinghy trail out of sight until I give the signal to get us," he called to Carla over the spray. "Hopefully it will only take fifteen minutes or so."

Carla nodded obediently. She wasn't feeling so good. She wasn't sure how much she could take of the pitching and rolling and was too nauseous to argue. She waited for him to climb on board before slowly letting out the rope. She felt even more alone bobbing helplessly thirty metres behind the boat. She gripped the handhold and settled down to wait.

Michael hoisted himself on board and crouched on the deck listening for anyone running toward where he was hiding. The deck remained deserted and there was no noise besides the lapping of the sea against the side of the hull. He looked back to make sure Carla had followed his instructions, and when he couldn't see the dinghy anymore, he gripped the kitbag and hid under the metal staircase leading up to the next deck.

His first task was to identify the boat. Leaving the kitbag under the steps, he made his way along the deck looking for a lifebuoy attached against the wall. When he found one, he read the name embossed on it: *The Mermaid*. A thrill of relief went through him. Isabella was not far away.

He returned to his hiding place and removed the explosives. He placed them strategically on the opposite deck and armed them. He patted the detonator in his pocket and took a deep breath. His next objective was to find Isabella's cabin and get her out. The explosives weren't very powerful, so wouldn't cause much damage. Their sole purpose was to create a diversion so that the two of them could escape in the confusion.

Keeping his head down, he crept like a hunchback toward midship. He wanted to first see how many crew members were on the bridge. Being a relatively small vessel, he doubted if there would be more than three or four of them. When he peered around the corner, he saw only one man at the wheel, which meant the others were probably asleep in their cabins. That was only a presumption, so he continued cautiously, keeping a sharp lookout for any movement.

When he entered the sleeping quarters, he counted four doors. He figured that Isabella's cabin would be the only one locked, so, with bated breath, he tried the first door. It opened easily and he quickly closed it without bothering to look inside. No sense in taking risks at this stage. He bypassed the next two doors and went straight to the last cabin. If he were holding a captive on his boat, he would keep the prisoner in the end cabin, the furthest point from the escape hatch.

He turned the knob but the door refused to budge. Removing the set of universal keys from his tunic pocket, he tried the first one. Nothing happened. The next one also failed to release the lock. He looked along the passageway in relief that it was still deserted but knowing that if anyone appeared he had nowhere to hide. He inserted the next key and fiddled with the lock. Suddenly he heard a faint snap as the bolt was released. He opened the door slowly and slipped inside. He still wasn't sure if it was Isabella's cabin. He saw a figure lying in the bunk with a blanket pulled up over its head. There was nothing he could do but approach the bed and lower the cover.

* * *

In the wheelhouse, the captain saw the blip appear on the radar screen again. He calculated the distance and recorded the position. It was exactly in the same place as before which, to his mind, ruled out the possibility of a passing ship in the night. He picked up the intercom and buzzed Carlos.

"The boat's back on the radar screen in the same position as before," he reported.

"Okay, I'll be right up."

When Carlos entered the wheelhouse, there was a puzzled look on the captain's face. "It's just slipped off the screen again," he said, frowning. "I swear it was there a moment ago."

"You sure? I hope you didn't interrupt my sleep for nothing."

"It was right here, I tell you." He pointed to a spot on the screen.

"Now that I'm here, go get some shut-eye. I'll keep watch."

"Thanks."

* * *

Gingerly, Michael lifted the cover off the head of the sleeping form in the bed. When he saw the long black hair draped over the pillow, his pulse quickened. "Isabella!" he called softly.

The figure stirred, then sat bolt upright and opened her mouth to scream. Michael covered her mouth with his hand.

"It's all right. It's me, Michael," he whispered.

She peered at him through the darkness. "Michael? Is it really you?" She threw her arms around his neck and clung to him like a baby. "How . . . ?"

"We don't have much time," he interrupted. "I'll explain later. How many are there on board?"

"Three."

"Good. Get dressed. We have no time to waste."

Isabella slipped into a pair of jeans and pulled a sweater over her t-shirt.

"Can you swim?" he asked.

"Yes," she replied, giving him a puzzled look. "Swim to where? We're in the middle of the sea."

"There's a dinghy thirty metres behind the boat. Carla is waiting in it for us. If there's trouble, jump overboard and follow the rope to the dinghy."

"And you?"

"Don't worry about me. I'll be right behind you." He took hold of her hand and led her to the door. "The tricky bit is getting out on deck." He opened the door and peered into the gloomy passageway. Suddenly he heard footsteps at the top of the hatch. He pushed Isabella back into the room. "Someone's coming," he breathed heavily. "Get back into bed in case they're coming to check on you." He crouched behind a chair in the corner of the cabin. It offered only limited concealment, but as long as the light wasn't switched on, he wouldn't be seen. He withdrew the knife from its sheath and held it ready. If it came to it, he wouldn't hesitate to use it. He was in the realm of self defence. Then he remembered he had left the door unlocked.

The Papal Secret

That might arouse suspicion.

He heard the door open and saw the figure of a man enter the cabin. He recognised him as the pilot in the wheelhouse he had seen earlier. That meant one of the others was now on duty. Two of them awake would make their escape much more difficult. On the other hand, he hadn't expected an easy time.

He watched the man walk over to the bed. He bent over Isabella and then straightened. Satisfied that she was asleep, he retraced his steps and went out into the passage, closing the door behind him.

Isabella sat up. Michael signalled to her to stay put until the intruder was well away. After five minutes, he got up and went to the door. There was no other choice but to open it and see if the way was clear.

"Let's go!" he said to Isabella.

They made their way safely past the other cabins and stepped out onto the deck. Holding onto Isabella's hand, he edged his way toward the stern where he could signal to Carla to come and get them. When he reached the staircase where he had unpacked the kitbag, he paused. To reach the stern they would have to cross the open deck. A solitary light burning on the bulwark above them was enough to expose them if anyone happened to look in their direction. It was the last obstacle before freedom.

Suddenly a man stepped out from behind the steps. The gun in his hand was pointing right at Michael's chest. "And you must be Mr. Frost," he grinned. "How enterprising of you to have found us and to board in such secrecy."

"This is Carlos, the madman in charge," Isabella told Michael.

"I trust you brought with you the memory stick that has caused all this trouble."

"It was delivered as per your instruction."

"I believe it was a decoy, Mr. Frost," Carlos hissed. "This is not a game we are playing." He turned the gun toward Isabella. "Now that you're here, I don't need her anymore. Let this be a lesson for your disobedience."

Their only chance was to create a diversion. Michael had the remote in his pocket and all he had to do was push the button to detonate the explosives he had hidden on deck. "Wait!" he said, holding up his hands. "I have it with me."

"Let me see it," Carlos hesitated. "Slowly, Mr. Frost. If I so much as see the butt of a gun appear out of your pocket, I swear I'll kill her."

Michael put his hand in his pocket and felt for the detonator. The charges had been placed against the wall not far from where they were standing. They were not strong enough to do much damage, but were designed to shock anyone standing close enough. As long as the explosion knocked Carlos off balance, they would have enough time to jump overboard.

His fingers curled around the device as he probed for the button.

"I'm waiting, Mr. Frost, or is this another one of your games?"

"It's not a game, I assure you," replied Michael as he pressed the button.

Both sticks of dynamite exploded simultaneously. The force of the blast threw Carlos against the bulkhead, and for a brief moment, the direction of the gun pointed away from them. Michael pushed Isabella toward the railing.

"Jump!" he shouted.

Before Carlos could recover his balance, Michael and Isabella vaulted over the railing and plunged into the sea. "This way!" he directed Isabella. They kept close to the hull so that Carlos wouldn't get a clear shot. Michael reached up and loosened the slipknot and swam toward the dinghy keeping a watchful eye on Isabella. He didn't want to lose her to the sea.

They followed the rope until they reached the dinghy. Carla was peering into the water at them. "Shit! I thought you were dead," she cried.

"Start up the motor!" Michael shouted, as he helped Isabella climb aboard. By the time he positioned himself at the helm, the dinghy had gathered enough speed to get far enough away from the boat to make an accurate shot impossible. They heard gunshots, but the bullets fell nowhere near them. They watched as the fire burned itself out on the port deck, safe in the knowledge that they were well out of sight of Carlos and his crew.

Michael signalled to Mario to come and get them. He was well aware that Carlos had a fix on the *Bella Mare* and would probably pursue them in an attempt to catch them before reaching territorial waters. He had no idea how powerful the engines of the *Mermaid* were, but once back on board his own boat, the radar would show the progress of the chase.

The *Bella Mare* had enough of a start to outrun the *Mermaid*. When they reached territorial waters, the pursuing vessel

The Papal Secret

broke off the chase and turned out to sea again, where they would be out of the jurisdiction of the Coast Guard.

For the first time since the ordeal, Michael was able to examine Isabella. "Did they hurt you?" he asked.

"No, they didn't bother me too much," she said. "I suppose they thought I had nowhere to escape to."

"I doubt if they would have let you go," Michael said. "They would have dumped you overboard after they received what they wanted."

Isabella shivered and moved closer to Michael. "Have you got something dry for me to change into?" she asked.

"I have my luggage with me," Carla said, taking her hand. "Let's go below and get out of these soggy things."

After they left, Mario turned to Michael. "They won't stop until they have what they want. None of you will be safe."

"I'm well aware of that."

"What are you going to do?"

"Spray insecticide into the holes and see what comes out of the woodwork."

"I hope the rodents are not bigger than you expect."

Chapter 22

Santa Margherita – August

"You're telling me this Carlos character kidnapped Isabella?" Inspector Conti looked quizzically at Michael. "Is this a red herring you're throwing at me to divert any investigation against you?"

For a moment, the humming of the ceiling fan was the only sound in the detective's office. Michael was not sure how much of the truth he should tell the inspector. Lying was not an option, but leaving out some of the facts would buy him some time to probe the affair a little deeper without police constraints.

"Obviously, the kidnapper is also the murderer you're looking for," Michael's voice rose over the blades of the fan.

"Is that right?" the inspector asked sardonically. "You're now a qualified expert on police matters?"

"As a matter of fact, I am," Michael replied. "You forget I was a practising criminal lawyer before I settled here. I know how warped minds work."

"So, let me get this straight." The inspector leaned back in his chair and had to quickly grip the front of the desk to prevent his chair from toppling backward. Regaining his composure, he continued. "It is alleged that Umbretti killed Rochi for information in his possession. Then he presumably pushed the unknown intruder over the balcony of the hotel to prevent him from getting it, and then conveniently disappeared into thin air. If he's the focus of attention, why on earth would anybody want to kidnap Isabella? Can you explain that to me, Mr. Frost?"

"I don't know the answer," Michael answered hesitantly, feeling trapped by the question.

"You don't know, or you're not telling? Or perhaps it is you and not Umbretti who has whatever it is the kidnappers want."

"Which is?"

"I don't know. That's why we're having this conversation—to find the answer."

The Papal Secret

Michael looked out the window. Two seagulls were perched on the sill preening each other. He marvelled at how clean these birds always were. There was not a blemish of dirt anywhere on their white chests. He turned away from them when the inspector's voice intruded into his thoughts.

"How much time do you need to fabricate a story? Surely the truth does not require such deliberation?"

Michael smiled. "You're right, inspector. You deserve the truth."

Inspector Conti leaned forward in expectation. He was not used to such complicated intrigue. As chief of police in a small town where hardly anything drastic ever happens, apart from a break-in or two, or a car being stolen, two murders in the same week affected him on a personal level. How he handled the investigation and the possible detaining of the culprits would change the way the townsfolk perceived him—hopefully with more respect than he currently had. Solving the case would enhance his reputation and attract the attention of his superiors in Milan. While he was trying to deter Frost from interfering in the case, he didn't want to lose the input needed to guide him toward a solution. He would allow Frost latitude to continue with his unofficial investigation while appearing to frown upon his interference. His plan was to stay close enough to the lawyer and step in at the opportune moment and bask in the credit of solving the crime. "I'm listening," he said eagerly.

"What I can gather," Michael said, choosing his words carefully, "Mr. Rochi was stealing money from the accounts of investors at the bank and Umbretti discovered the fraud."

"Go on."

"The trouble is we're living in a world where the integrity of those who are supposed to ensure that our moral actions are correct is sometimes also corrupt."

"So the thief stole from the thief?"

"It looks like it, only there seems to be a third party involved."

"The kidnappers and the dead man at the hotel?" Conti suggested smugly.

"Exactly, inspector. Now you know it all."

"Ah, but you have avoided telling me what it is you have that they want," the inspector gave Michael a long look.

"Until I can establish what it is, inspector, you will have to trust me."

Stan Miller

"Let me inform you that you are withholding evidence in a police enquiry," Inspector Conti said, rising from his chair. "I don't have to remind you that it is a criminal offence which carries severe punishment."

"Give me twenty-four hours to decipher the information. The task will save you time and manpower. By the end of tomorrow you will receive everything."

"Very well, Mr. Frost. Twenty-four hours it is."

Chapter 23

The Vatican – August

Cardinal Albertini never ventured outside the walls of the Vatican on foot. Whenever he had business in Rome, he travelled in one of the unmarked limousines belonging to the Vatican fleet. He preferred vehicles with darkened windows to ensure his anonymity remained intact. The world was a dangerous place and one never knew when some crazed imbecile would blow himself up in a public place or target a Vatican vehicle for some idiotic cause.

Today was a rare exception. He was meeting Fabio Mento to examine the old bronze gate which used to be the entrance from the outside into the Palace of the Archpriest. It had been permanently sealed after the Second World War and was showing signs of weakness. The locks had rusted, leaving them susceptible to forced entry.

Albertini wasn't really concerned with this apparent weakness in the security system. Mento was quite capable of solving the crisis himself, but he had chosen the place as an opportune moment to speak privately with the security officer. They had met too frequently in the gardens to risk another encounter that might raise eyebrows and attract interest; and the last thing he wanted was to arouse the suspicions of his inquisitive peers where he was concerned.

Albertini was not a man who endeared himself to people. He was straightforward and lacked finesse in his approach to others. He dispelled with tactfulness and didn't care if his words were hurtful. Usually respondents deserved his biting dialogue and he had little compassion for transgressors. Repentance was a personal matter between the sinner and God; his task was primarily to make sure his flock didn't follow him off the path of righteousness. That privilege he kept for himself because he felt he could handle it and justify any dubious actions on his part. Furthermore, he felt he had the ability to regain his footing on the straight and narrow anytime he chose to return to the Lord's ways.

He had not been a popular clergyman with his parish because the content of his sermons fell uneasily on their conscience, but he was a brilliant orator and worshippers kept coming back to listen to him. Such was his skill that it wasn't long before he attracted the attention of the Vatican and was ordained a cardinal.

The problem with Albertini was that his ambition proved stronger than his faith; it wasn't that he didn't love the Almighty, but he thought he could serve him better as his vicar on earth in his own way. The papacy itself was his ultimate goal.

The Vatican, like any other state, had its enemies. Secrets had to be protected and safety ensured. Cardinal Albertini was the perfect man for the job. Strong and energetic, he had the force of character to fulfil the role of protector like nobody else could. The pope was even once heard to remark, "Had Albertini been pope during the time of Henry VIII, England would still be a Catholic monarchy!" But Deputy Secretary of the Pontifical Commission was as far as the diocesan committee would allow him to progress. This, however, did not deter Albertini's ambition. He was prepared for a bitter struggle to reach the top and had collected secret files on everyone in the Vatican.

Mento was privy to the cardinal's ambition, so when he took him by the arm to lead him away from the group of locksmiths, he sensed trouble. He had failed his benefactor again and waited with bated breath for the tirade to begin.

"If it's discovered," Albertini said in an undertone, "that I was a recipient of Rochi's fraud, I'm finished here at the Vatican." He paused to make sure they were far enough away from the workmen not to be overheard before allowing his anger to raise the tone of his voice. "You failed to obtain the memory stick. The kidnapping was not a good idea because your actions have drawn the police into the case even further."

"At least we know Frost has it in his possession."

"Are you sure about that?"

"He must have it. Umbretti doesn't; otherwise, he would have blackmailed us by now with disclosure to get the money back."

"He may still do it."

"No, don't worry about him; he won't."

Albertini glared at Mento and said, "Money is no object. I want that stick found and brought back to me before Frost gets any clever ideas."

Mento had a pained expression on his face. He knew the cardinal's patience was running out and that this was his last chance to appease him. "Give me a few more days," he pleaded. "That's all I ask. I will go myself to Santa Margherita and finish the job."

Chapter 24

Milan – August

Carla opened her front door and looked down at the envelope lying on the floor. She stooped to retrieve it and froze when she saw the name of a law firm printed on the reverse side of the envelope. In that split second, she knew that Milo Umbretti was dead. She placed the letter on the kitchen table and made herself a cup of coffee while throwing furtive glances at the unopened letter. It was as if she could prolong Milo's life by not opening it.

She held the cup in her hands and sipped slowly from it. The hot liquid made her hands feel warm and, although it was a hot day outside, she felt comforted by the warmth. She was trembling as the letter lying in front of her beckoned to be opened. After several minutes, curiosity pushed fear aside and she picked it up in shaking hands. She knew what was inside before she ran the knife through the flap.

It was as he told her. The single photograph that fell from the envelope depicted seven soccer players wearing the colours of the Inter-Milan football club. She had no idea who they were although one of them looked familiar. She was not a football fan, but the city was full of fanatics. It would not be difficult to find someone to identify the players, and then she could equate a number corresponding to the numerical value of the first letter of each name. According to Milo's instructions, that would be the pin number to unlock his bank account.

Suddenly she felt very vulnerable and frightened. What if his killer was waiting for this very moment to rob her of the information she had just received and then kill her, too? Then common sense prevailed and she tried to convince herself that no one could possibly know the private arrangement between her and Milo. And no one knew where she lived, apart from the lawyer who sent the letter. All she had to do now was identify the players in the photograph and work out the pin number so that she could transfer the money as quickly as possible.

Then she would relocate to Paris, open a new banking account, and transfer the money there. She would keep a low profile and enjoy life in one of the most romantic cities in the world. Maybe even find a husband and settle down as a housewife and lead a normal life.

Suddenly her future prospects seemed good and her appetite returned. She opened a tin of smoked mussels, mixed some onions and tomatoes with it, and wolfed the meal down. Then she picked up the photograph and put it in the pocket of her cotton jacket. With her luck, someone would choose today to grab her handbag and run. The only barrier to her fortune was the identity of each player in the picture and until she found out who they were, the photograph was her most valuable possession.

As expected, it didn't take her long to get the names. The barman in the first pub she entered knew them all, and it only cost the price of one glass of wine. She spilt some of the liquid down her blouse in her haste to consume it so she could leave and return to her apartment.

Thirty minutes later, armed with the number scribbled on her arm, she made her way to the bank.

"This is a great deal of money you wish to transfer," the bank manager said. "Shouldn't Dr. Umbretti be doing the transaction himself?"

"My brother has two broken legs after a terrible car accident," Carla lied. "The money is urgently needed elsewhere and I'm only following his instruction. That is why he gave me the pin number which authorises the transaction."

"Nevertheless, I should phone him first," the banker smiled. "I'm only acting in his best interest."

"That won't be necessary," she said, authoritatively. "I have signing power." She pushed the letter from Umbretti's lawyer across the table and leaned back smugly. "And the secret pin number, I might add."

The banker read the document and looked up. "Let me make a copy of this letter stating that you have power of attorney and then we can proceed."

"Thank you." She entered the pin number and nearly choked when she saw the amount.

"You wish to transfer all of it?"

"Yes, we're relocating to France."

"The beneficiary, I notice, is you." The banker looked quizzically at her.

Stan Miller

"There's nothing illegal with that, is there?" She looked him straight back in the eye.

"Of course not, but I must ask. I have to protect the bank's interest as well. The bank would be responsible for restitution if it paid out money without making certain that it wasn't a fraudulent transaction."

"You have the documents showing that it is entirely legal." She leaned forward allowing her blouse to billow open enough to show him a generous amount of bosom.

"You'll have the full four hundred thousand Euros in your bank account within the hour," he informed her, wiping away a trickle of perspiration from his forehead. "Minus the service charge, of course."

Chapter 24

Santa Margherita – August

There are very few places like Santa Margherita, thought Michael, where the town itself offers an idyllic lifestyle to those who live in it. Of course, perfection is only an illusion which exists in nature's wondrous spectacle and the dream of humans to obtain a little of it. As Michael wandered through the seaside town bathed in sunlight and beauty, his mood was far from amiable. He had been given twenty-four hours to get to the bottom of a crime the inspector was struggling to solve, and all for the purpose of clearing his own name. The carefree demeanour of the people he passed in the street went unnoticed. He went straight from his meeting with Inspector Conti at police headquarters to his apartment where Isabella was waiting.

"The entry code only allows viewing," Isabella told him as he leaned over her shoulder to get a closer look at the computer screen. "The stick contains what looks like account numbers, but no names. It's meaningless to us. I don't know what all the fuss is about." She leaned back in the chair and massaged her temples.

"There has to be something overtly displayed that could identify one of the accounts," Michael said. "The possibility that someone's identity might be compromised is the reason behind all these recent events."

"Do you think my husband found out who it was?"

"More than likely," Michael agreed. "One thing is for sure, Umbretti is the key to all of this."

"And he's disappeared," Isabella declared.

"Carla should know where he is."

"Do you have an address?"

"No, but her phone number may be in your husband's diary. She was commissioned by him to woo Umbretti. Do you have it?"

"Yes, the police released his personal belongings to me."

She stood up. "It's in my case." Isabella returned a minute later with the diary. "We're in luck. There's no address, but her mobile phone number is here. Let's see if she answers."

"Hello," was the tentative reply.

"Carla, Isabella speaking. How are you, my dear?"

"I'm fine, but I have terrible news. Milo Umbretti is dead."

"Dead?" Isabella looked up at Michael and grimaced. "How did he die?"

"I don't know," Carla cried. "All I know is that he was murdered. He said they were after him."

"Who, Carla? Who did he say was after him?"

"He called them a 'pious group of thugs.' More than that, I don't know. All I know is that he is dead and I'm scared."

"Don't panic," Isabella tried to sound reassuring. "There is no reason for them to come after you."

"I was a passenger on the yacht," Carla said frantically. "You were also a passenger. We are all in danger; two murders out of the six of us so far. I'm getting out of here where nobody will find me." The phone went dead.

Isabella looked at Michael. "What do you make of that?"

"She's right. We are all in danger."

"Where does my husband's partner Martini fit in all of this?"

"I'd forgotten about him," Michael said. "Maybe it's time to find out."

* * *

Katherine Martini was waiting for them on the steps of the Duomo. She had chosen a public place because she said it would be safer. They approached the Gothic cathedral from the north through the Gallery of Victor Emmanuel, which contains some of Milan's finest shops. Michael had to tug on Isabella's hand to keep her in full stride. Built in the form of a cross, the Gallery is sheltered by a glass roof, so their eyes were already accustomed to the light when they emerged into the sunshine.

While waiting to cross the road, Michael looked up at the roof of the cathedral. He had read somewhere that over two thousand statues sat in niches in the walls that adorned the outside of the cathedral. Tarpaulin covers situated in some places where workmen were cleaning the white Carrara marble walls spoiled the resplendent sight. But the cathedral still

The Papal Secret

towered majestically over the Piazza del Duomo as they made their way to the foot of the steps where Katherine was waiting.

"I'm glad you came," she said, looking nervously around as if expecting unwanted company. "Let's go inside. We must not be seen talking together."

They entered the church and had to wait for their eyes to adjust to the dim interior. What stood out immediately were the windows telling Biblical stories in stained glass. It only took a moment for breathless admiration to give way to reality; they had not come to admire the art.

"What happened?" Isabella asked, as they slid into a pew beneath one of the windows.

"Franco has been getting threatening phone calls." Katherine looked around again. Even in the semi-darkness of the sanctuary she still felt unsafe.

"Would you care to explain?" Michael urged her to continue.

Katherine looked at Isabella. "You've probably already found out that your late husband and Franco were up to no good. They were stealing money from the bank."

"Yes, I know."

"Umbretti was sent to probe for proof, but greed got the better of him when he found it. He tried to conspire with Franco against your husband. Such a lot of money and the greedy crooks didn't want to share it."

"Was Franco in on my husband's murder?" Isabella asked angrily.

"No, I'm sure he wasn't," Katherine hastened to explain. "He just wanted the money, but when your husband stumbled on some information in Umbretti's laptop, things got aggressive. Giorgio threatened to expose Umbretti if he didn't give the money back. That's why he was killed."

"And your husband is innocent, of course?" Isabella said, not bothering to hide the irony in her voice. Michael laid a restraining hand on Isabella's lap. It wouldn't do any good antagonising the woman before she finished her story.

"Yes, innocent of murder, but not fraud. I'm afraid it doesn't end there, though. It seems that a third party became involved, someone with immense influence who will stop at nothing to protect his identity."

"Do you know who it is?" Michael asked.

"No, but we're not waiting to find out. We're too scared to go home. We're staying in a hotel until arrangements to leave the country are finalised."

"Where are you going?"

"Franco will kill me if I tell anyone, even you. When all this comes out, Franco will be a fugitive from the law. He is guilty of grand theft, you know, same as your late husband was. Be careful because they'll come after you next."

"They already have," Isabella replied nervously.

Chapter 25

Santa Margherita – September

The first of the month brought in heavy rain. Fabio Mento lifted the collar of his trench coat and lowered his neck into it like the head of a tortoise retreating into its shell. He had been standing under a tree across the road from Michael's apartment for two hours without seeing anybody go in or out of the building. He was not known in these parts so he figured it was worth the risk to go inside and make enquiries. Besides, he wanted desperately to get out of the rain.

"Who wants to know where Mr. Frost is?" the desk clerk asked contemptuously over the intercom.

"My boss wishes to hire his boat," Mento answered. "When is he due back?"

"Day after tomorrow," was the dry reply. "You'll find him on his boat. That's where he conducts his business, not here."

Mento retreated from the locked door and decided to call it a day. He had booked into a comfortable hotel compatible with the generous expense allowance given to him by his patron. No sense in catching pneumonia loitering about in the rain. He would return after dark and find a way in. Once inside, he would have the luxury of time when searching through Frost's apartment.

He treated himself to a sumptuous meal in the hotel's restaurant. He usually refrained from alcohol before a job, but the prawns were so succulent that it would have been sacrilege not to wash them down with a glass of white wine. He limited himself to a single glass, resisting all temptation to indulge further.

By the time he had finished his meal, the rain had stopped and it was a pleasant walk back to the apartment block where Frost lived. Without a security code to open the front door, he seized at the opportunity when a party of five people noisily approached the entrance. Mento ambled behind them and was relieved to see that the night watchman who greeted them in the foyer was not the same one whom he had spoken to that afternoon. The guard took no notice of him as they entered the building, thinking he was part of the group; Mento had his hand on the shoulder of the last man.

"Nasty bit of rain we had," he said jovially.

"A good bottle of wine helps to endure the discomfort," the stranger answered.

"That's the truth, my friend. Have a good evening." He followed them to the lift and broke off at a tangent when he reached the stairwell. He left the group to ride in the elevator while he used the steps.

When he got to Michaels's apartment door, he looked up and down the passage to make sure no one was watching before proceeding to pick the lock. He was an expert at opening locked doors, so it took only a few seconds for him to release the latch. He entered the apartment and quietly closed the door behind him. The curtains were drawn, so he switched on the entrance hall light and surveyed the interior. His first interest was examining the computer. There was no need to switch it on because he wouldn't progress very far without knowing the password. He had plenty of time to search for the data stick, but didn't want to linger for too long in case Frost returned unexpectedly. He had only the desk clerk's word that Frost would be away for a couple of days. The man had not taken kindly to him and might have been lying. But he wanted to look around first.

He went into the bedroom and opened the top drawer of the dressing table. He withdrew a pair of flimsy lace panties and buried his nose in them. He sniffed deeply and revelled in the fragrance of the garment. *Some men are lucky to have beautiful women in their beds*, he thought with envy. He put the panties in his pocket. *No harm taking a souvenir*, he thought. *The woman has plenty more.* He took delight in rummaging through her underwear. It aroused him just imagining her in them.

He finished exploring the bedroom and moved into the study. The computer desk would be an excellent place to start looking. Frost wouldn't be expecting his place to be broken into by an intruder and Mento hoped the flash drive would not be well hidden. He rifled through all the drawers but found nothing. Then he ran his fingers along the underside of the top drawer and felt something taped there. He nodded expectantly as if he had known all along it would be there.

The Papal Secret

"A popular hiding place for amateurs," he mused aloud. He removed the object and was delighted to see that it was a data stick. He switched on the computer. It wasn't necessary to gain access into the program but he would be able to ascertain whether or not the data stick was the one he was looking for. He leaned back and flexed his fingers.

The icon *Umbretti* came up on the screen and he knew he had what he wanted. He removed the stick from the USB port and dropped it into his jacket pocket. It was time to leave, but he had one more task to fulfil.

Had he taken more care, he would have seen the symbol drawn on a piece of paper attached to the clip on a message-holder standing on the desk next to the telephone. He would have removed it with the same fervour as the data stick.

* * *

"It's gone!" Michael exclaimed. The first thing he did on his return home was to retrieve the flash drive he had placed in the desk drawer.

"Are you sure that's where you put it?" Isabella asked.

"I know I'm not going crazy," he answered. "I never removed the screws from the side panel of the PC, either," He removed the cover and peered into the innards of the computer box. "Some bastard has removed the memory board. I have a brain-dead computer!"

"Let me check if anything has been taken." She disappeared into the bedroom. A second later she let out a yell. "The thief was a bloody pervert," she shouted. "All my underwear is scattered on the floor and my favourite pair of red panties is gone."

"Anything else missing?" he called. "Underwear you don't need with me around."

"Very funny," she mumbled. "No," she called back. When she returned to the study, she found Michael standing at the desk staring at a piece of paper in his hand. "What's that?" she asked.

"When I opened the data stick the other day, the only thing I couldn't make any sense of was this emblem." He handed the piece of paper to Isabella.

"I've seen this sign before," she said, screwing up her forehead, "but I can't remember where." She looked at the diagram more intensely, trying to joggle her memory. It depicted

Stan Miller

an ancient key next to the letter *V.* "It escapes me," she confessed.

"Seeing that it's together with a series of bank accounts, maybe the bank manager can throw some light on the enigma."

* * *

"Where did you see this emblem?" the bank manager asked, showing signs of distress.

"I'm not at liberty to say," Michael told him. "All I can tell you is that it was among some numbers which I'm presuming to be bank accounts."

"I see." The manager rose and closed his office door. "What I'm about to show you is highly confidential." He removed a file from a locked cabinet behind his desk. "I cannot allow you to read the contents of this letter, but look at the seal below the signature."

"It's identical!"

"What is it?" Isabella asked eagerly.

"It is a seal originating from the Vatican. I'm told that only a highly selective group of cardinals at the top of the Vatican hierarchy have the privilege of its use. No one dares challenge its authority."

Chapter 26

Vatican – September

Cardinal Angelo Pollini looked again at the internal memo which had just been handed to him. The Secretary of the Inner Council stood waiting for his response. It summoned him, most urgently, to attend a special purpose 'ancillary ecumenical' meeting to be held immediately in the small conference room adjoining the Papal Audience Hall. It had been called by Cardinal Albertini, and the secretary was there to escort Pollini to the meeting.

In normal circumstances any summons for such a meeting originated in his office and requested that the cardinals be present at the stipulated venue. This reversal of protocol was ominous indeed. It could only mean the gathering was being held without the knowledge of the pope because he was the issue of discussion. It was evident to Pollini that his escort was there to ensure he could not notify the pontiff in advance. The pope was currently in a meeting with the Israeli Ambassador and Pollini had a strong feeling that this was the reason for the unscheduled meeting.

When Pollini arrived in the CR, the other members of the council were already seated around the oval table. Albertini was standing at the one end, and it was evident by the way in which he curtailed his speech as Pollini entered that he was trying to solicit support for his proposition from the cardinals present before the meeting was actually opened.

"What is the meaning of this?" Cardinal Pollini stated his annoyance immediately. "Is this a conspiracy against the pope?"

"Not at all, Angelo," Albertini said, amicably. "There are just some concerns about His Holiness's bias toward Israel."

"I beg your pardon?"

"Was there a need to release a letter of apology to the Jews for his lifting of the excommunication order of a Holocaust-denying bishop?"

"It was not the Holy Father's intention to put strain on the reconciliation program between Christians and Jews by lifting the order, but it did unleash an avalanche of protest. Admitting the error helped to restore goodwill."

"The Vatican should be neutral in the affairs of other countries, and not show sympathy toward one at the expense of another."

"I suppose you are referring to the Israel-Palestine conflict?" Pollini had expected the discussion to veer in this direction.

"Yes."

"The Vatican supports peace and is strongly opposed to terrorism. The pope is not supporting one group over another; he is advocating peace."

"Then why is he consorting with the Israelis?"

"He is consorting with Israel, as you so debasingly put it, to find a solution for peace. Would you prefer if Hamas was sitting next door in the audience hall?" Pollini could not help raising his voice. "A terrorist group totally opposed to a peaceful solution?" He paused before continuing. "Tell me, Cardinal Albertini, what is the real reason for this meeting?"

Albertini took a deep breath and sighed. He had to be careful how he proposed going about casting doubt on the pope's recent behaviour; he did not wish to estrange himself from the support of the cardinals who admired the Holy Father for his outreach program.

"His Eminence has not been himself lately," he continued softly. "Something seems to be troubling him. Is he perhaps ill?" It was widely reported in June 2002 that Pope John Paul II refuted the speculation of his resignation due to failed health. In fact, no citation had been drawn up showing that he could not perform his duties. Albertini wanted to infer a parallel and cast doubt on Bandini's ability.

Pollini tried not to show any sign of alarm. He knew the reason, of course, but was not about to fuel the suspicion with a stray remark. "He is the spiritual leader of the Catholic world. As head of the church, it is a heavy burden to proclaim and instil what is to be morally accepted by all Roman Catholics as the teachings of Jesus Christ and his apostles."

"My point exactly," Albertini pounced. "But is he strong enough to carry out his responsibilities and is he doing it in the right way?"

"Vatican I was called by Pope Pius IX in 1869. It approved

The Papal Secret

the doctrine of papal infallibility in which stated that the pope can commit no error when he speaks as the head of the church in matters of faith and morals." Pollini banged the table with his fist. "How dare you challenge this edict? This is treason that you speak. You are all conspiring to commit treason! You speak as if we are in the throes of *sede vacante*. We are not in the middle of a papal interregnum! The Holy Father is alive and well and performing his duties admirably." He waved his arms across the table. "Adjourn this meeting at once and let me not hear another word of this kind of talk. Rather spend your time examining the good things our beloved Holy Father has done. You should all be ashamed of yourselves!" Pollini turned around and, with his cloak flapping about him as if suddenly stirred by a strong wind, stormed out of the room.

He had just stepped up to the edge of the precipice in defence of his pope. If the council knew the thoughts in his head and the heavy burden he carried in his heart as protector of such a profound papal secret, they would push him over the edge to die on the rocks below.

An hour later, he was seated opposite his pontiff sugar-coating the principal part of the concerns the council had with their leader's policies.

"I am the pope until the Lord, in his infinite wisdom, decides I've served my purpose in this world," Pope John Pietro I said calmly. "My term is not dependent on what the cardinals may think. If they are disgruntled, they only have themselves to blame. I was elected by the full vote of the Sacred College of Cardinals by ballot." He smiled and took a sip of tea Pollini had brought in with him. "You worry too much, my friend."

"I have much cause to worry, Your Eminence. To live with such a secret is not easy."

"You disapprove of my silence?"

"Of course not, Pietro," Pollini replied. "I respect your judgement, and I dare say I would have come to the same conclusion as you if the positions were reversed."

"Thank you, Angelo." Bandini laid a hand on Pollini's arm. "You are the only friend I can really trust. We may look up to heaven and pray to God for holy guidance, but politics is the dirt of this world and part of the equation. I want to be a good Catholic and make the world a better place. Do you think my Jewish blood will allow that?"

"The Jews have been the conscience of the world since

before our saviour. They have survived all the great empires who wanted to destroy them. Through them, God gave to the world moral instruction which they have adhered to for thousands of years. That kind of blood can do you no harm, Your Holiness."

* * *

Cardinal Vittorio Albertini vented his anger at the way Pollini had hijacked his meeting by striding aggressively across the Piazza del Forno. He had the common sense to realise that it would not benefit the integrity of the ministry to overtly display his feelings of anger too excessively in the presence of his peers, so he suppressed his foul mood until he reached his office.

Safely ensconced in the privacy of his office, he released his frustration by throwing the file he was carrying across the room. Sheets of paper floated down and settled on the floor like discarded mats that didn't fit together. It took him ten minutes to retrieve them and sort them into their original sequence—enough time for his temper to abate. Using his mobile phone, he called Fabio Mento.

"I want you to return to Rome immediately," he instructed the security officer.

"What about Frost and the woman, Your Eminence?" he asked. "They have just returned to the boat."

"Forget about them. I need you here."

"I have the data stick, but they may have accessed it. Wouldn't it be better if they weren't a factor?"

"I have a better way of dealing with them. Return at once!"

"I'll leave right away."

Albertini picked up another file and opened it. It was no coincidence that in his capacity as chairman of the Friendship Committee he had persuaded the members of the group to honour one of the most generous benefactors of the Vatican's Discretionary Fund. The money donated was used to support various charitable organisations, such as the Mandela Children's Fund.

As an expression of gratitude to the philanthropist, Albertini had commissioned Frost's boat to take the patron and his family on a seven-day cruise around the coast of Italy. Although the recipient of this gift could well afford to pay for such a cruise, he had accepted the gesture graciously and had informed the committee that he would be sending his wife and their two children and nanny on the excursion. Due to business commitments he would only be joining the cruise on the return journey.

Albertini didn't really care about the itinerary. If he had a pious conscience, he might have feared that God could read his mind and he would have prayed for forgiveness for harbouring such foolish intentions. But Albertini was piously defective, and he couldn't wait to put his plan into action. He had a much greater venture for the *Bella Mare*, one that would end in its destruction, together with its captain and holy guests.

Chapter 27

Rome – September

Michael Frost was pleasantly surprised when he received the invitation from the Vatican to present himself before the Friendship Committee that had commissioned his boat for a cruise later that month. He recalled something his agent had told him, that the boat had been reserved for a Vatican cruise, but recent events had caused the information to slip from his mind.

He looked up at Isabella sunning herself on the terrace. She was lying face down on the sun bed with her bikini top unfastened. Although he had seen her naked body on several occasions since they had met, he still couldn't help admiring her perfect form.

She opened her eyes and saw him staring at her. "What?" she asked, lifting her head and fully exposing the bulge of her breasts.

"Do you know that I love you?" he said.

She sat up, and with a glow on her face, replied, "Not as much as I have grown to love you." She got up and came over to him.

"Would this be an opportune moment for me to ask for your hand in marriage?" he asked hesitantly. A decline could cause complications in their relationship.

"It would," she smiled broadly.

"Will you marry me?"

"Yes!" she cried, and fell into his arms.

They hurried excitedly to the bedroom where, entwined together on the bed, they consummated their intention of marriage.

Much later, in the glow of gratification, she looked deeply into his eyes and offered a cautious condition. "We must keep our engagement a secret for the time being."

"But I want to tell the world," he protested.

"No; it's too soon after my husband's death. For the sake of decency, we must delay the announcement."

"Of course. I understand."

"For now, let's just be content with knowing that we are."

"How would you like to accompany me to Rome?"

"An engagement honeymoon?" she asked in surprise. "How quaint."

"I've been invited to the Vatican to discuss a cruise they've commissioned for the *Bella Mare*."

"Is that such a good idea? I mean, after all that's happened?"

"The cruise was booked some time ago. I don't think it has anything to do with recent events. Besides, with a little snooping around, we may discover who the strange seal belongs to. It's evident that someone there is involved in fraud, maybe even murder."

"Snooping around?" Isabella expressed shock. "There are only two things you can do at the Vatican. Behave yourself and admire the art!"

* * *

The Vatican was the only part of Rome Michael had never been to. On the two previous occasions he had visited the city, the queue into the Vatican was so long that he had given up waiting to gain admission. This time, with Isabella at his side, he headed across Saint Peter's Square with a more determined gait. There would be no waiting on this occasion. He looked up at the buildings above the northern portico as they passed the obelisk and twin fountains. The curving pillars embracing the square were impressive enough, but the great dome of Michelangelo dominated the entire scene.

They entered through the Bronze Portal to the right of the square and presented their credentials to an officer of the Swiss Guard. From there, they were escorted to a small reception room at the corner of the Cortile di San Damaso and asked to wait there.

"My apologies for having kept you waiting." A young man wearing the vestments of a bishop approached them. "Please come into my office. You'll find it more comfortable there."

They entered a small room, and apart from a few statues occupying several niches around the room, there was no other adornment. The wooden desk against the window had only one file on it.

"Please be seated," the young bishop said, opening the file. "I'm Father Augustus."

Isabella was wearing a long pleated skirt and a jacket to match, an outfit, much to Michael's chagrin, which entirely concealed her lovely figure. The cleric sitting opposite them didn't even look at her and she wondered if his stoic attitude would have remained intact if she were wearing something more revealing?

Father Augustus leafed through the file and then looked at Michael. "A very nice facility," he remarked. "The photographs and plans of the cabin layouts are most impressive. I am sure the accommodation will be entirely suitable for our purpose."

"I assure you, the yacht is one of the finest crafts of its class you'll find on the Italian Riviera," Michael said. "There is also the option of a fourth cabin should it be needed," he added.

"There are some details I wish to examine," the bishop said.

"I think I can fill in any gaps the file does not cover."

The bishop proceeded to complete his report as Michael spoke, and finally looked up in satisfaction. "I think I have all that I need. All that's left is to sign the contract." He pushed a document across the table.

The embossed seal in the top left hand corner was different from the one Michael had hoped to find. "Permit me to ask," Michael ventured, "but does each division of the Holy See have its own emblem?" He pointed to the crest.

"The Papal emblem is unique to the pope," the bishop answered with raised eyebrows. "As indicated here, it is *PP I*. The pope normally signs documents using the title "Papa," the abbreviated form being *PP* followed by the pope's numeral. There are, however, others assigned to different levels of the Vatican hierarchy. Why do you ask?"

Michael withdrew a piece of paper containing the symbol of the key and showed it to the bishop. The shocked look on the bishop's face told him he had hit a nerve.

"Where did you get this?"

"On a Vatican document," Michael lied.

"Impossible! That seal is for internal use only. It never reaches beyond these walls."

"This one did."

"Have you a copy of the document?"

"No, not with me."

"I must have it," the bishop insisted. "A breach of this kind could have serious repercussions for the security of the church."

"Can you tell me who the authority is behind the seal?" Michael asked.

"Certainly not. That seal denotes confidentiality of the highest degree. You should never have seen it." Bishop Augustus rose from his chair as an indication the meeting was over. His youthful face had grown pale. He wanted to report immediately that the secret seal had been compromised. "The guard will take you through the inside entrance to the Sistine Chapel. You cannot leave without viewing it." Bishop Augustus hoped to detain the couple within the walls of the Vatican in the event his superior wished to interrogate them further.

* * *

"What did you make of that?" Isabella asked when they were alone.

"I think we ruffled some feathers," Michael said. "Maybe we hit a nerve."

"Do you think someone here is involved in the murders?" Isabella said in an undertone. There was a strong echo in the Sistine Chapel. "Anyway, let's admire the view while we're here." She looked up and was mesmerised.

The ceiling was divided into three zones, but the zone running down the middle was their immediate focus of attention. The nine separate panels depicted episodes from Genesis, the most well known among them being God's creation of Adam as Eve watches from the shelter of his arm.

"This ceiling demonstrates the scope and power of Michelangelo's genius," mumbled Michael humbly.

"I read somewhere that," said Isabella, "according to Vasari, after four years of holding a paint brush above his head, for months afterwards he could only read mail from his father by holding the letters above his head."

For another forty minutes, no other thoughts entered their heads except trying to comprehend the magnificence of the maestro's work of art. Their admiration was interrupted by a tug on Michael's sleeve. It was Bishop Augustus.

Stan Miller

"The General Secretary of the Pontifical Commission wishes to meet with you in the garden," he said.

"Really?" Isabella gave Michael a quizzical glance. "I hope we've done nothing wrong?"

"Not at all," replied Augustus, "but Cardinal Pollini has a few questions he would like to ask."

"About the sign?"

"He will explain."

He ushered them out of the chapel through a side door into the Piazza del Forno and led them in the direction of the gardener's house. He stopped by a cluster of wooden benches and told them to wait there. It was not long before a man wearing a deep scarlet robe approached them. He was a tall man, lean, and walked with a straight posture. Isabella admired his strong, handsome features and guessed him to be in his early sixties. It was not fair, she thought, that men improved with age while women had to go to extreme measures to keep themselves looking good as they grew older and, more often than not, failed at it after reaching sixty. He greeted them with a warm smile.

"I am Cardinal Pollini," he said affably. "I know all about you. Nothing bad, I assure you." He smiled again. He gestured toward one of the benches and invited them to sit. "Excuse the venue. It is very pleasant outside, and I thought it better than sitting in a stuffy office. I trust you enjoyed the Sistine Chapel?" he asked. "It must have been painted by God himself through the divine inspiration with which he blessed Michelangelo."

"It is a miraculous achievement," Isabella agreed.

Pollini cleared his throat. "Just to put your minds at rest," he began, smiling broadly. He was pleasant, even jovial, and Isabella liked him at once. "The symbol you saw does not belong to any sinister organisation that carries out clandestine operations around the world." He laughed to emphasise the silliness of the notion. "Those secret societies are found in books and movies. The emblem is simply a Vatican seal used by three senior cardinals to ratify or reject minor proposals emanating from the Council of Priests. Three seals indicate approval. Less than that will refer the proposal back to the caucus for further debate and modification. The file will eventually land on the pope's desk only if it carries all three of the privy seals. The key is similar to the crossed keys found on the coat of arms of the Holy See. Pope John Pietro I

The Papal Secret

instituted a new innovation to his papacy. Something like the judges appointed by Moses to rule on minor disputes among the people to lighten his burden.

"Similarly, the pope appointed three cardinals as his privy council to deal with matters of lesser importance. The issue would only be presented to the Holy Father if all three keys appear on the document."

"What does the *V* in front of the key stand for?" asked Isabella, intrigued by the cardinal's explanation.

"The Vatican, of course," said Pollini. "You see, my child, we are not trying to hide anything."

"Who are the three members of the privy council?" asked Michael bluntly.

"That is something I cannot divulge," Pollini smiled patiently. "It is an internal structure and the privy seal carries no authority on a secular document."

"If the seal is used only internally," Michael asked, "why was it used externally to authenticate a money transfer?"

"As I said, a single key cannot authorise anything."

"Well, it seems that one of the three holders of the seal has made improper use of it."

"That is not possible, Mr. Frost," Pollini said icily, "and until I see proof of any evidence to the contrary, I think the matter should be forgotten." He stood up to indicate the meeting was at an end.

"Three people linked to this event have been killed," Michael concluded. "Our lives have been threatened. Be careful, Your Eminence; there may be a traitor in your holy triad."

Cardinal Pollini stood up. What he decided not to tell them was that each "seal of the key" had a subtle difference in design from the other two to prevent one seal from being used more than once on the same document. The one Frost had shown him had an identification mark which he recognised.

He signalled with his hand to the guard standing at the opposite side of the courtyard to escort the two visitors through the gate and out of the Vatican. He watched them go before walking back to his office, deep in thought. Those who passed him along the way stood aside for him, not wishing to disturb a priest so deep in meditation. But Pollini's introspection was not directed at the One above. He was thinking about what Frost had shown him. Besides himself, Cardinal Albertini and Cardinal Luca, the President of the Pontifical Commission, were the other two holders of the Privy Seal. He would have

165

ruled out the latter of any malicious intent; at eighty-four years of age his only ambition was to use his wisdom judiciously during the years he had left. Albertini, on the other hand, made no secret of his desire to be the next occupant of the Seat of Saint Peter and sometimes put politics ahead of his devotion to God. Pollini recognised the marking on the key as belonging to Albertini.

Pollini was of the opinion that it was generally accepted that either he, the Secretariat of State, or Albertini was the most likely successor to the present incumbent. He had not expected to be in a favourable position to be the next pope, and promised himself to oppose Cardinal Albertini, if for no other reason than to prevent him from being elected. Albertini was too selfish to hold such a lofty position. And now there was this latest development.

If Albertini was involving himself in schemes of enrichment from sources outside the Vatican, so be it; but murder could not be overlooked. However, if he probed too deeply, he might open up a can of worms that could nibble at his own secret. Above all, the pope had to be protected.

* * *

It had not escaped Albertini's attention that Frost had met with Pollini in the garden of the Vatican. He approached Bishop Augustus with the intention of finding out Pollini's sudden interest in Frost.

"The privy seal was compromised," the bishop told Albertini. "Pollini wanted to know how an outsider came to know of it."

Albertini's premonition of trouble rose easily to the surface, but before he had time to conjure up a suitable explanation, he was summoned to the secretary's office. He knew the reason and on his way up the stairs he decided to be forthright in his response to whatever challenge Pollini might throw at him. "It is entirely my fault that this lapse in security occurred," he confessed immediately.

Pollini was slightly taken aback, expecting a confrontation. "Indeed," he said slowly, "it is a most unfortunate error, but I suppose no harm was done apart from revealing one of our sacred rubrics."

"Frost probably came across it by chance."

"Perhaps, but the seal was revealed on a document you submitted to a bank."

The Papal Secret

"I have many dealings with banks concerning donations from wealthy patrons to the Vatican Charity Fund and, as you are aware, I have been granted the discretion of distributing approved amounts to our various charitable organizations. As a matter of fact, Frost was here to conclude arrangements for a cruise we are sponsoring in honour of the generosity of one of our benefactors."

"Frost claims to have seen a personal document of yours bearing the privy seal that has nothing to do with the Vatican."

"He must be mistaken," protested Albertini. "To what purpose would I use the seal to an external organization?"

"That's exactly what I told him," Pollini agreed. "Anyway, I urged him to forget the matter."

Albertini leaned back in the chair. "There is no reason why he shouldn't." He cupped his hands in pious rectitude and cleared his throat. "To digress," he said, "it seems that all is not well with the countenance of the Holy Father."

"I beg your pardon?" Pollini straightened in his chair.

"He has not been himself lately." Albertini saw a flicker of alarm in the eyes of the man sitting opposite him. Had he hit a nerve? He decided to press on. "Something seems to be troubling him. I ask again; is he ill?"

"The Holy Father is fine." Pollini recovered his composure. "He is just a little tired after his trip to Israel, that's all."

"Perhaps he would like to join us on the cruise for a few days?"

"I'll put it to him," replied Pollini, "but you'll need the Secretariat of State's approval first."

"The pope has full and absolute executive, legislative, and judicial power over Vatican City. The decision will ultimately be his. I'm sure you will be able to persuade him. The excursion will do him good." Albertini rose. "If you need to confide in me, you know you can rely on my discretion."

"I'll keep that in mind," Pollini shivered inwardly, wondering how long it would take Albertini's ingenuity to uncover the pope's secret.

Chapter 28

Rome – September

Fabio Mento peered through the darkness toward the Chambers building. Most of the office suites in the seven-story structure belonged to law firms. Surprisingly enough, only two security guards were loitering about in the foyer. Strange, thought Mento, seeing that every office in the building contained highly confidential information relating to the various clients the attorneys represented; one would have expected the place to be crawling with security personnel.

Mento lifted the cover of his digital wristwatch and noted the time: 01:00. He had waited long enough. The two guards were about to commence their routine patrol again. He had been observing them since ten o'clock and the beginning of every hour they spent twenty minutes checking the floors. One guard would start at the top and the other on the first floor. They would meet in the middle and then return to their station. He knew the routine; he had broken into Stendardi's office before.

Albertini had shown ingratitude when he reported what he had found out from a contact in Israel. The message he received was that the pope had visited a wealthy diamond merchant during his state visit to that country.

"Why am I only hearing of it now?" was Albertini's ungrateful response.

"My contact there only just found out."

"Who did he meet?" Albertini had asked.

"There were no names mentioned," Mento said, "but the visit was arranged by Tony Stendardi."

"The lawyer?"

"Yes."

That little conversation had precipitated his being at the Chambers that night dressed entirely in black. His sole objective was to discover the name of the man the pope had

The Papal Secret

met with. It had to be in one of the lawyer's files.

Mento crossed the road, but didn't proceed to the main entrance; there was too much light from within the foyer. Instead, he made his way to a small door situated on the east side of the building. It was the fire exit from the stairwell. The darkness made it the safest point of entry. He was an expert at picking locks in the dark and it didn't take him long to release the catch. He slipped inside and waited for his breathing to return to normal. He had to cross the foyer to get to the stairwell, but the guards were presently doing their rounds. He made his way upstairs to the fourth floor. The guards would not have reached this area yet, so he proceeded to Stendardi's office and quickly worked the lock.

Once inside, he crossed the carpeted floor of the reception area and entered the lawyer's inner office. He put on his rubber gloves to mask his fingerprints should anyone later suspect there was a break-in and call in the police.

The office was littered with files, but he decided to go straight for the jugular. Ignoring the stack of yellow folders on top of the desk, he stooped in front of the safe standing against the wall behind the desk. Putting his ear to the cold metal, he began turning the knob of the combination lock. It was an old safe and had a simple mechanism, and it only took him ten minutes to crack it. He was about to swing the door open when he heard a noise outside. One of the guards had stopped outside the office and was trying the door.

Mento was sure he had left no telltale signs that the lock had been tampered with. He had been trained to be careful, so he went to the door and locked it in case the guard decided to enter the outer office and check the place out. He waited for several minutes until he was sure the guard had retreated down the passage again. Turning back to the safe, he pulled it open. He was perspiring heavily in the hot air.

He withdrew a small flashlight from his pocket and switched it on. The narrow beam of light was not strong enough to be seen through the window because it had very little lateral width, but it illuminated the contents of the safe quite brilliantly. Albertini had warned him not to take anything, just to note the name and details of the Israeli. He hesitated while fighting to resist the temptation to stuff the pile of money resting on the bottom shelf into his pocket. But he adhered to the cardinal's instruction and only removed the documents on the top shelf. He carried them to the desk and began sifting through them. He wasn't sure exactly what he was looking for, and if he were caught perusing documents, he would spend the same amount of time in prison as if he'd stolen the money. The urge to take some of it was still very strong.

Suddenly, something caught his eye. A Star of David was embossed in the top left corner of a letter and he knew he had found what he was looking for. He carried the letter to the photo copier and made himself a duplicate. Then he carefully replaced the letter where he had found it and returned the documents to the safe. He took one last look at the piles of cash before shutting the safe and cursing his obedience to his patron.

In his haste to report his findings to the cardinal, Mento nearly got caught. He almost rushed headlong into one of the guards inspecting the fire exit door. He managed to stop himself and retreat into one of the toilets at the top of the stairs until the man had passed.

* * *

"A Mr. Grossman." Albertini looked up from the letter Mento had given him on his return to the Vatican. "Why would the Holy Father meet secretly with this Jew?"

"That still remains a mystery," Mento answered. "Unfortunately, the Israeli died a few weeks ago. We may never find out."

"We cannot be presumptuous enough and ask the Pope directly, but I'll find a way to make the lawyer talk."

Chapter 29

Rome – September

Tony Stendardi had a lunch appointment with an important client and he was five minutes late when he sat down at the table trying not to look too flushed. Dr. Alfred Beardley, a British industrialist, remained seated as Stendardi sat down opposite him. The Englishman held up a huge hand to silence the lawyer before he could offer an excuse.

"How good of you to join me on such short notice," Beardley greeted him. "I have taken the liberty of ordering a bottle of cabernet sauvignon. I hope you don't mind." He filled the space around him with an air of confidence which Stendardi knew stemmed from the fact that the man was extremely successful and wealthy.

"Not at all," replied Stendardi. "I have cleared my desk for the afternoon and once you've signed the document which you requested I bring with me, we can polish off the bottle."

"Good." Beardley smiled, and withdrew the gold Mont Blanc pen from his jacket pocket. "Let's get the business over with first before we order lunch." He quickly read the four-page document and signed both his copy and the duplicate document for the lawyer. "My intention is to establish an investment company with the objective of funding a trust to aid the Vatican's children's fund. You have met the pope, I believe?"

"Yes, on an entirely different matter, which," he smiled, "must remain confidential."

"Of course," replied Beardley. "Your business with the Holy Father does not interest me, only that you have access to his 'ear,' so to speak."

"Everything has been set up. I presume that it will be the proceeds from the capital of the investment company that will benefit the charity."

"Yes. My good deed is the forfeiture of any gains the investment realises."

"While leaving the principal amount intact?"

"Precisely, but let us just focus on the beneficiary, Mr. Stendardi," Beardley concluded, picking up the menu. "That is the only thing that should concern you."

Two hours later, after they had parted, Stendardi decided to enjoy a pleasant walk in the sunshine along the Lung Della Altoviti before returning to his office. He glanced along the Ponte Saint Angelo toward the Vatican as he passed the bridge and wondered for the first time in a long while how the pope was handling the revelation that had fallen upon him like the sword of Damocles. No announcement had been issued from the Vatican, so he guessed the pope was not yet ready to reveal his situation to the world. Such news would probably bring the papacy to its knees, and maybe bring some reluctant respect toward Jews. Or would it unleash another plague of anti-Semitism. He feared the latter.

Stendardi was feeling happy that afternoon. He had concluded a deal that would bring a healthy commission for administrating the fund for as long as the trust lasted, which could go on in perpetuity. The ox-tail had been rich but tasty, and the weather was perfect for this time of year. Satiated and content, he didn't notice a white sedan driving slowly behind him. When he paused to admire something, the vehicle also came to a halt. There were not many people walking along the pavement, as there were only a few shops in the area, and as the car got steadily closer to him, no one seemed to think anything was out of the ordinary.

When the vehicle drew alongside Stendardi, he noticed it for the first time. The driver stopped and beckoned to him. "*Scusa, signore*, I am looking for the Ponte Amedeo."

"You've passed it. It's over there." Stendardi smiled affably and pointed behind him. He didn't see the two men who got out of the back of the car on the other side. Suddenly they seized Stendardi and pushed him into the back seat.

Stendardi felt a large hand clamp over his mouth before he could cry for help. The door slammed shut and the car sped off toward the outskirts of Rome. Held down on the seat, Stendardi couldn't see where they were going. The two men had him pinned down and no amount of resistance could budge either of them. He had to stay like that for what seemed to be about fifteen minutes before he felt the car slowing down and easing into a garage. Suddenly the outside world disappeared.

"Let me go!" were the first words he uttered when the

assailant holding him uncovered his mouth.

"Shut up!" growled the driver.

Stendardi was pushed through an open doorway into a bleak room that looked as though it had not been lived in for a long time; it was musty and untidy. "Where are we?" he called desperately.

He was pushed onto an old sofa, which exploded in a cloud of dust as he landed on the dirty cushions. One of his assailants pointed a gun at his head.

"Are you going to kill me?" Stendardi's eyes were wide with fright.

"If you cooperate, you have nothing to fear; otherwise, your body would have already been dumped in the Tiber River."

"What do you want from me?" Stendardi stammered. "I have some money in my wallet. Take it, but don't harm me."

"Listen to me, Mr. Stendardi," the stranger spoke slowly. "Listen very carefully."

Stendardi broke into a cold sweat. The man knew his name. He feared his abduction was no ordinary mugging.

"I have two questions to put to you," continued the stranger. "Either you answer them or I put a bullet into your head. Do you understand me?"

"Yes, but what guarantee do I have that you'll let me go if I give you the answers to whatever it is you want to know?"

The stranger laughed cynically. "There are no guarantees in this business," he growled, "but the right answers might increase your odds of survival."

"A lot of what I know is privileged information between me and my clients," Stendardi said desperately.

"Do you see this gun?" the thug said, pressing the end of the barrel into Stendardi's forehead. "It doesn't know the law."

Stendardi said nothing.

"Shall we continue?" It was more of a statement than a question, for no answer was required. "Who is Samuel Grossman, and why did the pope meet with him in Israel?"

Stendardi felt as though the bullet had already struck him. He tried not to show undue shock. "Was," he said.

"Was?"

"Yes, he died a few weeks ago."

"Don't play games with me, you piece of shit. Give me an answer!"

Stan Miller

"Grossman was an Israeli diamond merchant and he wanted to bequeath some money to . . ." he thought of the lunch he had just had with Beardley, "to the Vatican's children's fund."

"You expect me to believe that?"

"It's the truth. Ask the Holy Father if you don't believe me."

"And what is your role in all of this?"

"To administer the trust fund. I have many clients like that. I have the document in my coat pocket," he said eagerly.

The two men were facing one another across a small coffee table. Suddenly the abductor got to his feet and leaned toward Stendardi. With his face inches away, he hissed. "You have until dawn to change your story into the truth, because if it doesn't check out, I'm going to splatter your brains all over the settee."

The three men left and he heard the bolt on the other side of the door click into place. Stendardi looked around. There wasn't even a window to escape through, but at least, for now, he was still alive.

Chapter 30

Rome – September

Rome lies on both banks of the Tiber River. The heart of Rome is around the Piazza Colonna; banks, hotels, luxury shops, and office buildings make the area the busiest place in the city. It was along the Via del Corso, the mile-long main street, that the hotel in which Michael and Isabella were staying was situated.

The Way of the Course, the street's English translation, runs through the Colonna Square and links two other squares to the north and south. The street got its name because it was used as a horse-racing course during the Middle Ages. The horses ran without riders while Romans cheered from the balconies lining the street. It was also the street where Tony Stendardi had his office.

Michael left Isabella in the shopping district to flirt with the designer brands filling every window while he continued to the lawyer's office building. He had decided to pay the lawyer a visit while in Rome to thank him for his intervention in prevailing upon Inspector Conti that holding Michael responsible for Rochi's murder was a miscarriage of justice. There was no motive, and common sense would have it that Michael would not be stupid enough to kill someone on his own boat while still at sea. Michael bought an expensive bottle of wine for his friend to show his appreciation.

"Mr. Stendardi didn't come to work this morning, Mr. Frost," said the dark-haired woman sitting behind the reception desk. Her blue eyes looked troubled beneath her worried frown. "I tried him at home but there was no answer. Was he expecting you?"

"No, I'm just a friend bearing a gift." He placed the bottle on her desk.

"He met with a client for lunch yesterday and I haven't heard from him since."

"Maybe he's taking the day off, miss . . . ?"

"Tina. You can call me Tina. He wouldn't do that without telling me. I can't understand it. He is very zealous with his time. He's already missed one appointment today and he's strictly punctual."

"Has his wife reported him missing?"

"She's in London visiting her sister." Tina began to get weepy. "What am I going to tell her?"

Michael handed the young girl a clean handkerchief and she dabbed the tears collecting in the corners of her eyes. "Have you informed the police that your boss is missing?" he asked her.

"No, not yet."

"Well, I think you should."

* * *

"I'm worried," Michael confessed to Isabella, half an hour later when they were seated in the restaurant. "I don't think Tony's disappearance is a coincidence. He was making enquiries on my behalf during your husband's murder investigation. Things are happening to everyone linked to it."

"What's that supposed to mean?"

"That the mastermind behind the killings is still watching those of us who are left."

Isabella shivered involuntarily and looked nervously around the restaurant at the other patrons to see if any of them were casting menacing glances in their direction.

"There's no need for paranoia," Michael cautioned her. "It's only a theory."

"That's supposed to make me feel better?" she asked cynically. "They've already grabbed me once!" Her whisper was ascending into a hoarse crescendo.

"Take it easy," Michael said, reassuring her by putting his hand over hers. "We just have to be cautious, that's all."

"I think we should leave your friend's disappearance to the police," Isabella voiced her conclusion. "If we get involved, we'll expose ourselves to a reaction from them."

"Maybe you're right."

"I know I'm right!"

* * *

The Papal Secret

When they returned to the hotel, Michael waited for Isabella to go into the bathroom to take a shower. When he heard the water running, he made the call.

"I gave you twelve hours and you've been gone for three days!" Inspector Conti's voice bellowed out of the receiver. "Where the hell are you?"

"In Rome."

"Great. I'm in the middle of a murder investigation and you're not off the hook yet."

"Oh come on, inspector," Michael said flatly, beginning to lose patience with the little bureaucrat. "Your murder case is over. You know that Umbretti killed Rochi and pushed that man over the balcony. Case closed."

"Ah, but who killed Umbretti?"

"Umbretti was murdered in Milan," Michael reminded him. "That's someone else's problem now." The silence on the other end of the line conjured up an image of Conti looking all forlorn, as if someone had just taken all his toys away. "How would you like to do a little sleuthing in Rome?" Michael invited him. "In an unofficial capacity, of course."

"Rome is way out of my jurisdiction, Michael." Conti's answer sounded hollow. "The local authorities will regard any offer of assistance as interference."

"Surely you have one or two contacts here to give us some sort of lead? A friend of mine linked to your case has disappeared. I need your help to find out what happened to him."

Conti thought about it for a moment. It would be an exciting challenge from his boring routine, and if he was able to contribute anything important to the police in Rome, it would enhance his reputation and raise his small-town status into the big league.

"I have a few days leave due to me," he said finally. "I'll fly down in the morning. Where are you staying?"

Michael told him.

"Book me a room."

Chapter 31

The Vatican – September

It was not difficult to check out Stendardi's story. Cardinal Albertini had only to make one phone call to Phillipe Vittorio, the manager of the Vatican Bank.

"Yes, an account has just been established in favour of the Children's Fund," the banker said. "May I enquire why you wish to know?"

"I require some details for a presentation to the council of cardinals later today," said Albertini. "On the agenda is the investment proposal for the children's fund.

"I cannot divulge the source of the donation, as you will appreciate. Our rigorous protocol does not permit it, especially when the benefactor wishes to remain anonymous."

"Of course," said Albertini politely. "I certainly wouldn't want to violate protocol."

"The amount, however, is recorded in the balance sheet and will be available for your inspection."

"Are you able to confirm that the trust is being managed by a law firm called Stendardi and Partners?"

"That is correct," replied Vittorio. "It is no secret."

"Thank you for your cooperation."

Albertini made one more phone call. "His story checks out," he said.

"What must I do with him?"

"Let him stew for a while. He may tell us something useful before we dispose of him. I'll let you know as soon as I've decided."

"He'll go straight to the police if we let him go."

"I know. Let me think about it."

Chapter 32

Rome – September

Inspector Conti arrived in time for a late breakfast. He sat down opposite Michael and Isabella and ordered a cheese and mushroom omelette. "I came against my better judgement," he told Michael. "Everyone associated with you and your boat meets with disastrous consequences."

"The conspiracy may reach into the Vatican itself," Michael added.

Conti dropped some egg on the white tablecloth before it could reach his mouth. He gave Michael a hard stare. "Be careful what you say," he exclaimed. "The Vatican is off limits and crazy accusations like that will land you in serious trouble."

"Do you recognise this?" Michael slipped a diagram of the Privy Seal in front of the inspector.

"No. Should I?" asked Conti looking puzzled.

"Not according to a senior source in the Vatican." Michael went on to explain what he had learned during his conversation with Cardinal Pollini.

"I'm surprised he explained anything to you at all."

"He wanted to put our minds at rest."

"Good advice," said Conti. "I agree you should drop that line of enquiry. You're treading on sacred ground, if you'll excuse the pun."

Isabella smiled. "Can you help find the missing lawyer?" she asked.

"I can ask around. I have a few friends in the right places, but if the police can't find him, I don't see how we can." Conti dabbed his mouth with a paper napkin while considering a second helping of bacon and eggs.

"To them, it's just one case among many," Michael said.

"We can focus all out efforts on finding him. All we need is a place to start."

* * *

Later that afternoon, Inspector Conti met Michael and Isabella at the hotel pool. Seeing Isabella reclining on the chaise longue clad in a skimpy bikini took his breath away and it took him almost a minute to find his vocal chords again.

"I have a bit of news," he said, failing miserably in trying to keep his eyes off Isabella.

"Something we can work on, I hope?"

"It's not much," Conti confessed, "but it's a start." He examined the notes he had written in his pocket notebook. "A witness says he saw a man fitting Stendardi's description being bundled by two men into a white sedan."

"Did the witness get the registration number?"

"Surprisingly enough, he did. It's registered to Avis."

"A rental. It figures."

"It was hired by a Mr. Peter Salvatori, who happens to be a clerk in the Swiss Guards."

"Has he been detained for questioning?"

"He hired the vehicle for a priest who was visiting the Vatican." Conti rolled his eyes in despair. "Mr. Salvatori says it disappeared from the parking area before it was given to the recipient."

"Do the police believe him?"

"The fact he reported it stolen before the abduction suggests he had nothing to do with it. If he were guilty he wouldn't have hired it in his own name."

"Now do you believe me?"

"I'm afraid I'm beginning to, but it doesn't change the fact that I have no authority to enter Vatican territory; neither do the police. We have to solve this without involving the clergy."

"But if a clergyman is involved?"

"We'll have to hope he does something to incriminate himself. God knows, we can't probe too deeply. If anything comes up, we'll accept it as a fringe benefit."

* * *

The only clue they had was the white Toyota, which was seen driving north along the Via Flaminia.

"They could be in Milan by now," Conti remarked. "The police are looking for the car. When they find it, my contact will let me know. Until then we may as well go sightseeing!" Conti's mobile phone rang as he was speaking. "Yes? I see. Thanks for letting me know." He looked at Michael and smiled. "The Coliseum will have to wait. They've just found the car."

* * *

They pulled into the visitor's parking area twenty minutes later. The Villa Borghese, which was once owned by a wealthy family, is one of the finest parks in Rome. Its hills, meadows, and woods are ideal countryside to host the city zoo.

The white Toyota was fenced off by a yellow police ribbon keeping onlookers away from the investigating officers. Inspector Conti crossed the police line, flashed his badge, and was allowed to proceed to the car. Michael and Isabella had to be content with standing and watching the proceedings from the other side of the line. Conti singled out a young detective and drew him aside. "What can you tell me, Tony?" he asked.

"Not much. There's no evidence of any blood. The car's clean, although we did manage to lift some fingerprints. They may not belong to the perpetrators, but we'll run them anyway and see who comes up through the system."

"You'll let me know?"

"Sure," Tony leaned closer to Conti, "as long as you call me if you find them first. It's time I got a promotion."

"That's a deal." Conti retraced his steps back to where Michael and Isabella were standing. "They found fingerprints. By this evening we should know if they belong to anyone with a record."

Chapter 33

The Vatican

Pope John Pietro I lowered the newspaper he was reading and rubbed his tired eyes under his spectacles. Would there ever be peace in the world God created? The report stated that the Israelis had approved plans for additional settlement construction in the West Bank. The Palestinians now insisted that they would not rejoin peace talks until Israel completely froze settlement growth in their area. Bandini laid out a map of the area of conflict on his table. He had taken a keen interest in the latest developments because an idea was already forming in his mind. He reached for the phone.

"Angelo, arrange a meeting with the Israeli ambassador and the representative for Palestine," he told Pollini. "They're both still in Rome, I understand."

Surprisingly enough, they were both eager to meet with the pope and the meeting was scheduled for that afternoon.

"At least they've agreed on something," muttered the pope.

In the corporate world, the chairman or president of a company is usually the last to arrive at a meeting, to give time for the board members sitting around the table to get nervous. With delegates at a disadvantage, the chairman could be more assertive. In the Vatican, protocol calls for the Holy Father to be already seated in place when his visitors arrive.

When the two rival politicians arrived at the Vatican Palace, they were ushered into one of the reception rooms where the pope was waiting to receive them. Pollini was in attendance, of course, as well as the Secretariat of State of the Vatican.

"There are many opposing forces in the world and not enough intermediaries," the pope began in a soft tone. He found that a pleasant timbre to the voice often modified excitability. "My function is to offer fair advice so that we can work toward an amicable solution."

"We can never have peace in the Middle East if the Israelis

The Papal Secret

insist in pursuing a land-grab policy," Anwar Attar opened his case.

"Judea and Samaria belonged to Israel long before the Arabs arrived," countered Moshe Eban.

"Gentlemen," the pope said raising his hand to silence them. "I am well aware of the problem. We are here to solve it."

"Continued settlement activity in the West Bank is inconsistent with a desire for peace. Tearing down their constructions would solve it," the Palestinian said.

"Peace!" answered Eban, raising his voice. "Look who is advocating peace! How do you expect peaceful coexistence when you have an army of suicide bombers continuously attacking our civilian population? Retreating from our land won't achieve anything."

Bandini was fully aware of their individual complaints. They had been discussed and argued over for so many years. It was time to silence the two antagonists sitting opposite him, and he suddenly brought his fist down on the table. This uncharacteristic behaviour of the Holy Father brought an abrupt end to their quibbling. "Enough!" he said in a raised voice. "You are not children fighting over a ball. Please listen to what I have to say."

Silence descended in the hall. Only the echo of the pope's admonition was heard rebounding off the walls. Pietro Bandini unrolled the map he had been studying and anchored the corners with four paperweights. They were four fragile glass figurines used purposely for this occasion to deter his visitors from suddenly picking them up and throwing them at each other. Using a pencil, he pointed to an area on the map which he had shaded in.

"Here is the settlement protruding into the Arab section of the West Bank." He looked up to make sure the two adversaries were looking at the same place. "As you can see, there is a river running along the one side of the settlement. My proposal is to build a man-made lake spanning the river to divide the two sides. To the south, the river runs into Israeli territory. I suggest that Israel hand over that section to the Palestinians in return for keeping the land encroaching onto the Arab side where their settlement is being built. It will make a natural border where you can both build your housing projects and remain separated by the lake. Eventually, and this has to be agreed upon, an imaginary line drawn down the middle of the lake will become the official border when Palestine one day chooses independence."

The two men studied the map in context of the pope's proposal, looking intently for disadvantages. Their pensive mood lingered for a long time. Bandini was happy; the longer they remained silent, the more confident he was of an agreement being reached. He decided to push a little bit more.

"A modern shopping centre on either side of the lake would be a lovely attraction for the people living there. Even if you sit at the waterside cafes drinking coffee and looking across at each other with unfriendly eyes, it will be better than war."

It pleased the pope to see Eban nodding. "It could work," the Israeli finally admitted.

"But how will we finance such a scheme?" Attar asked suspiciously. The Israelis had plenty of money; the Palestinians didn't. They existed on hand-outs and hoped the same would be offered in this case. He wasn't disappointed.

"The Vatican is prepared to assist by making funds available," the pope announced. "If this pilot scheme works, and I don't see why it shouldn't, it may be the forerunner for a peaceful coexistence of two separate states. We can plan similar projects along the rest of the border. All people really want is to feel safe and be happy."

"I will put your proposal to our prime minister," Eban said. "He desperately seeks an equitable solution to the problem." He leaned back in his chair, satisfied with having lobbed the ball into the opposition court.

"The Palestinian Authority Chairman has the final say," was Attar's response.

"Don't let this opportunity pass," said the pope, looking from one to the other. "For whoever rejects it is not in favour of peace."

When Pollini was alone with Bandini after the others had left, he put a loving arm around his friend's shoulder. "Divine wisdom and Jewish chutzpah work well together, my friend," he said.

Chapter 34

Rome

Inspector Conti received word from his contact much sooner than expected. Sometimes his colleagues could get off their backsides quickly if they wanted to, he mused. Michael and Isabella were out somewhere, so he left a message at the reception desk for them to meet him in the hotel bar. He was officially off duty in Rome and it was late enough in the afternoon to enjoy a strong drink. He was just starting his second glass of imported scotch when Michael walked in.

"The last place I thought I'd find a police officer," Michael said when he found Conti leaning on the bar counter nursing his drink, "is in a place where temptation is difficult to resist."

"Aren't policemen allowed to be human?" he replied, taking a sip of his drink without conscience.

Michael ordered a Miller beer and sat on the stool next to Conti. "Any news?" he asked.

"The surveillance camera showed only one man getting out of the vehicle. The kidnappers must have taken the lawyer to a safe-house first before abandoning the stolen rental."

"Have your friends at the precinct matched the fingerprints yet?"

"They're still working on it. Given the time frame when the witness reported having seen the abduction and the discovery of the car, we can assume they are holed up somewhere in the vicinity of the Villa Borghese."

"It's still like looking for the proverbial needle in the haystack," added Michael.

"Unless the fingerprints yield something, I'm afraid there's nothing much more we can do; except wait."

"Wait for what? A body?"

"Hope not," sighed Conti. "We have to wait for a ransom demand; then we can follow the trail."

"If it's ransom they want."

"They want something. They always do, and if they wanted him dead, they would have killed him then and there on the street."

"Unless he has information they want," Michael suggested. "That will mean they have no need to contact anyone else."

"Well, there's not much we can do at the moment. His wife is on her way back from London. Let's hope it's a ransom they want and that they contact her. She'll be under police protection until we find out what's going on."

"Let me get you a refill," Michael offered. "Thank you for your help in someone else's jurisdiction."

"No problem. I needed a break from paradise."

* * *

Isabella stood on the balcony of their hotel suite and gazed across the rooftops of Rome. There wasn't much colour in the city: grey stone buildings, interrupted by domes and church steeples stretching as far as the eye could see. In the distance, the hills were green and the river offered a pleasant diversion from the crowded streets.

Her thoughts turned to Michael's meeting with Inspector Conti in the hotel bar downstairs. It had surprised her how quickly her love for Michael had developed, but it was the sequence of accidental circumstances and a strong attraction that had resulted in their intimacy. Their brief affair before her husband's murder was out of character and she shouldn't have done it, but she was not sorry. She had been drawn to him from the start. Maybe it was his attentiveness—something she very rarely got from her husband; maybe their relationship was spurred out of her unhappy marriage. Her love for Michael was not perfect, of course. There were still issues that had to be settled. Although she had fallen out of love with her husband even before his death, she hadn't quite come to terms with his demise. Perhaps it was guilt that made her feel this way; guilt for betraying him with another man before he had died. But then, she deserved to be happy, a feeling she had not had for a number of years, until now.

Michael came from a different background, yet they were compatible. She tried to imagine her life with him. He was an adventurer; most often away on his boat. He also had his own baggage, dealing with a wife who had been killed. Isabella was a city girl who loved fine things and cherished a home of her own. Could they remain satisfied with each other? Then she thought of her life without him and shivered.

The sun was beginning to set when she heard the door open behind her. She turned to see Michael walking toward her. "Any progress in the case?" she asked, trying to mask the intense desire to make love to him.

"Not really," he said. "The police are hoping for a positive lead. Until then, we wait." Michael watched her as she stood in the golden glow of dusk. Her olive skin blended perfectly with the magnificent backdrop of the setting sun and the light behind her shone through the material of her sundress, revealing the perfect shape of her body. He told himself that he would never tire of her. A terrible thought entered his mind: what if she decided to leave him when all this was over? He opened his arms and she easily slipped into them.

She clung to him tightly, as if some unseen force was trying to pry them apart. He sensed her intensity and responded with the same alacrity. Her tongue explored his mouth as her fingers ran through his hair. She could taste the beer on his breath, but it only enhanced her desire.

He felt her fingers unbuttoning his shirt. In seconds it was open and she was running her long fingernails over his chest. He loosened her sundress and lifted it over her arms, letting it fall to the floor; she was naked underneath. She lowered her hands and untied his belt. Then she reached for him and guided him inside her.

Leaning against the wall, with the whole of Rome beneath them, they confirmed their love for one another by pushing their nakedness passionately against each other.

"I love you, Michael," she said, hardly drawing her mouth away from his.

"I never imagined I could love like this again," he breathed into her mouth. "I want to be part of your life from now on."

"And I want us to be together for the rest of our lives."

Chapter 35

Rome

They had a suspect. The fingerprints matched a known ex-con and an arrest was imminent. Inspector Conti was confident that the rogue would squeal and they would soon have an address where the lawyer was being held. But first they had to find him.

"These thugs usually frequent the same old disreputable joints," Conti told Michael. "Birds of a feather', and all that shit. As soon as he's spotted in one of the bars, the police will nab him."

"I hope it's soon," Michael said in subdued expectation. "If he's involved and knows where Stendardi is being held captive, his boss won't let him run around loose. Do you have his home address?"

"Yes, but he'll keep away from there."

"He doesn't know he's been identified. He's probably not even aware we're looking for him."

"Good point. I'll drive."

The part of the city they drove into looked like a breeding ground for rats. Leaking bags of garbage lay strewn in the narrow street. The stench was terrible and Michael wondered how human beings could live with it. He held his nose as they walked up some steps to the front door of an old house.

"No point in knocking," Conti said, and fiddled with the lock. The door creaked open and they entered a darkened hallway. They moved slowly across the dining room toward the only door which was closed. Conti picked up a stone ashtray. "I'm unarmed," he confessed.

"Great!"

Suddenly the door opened and a figure dashed out of the darkness. Conti swung wildly with the ashtray and missed. Michael charged after the fleeing man and prepared to tackle him. If he reached the front door, they would lose him for good.

The Papal Secret

He dived at the man's feet and tripped him. Both of them crashed against the wall. In the darkness the only thing Michael could make out was the man's glistening bald head. In the next instance, the ashtray came down on the man's head and the sweat turned into blood. The man lay motionless on top of Michael.

"You killed him!" Michael moaned.

"Nonsense! The man's skull is harder than Carrara marble. He's only dazed."

"What the fuck do you want?" the bald head asked groggily as he regained his senses.

"What did I tell you?" Conti held the ashtray aloft as a warning that he would use it again if necessary. "Check if he's armed."

Michael pushed the bald-headed man off him and quickly frisked him. He noticed that the man's eyes were glancing in the direction of the kitchen.

"He's clean, but you'll find his gun on the kitchen table," he told Conti.

Conti went to retrieve it. "Not bad for an amateur," he smiled, brandishing the weapon in his hand. "How did you know?"

"I've dealt with low life before. I know the signs."

Conti turned his attention to their prisoner. If they had found this place, it wouldn't be long before the police arrived. They would take the bald man down to the station and interrogate him over a cup of coffee until his lawyer arrived before letting him go. You never learned anything with that approach; he shook his head sadly. A direct attack was best and, as he was working outside the law, force would bring quicker results.

"Where have you taken the man you kidnapped?" he asked gruffly, slapping the man hard across the face.

"Are you cops?"

"No, we're conducting a survey for fashion week, you stupid prick! Answer the question or I'll put one of your own bullets into your foot and work my way up to your balls."

"Fuck off!"

Conti squeezed the trigger and blew off the bald man's big left toe. "Your knee's next," he added, pointing the gun at his knee.

"The Villa Glori in the old woodcutter's cottage," he said,

grimacing in pain. "Don't tell them you heard it from me, otherwise I'm a dead man."

When the police arrived a few minutes later, Conti met them at the door. "The bugger shot himself in the foot," he told Captain Corda. "No doubt he'll blame me. He says they're holding the lawyer in the woodcutter's cottage at Villa Glori."

The captain eyed him suspiciously. "I told you not to interfere," he said.

"I'm not interfering," replied Conti. "We were just passing by and we decided to help."

The Villa Glori, a park honouring Italy's war dead, is situated to the north of the zoo where the abandoned car was found. It was thickly covered with pine trees and offered ample concealment for the police squad as they moved toward the cottage. The captain wanted to wait until nightfall, but time was of the essence and it was decided to move in without delay before the abductors had a chance to kill their hostage.

Michael and Inspector Conti remained behind the main attacking force led by Captain Corda. When they approached too near the backmarker, the last man waved them back with a flick of his hand.

Through the trees, Michael could see the police advancing toward the house. "Easy," Michael breathed. "Don't go charging in like a team of ten-year-old soccer players all chasing after the same ball." He relaxed when he saw them spreading out and flanking both sides of the house.

The gunfire ahead echoed in his ears and he dropped next to Conti in the undergrowth. He prayed that Stendardi was still alive and that the kidnappers had not killed him as a last resort. There was nothing more he could do but watch.

The young police officer next to Corda took the first hit. He spun backward and lay on the ground holding his shoulder.

"Are you okay?" Corda bent over him.

"Yes, captain, I took one in the shoulder; it's nothing."

"Back off and wait for a medic," ordered Corda.

The two-way radio on his belt crackled. "Captain, we've gained access," the sergeant he had sent around to the back of the house reported. "We've got two of them. There's one more at the front door on your side. No sign of the hostage."

"We're going in now." The captain signalled to the two men with him to take up positions on either side of the door. "Cover me," he whispered. He swung the door open and rushed

The Papal Secret

inside. It took him only seconds to see the gunman standing on the top of the stairs. He aimed for the man's head and shouted. "Drop your weapon, now!" The man didn't move.

All Corda heard was the roar of a gun. A moment later, the gunman's body hit the floor and rolled down the steps to land at his feet. He bent down and examined the body. The man was dead.

"He was going to shoot you, sir," one of the policemen said. "I had to do it."

"You did the right thing. Thanks." Corda was annoyed with himself for hesitating. It could have been him lying dead on the floor instead of the perp.

Another three members of the squad arrived. "Downstairs is all clear," one of them said. "The hostage is locked in the attic upstairs. He's alone, if you can believe what these bastards are telling us."

Corda went cautiously up the stairs and stopped in front of the only door on the second level. "Stand back!" he shouted and blasted the lock. The door swung open and when he entered the loft, he saw a man sitting in a chair. His arms and legs were tied and there were bruises on his face.

"Thank God you found me," he said, trying to smile.

* * *

Michael found Stendardi leaning against one of the police vehicles. A young nurse who had attended to him was packing away her medical bag. Turning to her patient, she said, "You'll be okay now, Mr. Stendardi. The bruises will heal in a few days."

"Thank you, my dear," Stendardi said. Turning to Michael, he added. "What are you doing here?"

"Lighting fires under bureaucratic arses," he replied. "Sometimes the cops require civilian motivation before they get going. What did the kidnappers want with you?" Michael looked around hurriedly. It was only a matter of time before he was told to leave.

"Information."

"What kind of information?"

"I can't tell you exactly, but it is a very delicate matter."

The arrival of Captain Corda put a stop to any further conversation.

Stan Miller

"Mr. Frost, I must ask you to leave. This is police business now and I have to take Mr. Stendardi down to the station for debriefing."

As Michael got up to go, Stendardi whispered in his ear. "I think I know who put these guys up to it. Meet me at my house at ten."

Chapter 36

Rome

The car continued on harmlessly. Michael eased away from the shadows outside the gate of Stendardi's house and watched the vehicle disappear down the road before ringing the bell. It opened silently and he went in.

"Were you followed?" Stendardi asked, closing the door behind him after a brief look up and down the street.

"I don't think so, but I was paranoiac enough to look suspiciously at a cat skulking behind me when I arrived."

They went out onto the terrace overlooking the garden. There was no wind and the trees on the other side of the lawn were still and silent; not even the leaves rustled. It was as if the foliage itself was also waiting for an explanation. A perfect night, thought Michael, but the ensuing discussion would change all that.

"Thank you for rescuing me," Stendardi said. "I believe it was through your insistence that the police reacted so quickly."

"You're safe now."

"Yes, for the moment. I asked you here because there seems to be a common factor linking our two cases." He paused, holding Michael with his eyes.

"Go on."

"You told me that your own investigation concerning the murder on your boat is linked to a fraudulent action involving someone in the Vatican?"

"Yes. An emblem was used on a bank transfer document which, as I found out later, was the privy seal of three senior cardinals at the apex of the papal hierarchy. I spoke with Cardinal Pollini, the General Secretary of the Pontifical Commission, and he confirmed it."

"He told you that?"

"Yes, he said the seal was only used in internal matters and that I shouldn't concern myself over it."

"Pollini is beyond reproach. His loyalty to the pope is unquestionable. I would trust him with my life."

"You know him?" Michael asked in astonishment.

"That brings me to the reason for my abduction," Stendardi's face changed abruptly. He was a serious man most of the time, but the intensity of his countenance became even more resolute. "I was kidnapped for information they wanted concerning one of my recently deceased clients."

"Lawyers have many enemies, but would they go that far?"

"They wanted to know the nature of my client's business with the Holy Father." Stendardi paused while he poured two glasses of wine and handed one to Michael. "Of course, the information they wanted me to divulge is privileged. I can't even confide in you, but I can tell you that it would be very valuable in the hands of the pope's enemies."

"And you think we are both looking for the same man?"

"It looks like it."

"Then it must be one of the three holders of the Privy Seal."

"It will be impossible to get any names out of the Vatican. Their secrecy is worse than lawyers'." Stendardi gave a rare smile.

"You must inform Cardinal Pollini right away of our suspicions. He will know what to do."

* * *

It wasn't until late the following afternoon that Stendardi was able to meet with Pollini. He had stressed the importance of meeting somewhere outside the Vatican, where he would explain the importance of secrecy. If indeed there was a rogue prelate inside the Vatican responsible for his abduction, it would jeopardise the safety of them both if they were seen together.

The venue for their meeting was across the Tiber River at the Gallery of Modern Art. Although Pollini was not an admirer of the post-Renaissance genre, the curator of the gallery was a personal friend of his who knew how to be discreet. He made his office at the back available to the two men and quietly retired to do some work elsewhere in the building.

The Papal Secret

"What is so important to draw me away from Michelangelo's frescoes?" Pollini asked, closing his eyes as if trying to recall those beautiful images that he loved so much.

Stendardi could speak freely with Pollini because he had also earned the respect of the pope for keeping silent about his knowledge of the pontiff's heritage. He was a man both clerics knew could be trusted. He told the cardinal of his abduction and how he had been rescued before he could be coerced, through torture, into telling what he knew about Grossman's business with the Holy Father. He also related to Pollini the content of his conversation with Michael. At the mention of Michael's name and what he knew of the privy seal, Pollini sucked in his breath and hurriedly crossed himself, more out of distress than devotion. When Stendardi stopped speaking at the end of his discourse, Pollini stood up and moved around the room, deep in thought.

"Thank you for informing me," he said at last. "If the Holy Father is in danger, it is better to be forewarned."

"Is it possible for Your Eminence to reveal the names of the holders of the privy seal?" Stendardi dared to ask.

"I'm afraid that is impossible. It is privileged information. You, of all people, can appreciate that."

"Fair enough, but our lives are also in danger. How are we to protect ourselves if we don't know who it is that threatens us?"

"Even if it is true what you claim, knowing who it is will not help you. A man in that position has hired hands to do the dirty work. The threat could come from anywhere. Just be careful and be aware of who's around you." He bent forward until his mouth was close to Stendardi's ear. "Is our secret still secure?"

"Yes."

"Then I will attend to my own investigation within the walls of the Vatican, and if I find out who might be posing a threat to anyone, I will deal most severely with him before he can do any more harm."

* * *

The Holy Father looked tired, thought Pollini, and it pained him to think that what he had to tell him would add to his burden. They were in the little private chapel near the pope's bedroom. Members of the papal household had already retired to their quarters, leaving them both alone. The two men were sitting together against the back wall of the chapel.

"Has Sister Francesca retired to her room for the night?" asked Pollini. The nun had been in the service of Pietro Bandini for many years and still carried out her humble chores, fussing over his welfare. She was often heard humming a happy tune as she walked down the dimly-lit corridors in the morning carrying a tray of steaming hot coffee and some biscuits for the pope. "She knows nothing of our secret, I presume?" He wasn't sure how far the pope would go in confiding in her; they had known each other for a long time.

"Of course not," replied Bandini. "She doesn't take confessions."

"I'm afraid Albertini is becoming a handful," Pollini continued, underplaying the seriousness of the situation. There was no need to tell him about events that had recently happened outside the Vatican which Albertini was alleged to have been involved in. Suffice to warn the pontiff that Albertini suspected collusion between the Holy Father and Grossman and seemed determined to find out what it was.

"Is it possible for the secret to become compromised?" Bandini asked.

"Not at all," Pollini tried to reassure him. "The only proof is in your possession."

"It is safely hidden."

"It must remain so, until you are ready."

"It could take the rest of my life to make that decision," the pope said sadly.

"Albertini would love to unseat you, Pietro. You must be careful."

"Promise me one thing, Angelo. If anything should happen to me, I want you to oppose Albertini in an election for the papacy. We don't want another Borgia dynasty."

"You have my word, Your Holiness."

* * *

Cardinal Albertini may have strayed off the path of righteousness, but he loved the Vatican to a degree of obsession and he was beginning to feel uneasy. Perhaps in trying to find some way to discredit the reputation of the pope, he had overplayed his hand. The kidnapping of the lawyer and his subsequent escape required greater discretion on his part.

The Papal Secret

His inadvertent use of the privy seal in a private communication had made Frost suspicious of Vatican involvement in the yacht murders. He cursed his recklessness.

Questioning the lawyer about Grossman had been a mistake. With Stendardi free, Pollini would get to hear of the abductors' interest in the Israeli and begin to wonder who they were working for. The only positive outcome to the botched kidnapping was, if there was a cover-up between Grossman and Pollini, and Stendardi knew about it, ruffling some feathers might lead to mistakes being made, and it would only be a matter of time for the secret to be chipped away and exposed. However, it was not his intention to bring the Vatican into disrepute and tarnish its image, no matter how fiercely his own ambition burned within him to become the next pope. Discretion would rule his actions from now on.

Chapter 37

Santa Margherita

Michael looked across the vast expanse of water and wondered why he was involving himself in matters that really weren't his concern. Let the police sort the mess out. He felt good standing on the deck of his boat listening to the shrill sounds of the seagulls and the gentle lapping of the waves against the hull. For him, the sea represented an uncluttered world in which he could think freely. Unconstrained by the mundane problems of daily life, once on board, he had only the wind and the rain to contend with. That is, until he looked at the manifest of the forthcoming cruise that had been booked and saw Vatican involvement again.

Isabella had returned that morning from her home in Milan. It had taken Michael's entire repertoire of persuasion to convince her to return to the boat. He had to repeat several times how much he loved her before she happily relented. The ten days apart had been lonely and meaningless.

He had felt the same loss of companionship after the death of his wife. But then, the tragic event had dulled his senses and robbed him of any feeling whatsoever. The reality that his loss was final had plunged him into a state of nothingness for a long time while he tried to cope with what had happened. Now, love had ignited his *joie de vivre* and his craving for a companion once more.

"As idyllic as this life seems to be," Isabella moaned as she dipped a mop into a bucket of soapy water, "it's not as satisfying as standing on a veranda that doesn't move and with servants to keep it clean!"

He looked up and smiled at her. "Who said being in love was easy?" he teased.

"I probably read it in the *Idiot's Guide Book to Marriage!*"

"There's no such publication."

"Well, there should be," she insisted, and ran the mop once

The Papal Secret

more over the deck where she was standing. "Why don't we just wait for rain?" she asked. "Then the entire boat will be cleaned in one go."

"Get on with it, or you'll be fired."

"Don't tempt me to provoke you any further," she warned.

Their attention was suddenly diverted by the sound of a commotion on the dockside. A Mercedes 600 was trying to force its way onto the quayside where the *Bella Mare* was berthed. Several dockside workers were standing in its path blocking the entrance.

"You can't drive your vehicle onto the pier!" one of the workmen was shouting. "Reverse back into the parking area."

The driver of the sedan was taking no notice of the instruction and continued inching through the crowd blocking his way. A tirade of insults was thrown at the driver until the car stopped and a man got out. He was holding a gun in his hand and was waving it furiously over his head. The men jumped back and, like a well-drilled platoon of soldiers, opened the way for the Mercedes to continue.

Much to the chagrin of Michael, the vehicle stopped alongside his boat.

The man with the gun walked up the gangplank and approached Michael. "My name is Fabio Mento and I'm an officer in the Surveillance Corp of the Vatican," he said in a steady voice.

"You're a long way out of your jurisdiction, so unless you intend using that weapon, I suggest you put it away," Michael said without trying to hide the contempt in his voice.

"Oh, I'm sorry," said Mento, replacing the gun in his pocket. "I only brandish it to get quick results. It usually prevents the necessity of an argument." He extended a hand, which Michael shook reluctantly. "You must be Captain Frost?" he added.

"Yes, this is my boat."

"Excellent, then we can get right down to business." He placed his briefcase on the table and withdrew a folder. "I have here the details of the Vatican cruise. Quite satisfactory, I assure you, but I am here to discuss a few changes to the arrangements, and to inspect the boat."

"The pamphlet you have covers all the facilities on board, as well as the accommodation. What more do you wish to know?"

"There is nothing like seeing things for yourself, wouldn't

you agree, Mr. Frost, especially when the people you are responsible for are so important?" He opened his briefcase and extracted a folder. "I need to know everything about the course you will be navigating and the personal profiles of your crew." He withdrew a gold fountain pen from his jacket pocket and opened his notebook. He looked up expectantly at Michael as if waiting for dictation. "Including you, how many crew members will there be on the cruise?" he asked.

"Three."

"Isn't it a bit risky sailing with only a crew of three?"

"We're not crossing the Atlantic, Mr. Mento," Michael told him.

"Fair enough; less of a security problem then. How well do you know them?

"The one has sailed with me since I started," Michael said. "The other is my fiancé."

As if waiting in the wings for her cue, Isabella entered the stateroom. She was still wearing the shorts and t-shirt she had on while mopping the deck.

Mento had the good manners to rise and bow slightly. "I see the ship is in good hands," he said.

"This is Isabella," Michael announced.

"Delighted to meet you," he said, giving her a good look, "which brings me to the purpose of my visit. The pope will be joining the cruise for one night when you berth in Fiumicino. It will be my responsibility to see that nothing goes wrong while he is on board." He turned to look at Isabella again. "As much as I admire your exquisite beauty, signora, I must request that you dress modestly in the presence of the Holy Father."

"Of course," she smiled. "I keep my finery for when we are at sea."

"Naturally," Mento bowed.

"There are only three luxury cabins on the *Bella Mare*, and you have already filled them."

"Dr. Alessandro Riva's family will be spending the night ashore when the pope arrives. The philanthropist and the pontiff have business to discuss. They will be alone, apart from Cardinal Pollini, Cardinal Albertini, and me."

"It's your cruise."

"Good, then it's settled." Mento stood up. "Now, if you would care to first show me around, I'll leave the two of you to continue preening your ship."

Chapter 38

The Vatican

Cardinal Albertini stood at the window of his second-floor room watching the shadows lengthening across the courtyard. Birds had gathered on the lawn, picking at blades of grass and extracting whatever it was they were feeding on. The afternoon was swiftly coming to an end and he could hear the shuffling of feet outside in the corridor as everyone was making their way to the communal chapel for evening prayers. Albertini didn't turn away from the window but continued watching the birds. *Such carefree creatures*, he thought. *The Lord should have created the earth only for them.*

The Grossman connection was still troubling him and the more the enigma perplexed him, the more furiously he pressed on the white beads of his rosary. What frustrated him even more was that he could not invest the question with a degree of prayer. What he was proposing to do was to pluck the apple from the forbidden tree!

If there was some strange secret the pope was keeping, learning what it might be could hasten the day of his apostolic succession to the papacy. Unfortunately, that information was probably secured in only one place, the papal safe.

Albertini arrived at his decision as a large bird landed amid the flock of smaller creatures and chased them away with a flurry of its wings. *Even paradise has its blemishes*, he thought wryly.

The evening Mass was always attended by the Holy Father and his secretary, Pollini. That would keep them in the abbey for at least an hour. *Enough time*, thought Albertini, *to do a little snooping.*

He turned away from the window and went to his desk. Lying on top of the wooden table was a small black tool case. He opened it carefully and selected a few skeleton keys that Mento had told him would open the most bothersome of locks.

Stan Miller

He had almost an hour to crack open the safe.

Albertini opened the door to his room and peered out. As expected, the corridor was deserted and dimly lit by low-wattage wall lights. He made his way carefully to the papal quarters, and with a hasty look around to ensure that nobody had lingered in the vicinity, he crossed the outer office and went directly to the pope's door. It was unlocked; there was little need for tight security within the walls of the Vatican.

It was highly unlikely that the pope was still in his study, but he had taken the precaution of preparing a cover story that would explain the reason for him being there; he was carrying a document with him that required the pontiff's signature. Albertini hesitated in the corridor, listening carefully for any sounds coming from the office he was about to enter. There were none.

Hesitantly, he turned the handle and opened the door. He entered the room quickly and closed the door behind him. The only light that burned in the room was a desk lamp which gave enough illumination to avoid having to switch on the main overhead light. Albertini glanced up at the crucifix hanging on the wall behind the pope's desk and instinctively crossed himself.

He diverted his gaze from the cross, knowing that what he was doing was unethical, and examined the large safe standing in the corner opposite the window. On his knees in the stillness of the study, he kept his eyes away from the figure on the cross and inserted the first key. It failed to engage. He tried the next one and it too didn't release the lock. He glanced up at the figure of Christ as if imploring divine assistance, but he was sane enough to know that if it came it would not rule in his favour.

After fifteen minutes of failure, he rose to his feet and rubbed his sore knees. He found himself pacing the floor to rid himself of the stiffness in his legs before kneeling once again in front of the safe. This time the lock finally succumbed to the seventh key.

The safe was packed with papers. He carried them over to the desk and without the slightest feeling of guilt at this intrusion on another man's privacy, began a careful scrutiny of each document. His attention was drawn to a sealed envelope lying on its own on one of the shelves. He read the inscription and his heart went cold. "To be opened in the event of my death," he read out loud. He knew this was the moment of truth. If he broke the seal now and opened it, the

The Papal Secret

pope would know the letter had been tampered with.

He looked around the room. A small kettle stood on a coffee table against the wall by the window. He went over to it and checked that it was filled with water. Then he switched it on and waited for it to boil. When it began to steam, he held the envelope over the hot vapour and waited for the glue to soften. Carefully, he pried open the flap without tearing it. He switched off the kettle and went to sit at the pope's desk.

Albertini had to read the pope's confession three times to make sure he wasn't hallucinating. He leaned back in the chair and closed his eyes. The revelation was beyond credulity and he needed time to think and digest what he had just learned. He wasn't worried that the pope might enter at any moment; the letter in his hand had just made him the most powerful man in Christendom.

Although somewhat misguided, Albertini was still a pious man. His first concern was the impact this revelation would have on the church. Strangely enough, his worst fear was not that the world would be shocked, but that the Jews might gloat.

Finally, he made his decision. He tore a blank page from the papal note pad and folded it exactly like the original. Then he placed the blank piece of paper in the envelope and resealed it with a touch of glue. Satisfied there were no signs to suggest that it had been tampered with, he placed the envelope precisely where he had found it. The instruction on the envelope meant that it wouldn't be opened until it was too late. Let the College of Cardinals figure out why the deceased had left a blank piece of paper to be read after his death. He smiled cynically and placed the pope's letter in his pocket and let himself out of the office. Glancing up and down the corridor to make sure nobody saw him leaving the papal quarters, he went straight to the chapel, arriving moments before the conclusion of evening prayers.

He mingled politely with as many worshippers as possible so that his attendance would be noted, and retired to his chambers to deliberate further on the issue before the evening meal was called.

Chapter 39

Nelspruit – South Africa

Franco and Katherine Martini had chosen a new life of anonymity in the town of Nelspruit, situated in the north eastern part of South Africa near the Kruger National Park. They felt safe and secure in their new home and, with the money Franco had salvaged from the Rochi embezzlement scheme, had enough in the bank to ensure a comfortable life. They had restricted their socialising to a few friends and preferred to maintain a low profile.

But it is difficult for a newly-arrived Italian couple to go unnoticed in a predominantly black town with a large white Afrikaans-speaking community, and it wasn't long before Fabio Mento learned of their whereabouts. Mento had contacts everywhere in the world except, by his own admission, in the Middle East where information-gathering on prominent Catholic families was a little more difficult. He had compiled his dossier on men of influence from whom he could either solicit favours or blackmail, whichever was applicable to further his own interests. His Vatican salary was not enough to support a spendthrift wife and her lavish lifestyle, and his job in security opened many doors that would otherwise be closed to him.

Mento had a talent for accruing large sums of money through nefarious enterprises; he already had false documents prepared claiming beneficiary rights to Martini's fortune should the couple meet with an untimely end. He would also be doing the *patrone* a favour tying up more loose ends if the couple were to disappear for good.

When Franco Martini made arrangements to take his wife on a vacation into the Kruger National Park, Mento seized his opportunity. It only took one call from his mobile phone in Rome to dispatch the two assassins to the game reserve. His only instruction was to make it look like an accident.

Franco and Katherine went straight to the observation deck after they had checked in at the lodge. It was too late to venture into the park itself so they sat at a table on the terrace overlooking the watering hole. They ordered a bottle of wine and settled down to watch what was happening below them.

What made Africa different from whatever they had experienced before was its scent. A dusty aroma of dry grass and bushveld shrubs blending with the pungent smell of a herd of wildebeest drinking at the edge of the waterhole gave the air its bittersweet fragrance. The monotonous tones of different shades of green gave the landscape a beauty of its own, but when a flock of pink flamingos settled near the herd, the whole world seemed to explode into colour.

Franco sat mesmerised by the scene on the other side of the fence. It was as if he were watching the creation of the world unfolding in front of him. Some giraffe approached the waterhole on tentative legs and cautiously found a place for themselves away from the noisy herds of wildebeest and zebras. From their lofty height, the giraffe surveyed the high grass surrounding the water for any signs of lions or other predators that might have encroached into the vicinity in search of food. When satisfied that no danger was overtly present, they spread their gangly legs apart like arthritic sufferers and lowered their heads to drink.

At the end of the day, when the sun seemed to touch the horizon in a hue of golden-orange, bringing the sharp serration of thorn trees into focus, the animals moved away from their drinking places to find refuge in the long grass during the hours of darkness. Only the shrill sound of birds and crickets indicated that the land was still alive.

Night comes suddenly in Africa and the darkness around them was complete. Katherine looked up at the stars and was surprised to see how many there were; the pinpricks of light stretched from horizon to horizon.

They ate dinner in the camp restaurant and retired for the night. The gates of the camp opened at six a.m. and they wanted an early start.

* * *

On their first day, they decided to take the safari bus tour into the game reserve. Sometimes, the animals were so well camouflaged in the high grass that they weren't seen until the guide pointed them out. A pride of lions rose majestically to their feet and emerged out of the undergrowth like wisps of vapour rising into the air. The lions sauntered toward the bus, which had stopped at the side of the road.

Suddenly, a belly roar emanating from the throat of the fiercest looking beast broke the nervous silence on the bus, causing the passengers to instinctively lean away from the windows. Moments later, the pride ambled off, and all that remained of their intrusion into man's proximity were the bewildered expressions on the faces of the onlookers.

Later that afternoon, they saw another rare sight. A cat-like creature emerged into view; its foreshortened jaw and feline face gave it an innocently beautiful appearance as it stalked slowly through the grass. Ahead, an unsuspecting gazelle that had become separated from the herd was grazing quietly on its own. The spotted cheetah, recognising the vulnerability of its prey, sprang into action. Only then did the little buck look up and realise the danger it was in. Terrified, it tried to outrun the cheetah. The chase was of short duration. With a mighty swipe of its paw, the cheetah felled its victim and gripped it by the throat.

"Look at the cheetah's elongated legs," explained the ranger. "Its powerful hind legs can propel it to twice the speed of a racehorse. No animal can outrun it."

The buck did not take long to die. It kicked and thrashed about for a while trying to free itself from the asphyxiating grip on its throat until the struggling ceased and the feeding began.

Katherine noticed that the white stomach of the buck was left intact.

"Unlike most other predators," the ranger explained, "cheetahs leave the stomach of the kill untouched. You'll notice how carefully they are eating around the gut so as not to puncture it and soil the meat."

High in the sky above the kill, several large vultures were hovering, waiting for the cheetahs to move away so that they could swoop down and devour whatever was left of the carcass. The beauty and savagery of Africa was juxtaposed in a single moment of time.

Katherine couldn't help shivering as a terrible sense of foreboding overcame her.

Chapter 40

Kruger National Park

Early the next morning, Franco and Katherine set out in their own car to explore the wild at their leisure. They had no reason to suspect they were being followed and failed to notice a grey Jeep following at a distance behind them. When they stopped at a small waterhole, the Jeep carried on past them.

Franco pointed to a fish eagle swooping down and shimmering across the surface, dipping its talons into the water and then soaring upwards with a fish gripped in its claws. *Existence in the wilds*, thought Franco, *is fraught with danger from stronger predators.* Survival was a common instinct shared by all species.

They continued their journey in an expectant mood, until the road curved sharply to the left and the grey Jeep was blocking their path. Franco slammed on the brakes. A man was standing next to the Jeep.

"*Dove vai, signore* Martini?" asked the man with the gun.

"What do you want?" Franco asked.

"Park your car behind that tree," the man said. "You are both coming with us."

"Who are you and where are you taking us?" Franco was beginning to panic. The motive for this ambush was not robbery. They knew his name.

"Get in the Jeep!"

Franco looked at his wife and then at the gun pointing toward him. "We'd better do as they say, Katherine."

The Jeep turned off the main road onto a dirt path hardly wide enough to drive along. The driver ignored the large sign forbidding entry. As they drove, thorn bushes scratched the sides of the vehicle, which the driver didn't seem to mind. *Probably a hired car*, thought Franco.

They drove for about five kilometres until they came across a mass of moving grey shapes. With their heads lowered, the wildebeest were galloping past in a determined rush to get away from something that had evidently frightened them.

"Stop the Jeep," the man with the gun told the driver. "This is a perfect spot." Turning to Franco and Katherine, he gave one more command. "Get out!"

"You can't leave us here," shrieked Katherine. "This is lion country!"

"Precisely. Now get out or your husband will die right here with a bullet in his head."

Franco got out of the vehicle. "Come, Kathy; we'll stand a better chance away from these two thugs." Franco took hold of his wife's hand and moved into the bushes.

"How sweet," laughed the man with the gun. "Enjoy your lover's stroll in the wilderness. It will be your last." He climbed back into the Jeep and laughed sardonically as the sound of a roaring lion came from the other side of the clearing. The Jeep sped away in a fanfare of dust.

"We'll stay close to the trees," said Franco, making it sound like the perfect plan. "That way we can climb to safety should the lions approach."

"Don't they climb trees?"

"Not as a rule."

"Do they know the rules?" she asked, not intending to be humorous. She had read somewhere that lions liked to stretch out in the branches of trees for a quiet nap in the shade. "I suppose it will be safe if we climb high enough into the tree where the branches are too thin to hold their weight."

Franco tried to take a bearing. He thought they had driven south from the main road where he was forced to leave his car. That being the case, if they kept the sun to their right, they would eventually come across the road where they could stop a passing motorist and get a lift back to camp. But that was five kilometres away and they still had to break through the gauntlet of hungry lions. The periodic roar of a lion reminded them that the beasts were not too far away. "Perhaps we should get downwind of them," he suggested, "so they won't smell our presence."

"Downwind of whom?" asked Katherine. "You don't even know where they are."

They walked on in silence, hugging the line of trees. When they reached a baobab tree, they paused to rest under it. The large trunk was partially split down the centre, offering a foothold to the higher branches if they needed to climb up in a

The Papal Secret

hurry. Katherine sat down, leaning her exhausted body against the broad trunk. She removed her shoes and massaged her blistering feet.

"We should never have come to Africa," she moaned. "This place is alien to us."

"If they found us here, we wouldn't have survived very long in Europe."

"Why do they want us dead?"

"I'm not sure," he shook his head sadly. "Perhaps they think we know who's behind the killings in Italy."

"What did you get yourself involved in?"

"Giorgio was siphoning small amounts of money off hundreds of investment accounts. It wasn't supposed to get out of hand."

"Breaking the law is already out of hand."

"You didn't complain spending the money."

"You don't have to be crude, Franco."

They both fell silent. This was not a time to argue. Their life in Milan had not been that bad until greed got the better of him. Rochi's scheme seemed so simple—a few Euros siphoned from clients' investment accounts that would not mature for years would hardly be noticed, especially if huge dividends were eventually declared. That is, until Umbretti latched onto the scheme and wanted some of it for himself. It was a bad move bringing in the big boys like he had. They wanted everything for themselves.

Suddenly, Katherine gripped his hand so tightly that her wedding ring ripped open his skin. "Franco," she croaked, fear choking her voice. "It's there, at the edge of the clearing."

Franco looked up into the eyes of the beast. Its shoulders and forelegs were tremendously muscular, even as it stood motionless, watching them through gold-coloured eyes. Franco stared in horror at the long, sharp teeth, saliva dripping from its open mouth.

"Don't make any sudden moves," he warned her.

Katherine had already shuttled to the other side of the tree. She stood up slowly and began climbing into it. Franco decided to follow her before the lion charged. As if knowing Franco's intention, the lion launched itself into attack.

Summoning extra strength from the surge of adrenalin coursing through his veins, he hoisted himself into the tree and began climbing upward.

Stan Miller

The lion was swift for its three hundred and fifty pounds, and it crashed into the tree with such force that Franco lost his footing. The lion clung to the tree trunk and embedded its claws into Franco's trailing left foot.

It wasn't the pain that caused him to scream, but the force with which the lion dragged him downward. His fingers began to lose their grip on the branch above and he realised that if he could not escape the grip the lion had on his foot, he would be doomed. Katherine was reaching for his hand in a vain effort to prevent him from succumbing to the lion's clutches.

In the end, Franco could not hold on any longer and dropped to the ground next to the lion. Two other lions appeared and joined in the frenzy. Franco's body was ripped apart in seconds and no amount of screaming from Katherine deterred their determination to eat. They dragged his body into the long grass and continued to gorge on his body, blessedly out of Katherine's sight.

An hour later, the lions moved off and left Katherine sobbing hysterically in the tree. Now she was alone and didn't know what to do. She remained in the tree for another hour before lowering herself to the ground. She began running in the direction they had been going. She didn't fear the lions anymore. What she had witnessed had driven out all emotion; all she wanted was to get as far away as possible from this cursed spot.

* * *

Sergeant Alan van der Westhuizen picked up the yellow file for the last time. The coroner had issued a verdict of death by misadventure. There were signs all over the park warning people not to get out of their cars, so the tragic deaths of the man and woman were brushed aside as carelessness.

The sergeant, however, was not entirely convinced. The victims' car was found too far away from what was left of their bodies to suggest careless wandering, and a second set of tyre treads indicated that there had been another vehicle present. His superior had scoffed at his opinion. "Even in the unlikely event that it was some sort of bizarre revenge killing," he was told, "the perpetrators would be gone by now and probably safely back in Sicily. Better to concentrate on local problems."

The issue concerning him now was the pending protest march on the municipal offices by disgruntled residents over bad service delivery which had been allowed to continue for too long. And he hadn't even mobilised his troops yet.

He shrugged his shoulders and stamped the file, dropping it into the *case closed* tray on his desk.

Chapter 41

Santa Margherita – Italy

Michael had made a phone call the previous afternoon which prompted a visit the next morning to the *Bella Mare* from Tony Stendardi. The lawyer was dressed casually for this occasion, which meant he had disposed of his tie. He removed his navy blazer and took a seat opposite Michael on the aft deck, where there was enough shade to keep them cool.

"Thank you for inviting me to sail with you during your sea trials," he said. "A couple of days break will do me good."

"We have a lot to talk about while you assist me on the bridge," Michael reminded him.

"I'm well aware there's no such thing as a free lunch, so whatever it is that's troubling you, I'm more than willing to help; pro bono, of course," he smiled.

"I know you have your contacts at the Vatican," Michael began.

Stendardi raised his eyebrows and waited for his friend to continue.

"Everything that has happened this past month to the passengers on my last cruise has indicated a Vatican connection. I'm not saying that there is corruption in the clergy," he hastened to add, "but someone there seems to be involved in illegal activity. The privy seal on a document submitted to an institution outside the holy walls seems to suggest that something is going on, especially when the seal appeared on a fraudulent transaction."

"The bank embezzlement Umbretti was investigating?"

"Yes."

"A Vatican seal doesn't prove anything, Michael. It could have been mistakenly used by someone or misappropriated by an unauthorised party. One would have to locate the destination of the transfer in order to implicate the culprit. Have you been able to do that?"

The Papal Secret

"Of course not," replied Michael. "I don't have the authority to investigate a crime of that nature, especially if someone in the Vatican is allegedly involved."

"It's a powerful state, run by ethical standards. Vatican City is a recognised natural territory under international law. They have their own gendarmeria responsible for public order and law enforcement. Italian law is an outside factor, but they do fear God, who is omnipotent. They know they cannot hide anything from the creator. As a rule, they are all good men."

"And what about the secular staff, such as gardeners, drivers, security personnel?"

"They have all been screened thoroughly."

"So have corrupt cops."

"Well, if I were investigating a case like this, I would start with the security staff. You know the adage: who watches the watchers?"

"Actually, I'm not really concerned who is on the take," Michael said. "My main concern is for the safety of Isabella. Did you see the morning papers?"

"It's in my case. I haven't had the chance to read it yet."

"Another two of my passengers on my previous cruise were killed in South Africa."

"Really?"

"Yes; Franco Martini and his wife." Michael handed the lawyer the morning newspaper.

Stendardi read the report and looked up at Michael. "But the report here says it was accidental, that they were warned not to leave their vehicle while in the game reserve."

"Killed by lions five kilometres away from their car? Not bloody likely."

"Maybe you're over-reacting. It could be coincidental."

"I'd like to believe that, but I can't," whispered Michael. He looked at Stendardi. "They were silenced because they knew too much."

"And does Isabella know too much?" asked Stendardi cautiously.

"I beg your pardon?"

"I intended no disrespect," Stendardi was quick to counter, "but for her own safety I need to know all the facts."

"Her husband did not confide in her—probably because she is a good woman and wouldn't have tolerated his misdeeds had she known."

"What about the call girl, Carla?" asked Stendardi. "She was close to Umbretti."

"Physically; that's all. She was so shit-scared when all this started happening, she took off." He paused and frowned. "She went to Australia or New Zealand, I believe. At any rate, she's gone."

"Which leaves only Isabella left from the original passenger list?"

"That's my point," Michael nodded. "Yet she's no threat to anyone."

"They obviously don't know that."

"I need your help," said Michael. "You have contacts at the Vatican and the privy seal is my only clue. I have to stop whoever is endangering Isabella."

Stendardi sipped his drink. He was thinking of his own ordeal at the hands of the kidnappers. Their interest was the connection between the pope and Samuel Grossman, a secret that had to be preserved at all cost. Was there a connection between the two cases? Possibly, and it would do no harm to probe a little. His thoughts were interrupted by Michael.

"I had an interesting visitor yesterday," Michael said. "Do you know of a man named Fabio Mento?"

Stendardi jerked upright and spilled some of his drink in his lap. "Damn!" he said, brushing a hand over the liquid. "Fabio Mento?" he repeated in surprise. "He's a senior security officer at the Vatican. Why was he here?"

"My cruise next week is for the family of a well known philanthropist in appreciation for money donated to the Church. The trip has been sponsored by the Vatican and Mento came to check out safety measures and security on the boat."

"Is that usual?" asked Stendardi, "I mean, for clients to make security arrangements?"

"Only if the Holy Father himself is due to board the boat."

"The pope is sailing with you?" Stendardi asked in disbelief.

"Only for one night. Apparently he has business to discuss with the millionaire."

"Most irregular," said Stendardi, and made a mental note to ask Pollini the reason for such an outing. How could anyone safeguard the life of the pontiff on a small boat at sea? "Strange, very strange," whispered Stendardi.

"Well," said Michael, rising from the chair. "I suggest you change into something more appropriate for sailing. We're leaving in half an hour."

The view from the deck was impressive as they moved swiftly across the waters of the Ligurian Sea. They were only a couple of hundred metres away from the shoreline as they passed the small town of Portofino. The green coastal mountains rose sharply toward the blue sky, and above the little harbour, the pink and yellow houses brought colour to the verdant landscape. Then the boat turned westward and moved away from the coastline.

* * *

The *Bella Mare*'s departure was noted by a man standing at the end of the pier. Stendardi's presence was also acknowledged when the boat departed with him still on it. What concerned the observer most was not that the boat had put to sea, but rather with the passenger who had sailed in it. He dialled a number on his mobile phone and waited for an answer.

"Pronto," he said into the instrument. "Fabio, the *Bella Mare* has sailed with signor Stendardi on board."

"What's he doing there?" came Mento's anguished reply.

"I have no idea, *mio capitano*."

"Then find out!" insisted Mento.

The man checked with the port authority and when he was told that the *Bella Mare* was conducting sea trials and would return in the morning, he shrugged and went back to the *pensione*. No sense sitting and waiting at the edge of the pier. He looked at his wrist watch; it was time for his afternoon aperitif. He sat down at the bar and ordered a Campari and soda. He had no qualms about mixing business with pleasure. He patted the gun in his pocket. Perhaps Fabio would instruct him to use it when the boat returned in the morning.

* * *

"Someone noted our departure," Michael said, as the three of them were sitting down to dinner on the foredeck. He had chosen the smaller deck so he could keep a look-out for the lights of other ships that might intersect the course ahead of them.

Isabella looked lovely as usual, dressed in white slacks

and a yellow blouse. For a moment he wished they had sailed alone so he could make love to her under the stars with a faint breeze from the west to cool their naked bodies. But he planned to spend the rest of his life with her, so there would be plenty of other opportunities to express his love in the most desirable way.

"You mean someone was spying on us?" asked Stendardi. "I think your previous concern is well founded. Both Isabella and I have been targeted by abductors. It seems that their interest in us hasn't waned."

"There was a man at the end of the pier who was a bit out of place. I know the type of folk in Santa Margherita and he was not one of them," Michael said. "I saw him make a phone call as we left and he never took his eyes off the boat."

"Then he must know I'm on board?"

"Is that a problem?" Isabella asked.

"Not if it's just a precaution before the pope's cruise."

"We both have a finger on some kind of Vatican conspiracy," Michael went on. "What if the source is the same?"

"I can't divulge the details of my case, but I can tell you that one of the cardinals is opposing the pope's outreach program and wants to prohibit close relations with non-Christian religions. You may be aware that the Holy Father has extended a hand of friendship to the Jews and is trying to end the ancient belief of Jewish culpability for the death of Christ. If he is able to discredit the pope in any way, it may hasten the day for him to become the next pontiff. There's also the probability that this cardinal will need lots of money to negotiate support through political influence. He would also want his own candidates to fulfil certain positions in the Vatican."

"So tapping into Rochi's scam through Umbretti would serve that purpose?"

"Most certainly."

"Then it seems we do have a common adversary."

Chapter 42

The Vatican

Cardinal Pollini left his office in a daze. The fact that the pope was embarking on a cruise of friendship with the philanthropist Dottore Alessandro Riva and his wife Sophia was not as disturbing as the news that Cardinal Albertini and Fabio Mento would be accompanying them. It was no secret in Vatican circles that Albertini and Mento worked closely together, but what was not known was the conspiratorial nature of their association; only Pollini suspected it. He wished the boat were big enough to take a few of his own security personnel to neutralise the presence of the other two. To make matters worse was the continual smirk on Albertini's face whenever they were together, almost as if he was savouring some secret against him.

He crossed the richly decorated Clementine Hall, descended the papal stairway and left the building. He made his way to the courtyard of the Swiss Guards near the Gate of Sant'Anna and proceeded to the office of Roberto Silva, a captain in the Corpo della Gendarmeria, sometimes referred to as the Vigilanza, in charge of law enforcement.

Roberto Silva looked up in delighted surprise when he saw Pollini standing at the door. "Your Eminence, please come in. May I offer you some espresso?"

"Thank you, Roberto," Pollini said, taking a seat on an easy chair beneath the high-set window. "I have a rather delicate matter to discuss with you, one that must remain between us for the time being."

"You can rely on my fullest cooperation," Captain Silva said sincerely. "And my discretion," he added.

"Thank you, Roberto," replied Pollini. He paused before carefully choosing his next words. "How well do you know Fabio Mento?"

Silva leaned forward as if waiting for an explanation to the

Stan Miller

strange question. When none came, he answered, "He seems to be doing a good job in security. We are not friends, of course, as we have nothing in common. He prefers to work alone and delegates without consultation with anyone."

"Do you trust him?"

Silva hesitated. Although he had an immediate answer to the question, he wasn't sure how Pollini would react to a derogatory remark. He had always been totally honest with the cardinal and respected his motives without question. This was not a time to sugar-coat a response. If the cardinal wanted to know, there must be a good reason for asking.

"I don't like him," Silva finally replied. "Mento was never one for correct procedures, and underlying everything he does is a personal agenda which seems to affect his decisions. He runs his division within the Vatican State with a degree of secrecy, and I run mine within these walls according to the charter I swore to uphold. Mento and I have little to do with each other."

"I need an unusual favour," Pollini said.

"If it's within my capability, you have it."

"Mento works closely with Cardinal Albertini, who, as you may well know, has considerable influence in Italy and is deemed as a suitable candidate one day for the papacy. Next week the pope is due to board a private yacht for a meeting with Dottore Alessandro Riva, who contributes a great deal of money to Vatican charities. Cardinal Albertini and I will be present, together with Fabio Mento who, at the cardinal's insistence, will take care of papal security. It's a small boat, so Mento will be the sole protector of the Holy Father while he is on board."

Pollini got out of his seat and went across to the window. He looked out and saw grey clouds gathering to the west. Another storm was approaching and the pending downpour served only to deepen his sombre mood. "I don't like it," he added, turning to face the police captain.

"I see," said Silva. "What do you want me to do?"

"If anything should happen to the pope, Albertini . . ." He didn't finish his thought. If the pope were to die, God forbid, Albertini was the most likely successor and all of Pietro Bandini's liberal decrees would be nullified. "I want you to sail with us, to keep an eye on things and prevent anything untoward from happening."

"You want me to spy on Mento?" Silva asked in surprise.

"I want you to protect the pope."

Chapter 43

Portofino

The *Bella Mare* dropped anchor silently in the early morning light of the tourist fishing village of Portofino. As a precaution to being seen leaving Santa Margherita the previous day, Michael wanted to discharge his guest in the nearby port to avoid further surveillance from any undercover observer.

"This Mento character from the Pontifical Swiss Guard displayed a supercilious attitude during his inspection of my boat, which did nothing to ingratiate him to me," Michael said as Stendardi was preparing to disembark. "Being sole protector of the pope while they're on board worries me."

"Was there no talk of a flotilla of accompanying security craft?" asked Stendardi.

"That's my point. I'm sure we will be accompanied by escort vessels, but the pope's safety on board my boat will be in the hands of one man: Mento. That places a terrible responsibility on me as captain. If anything should happen . . ." He left the rest unsaid.

"That gives us only a few days to establish the identity of the bearer of the privy seal involved in all of this."

"Cardinal Albertini has shown signs that he is probably the one we seek." Michael was almost sure of it but if it was someone else and they failed to find out in time, the results could be catastrophic. "We have to make sure."

"And how do you propose doing that?" asked Stendardi, his eyes searching the harbour for any suspicious-looking characters.

"Cardinal Pollini knows. All we have to do is ask him."

"I thought he made it quite clear that such a topic was taboo."

"The question may not receive an answer, but it could alert him to the danger."

"I'll make the call."

* * *

Cardinal Pollini was not surprised by the content of Stendardi's phone call. He already had a bad feeling about Cardinal Albertini. Pollini and Stendardi were each bonded to the other by the secrecy of the Grossman revelation, so had established a mutual trust which allowed them to speak frankly with one another. Though he was not prepared to overtly violate the Vatican's code of secrecy by divulging the names of the holders of the privy seal to any outsider, he did agree to look into the matter and regard the information as a forewarning.

Some years before, the head of the Vatican body investigating abuse by priests argued that accused clergymen should not be handed over to secular authorities, but rather, they should be investigated under stringent secrecy within the church. Under normal circumstances, any matter regarding suspicious or unethical behaviour was reported directly to the president of the Pontifical Commission, who would delegate the complaint to one of his secretaries for further investigation. Cardinal Albertini, however, was the recipient of such a complaint and also the Deputy Secretary of the Commission. Although Pollini was the more senior official, it would be difficult challenging Albertini without appearing to have a political motive behind a confrontation. As yet, Albertini was guilty of no known transgression. Pollini took it upon himself to go directly to the pope and express his anxiety.

"You worry too much, my friend," the pope smiled at Pollini, "even if it is out of concern for my safety."

"Albertini knows something, and I don't like it."

"The only thing that could possibly harm me is safely locked away in my safe."

"His mannerisms suggest that he is holding a trump card."

"The trump card, as you put it, is only for me to play should I wish to do so."

"He'll do anything to discredit you and force you to resign, Pietro."

"According to the Code of Canon Law, my resignation cannot be forced upon me by anyone."

"I have a greater fear than your abdication," Pollini said solemnly. "In 1978, Pope John Paul I died under mysterious circumstances, just a month after his accession. Some suspect he was murdered."

"It was never proven he was poisoned."

"All the more reason for concern." Pollini looked worried.

"I suppose you are referring to the yacht cruise?"

"An unwise decision, if you permit me to say so. Security will be at a minimum. You will be too vulnerable while at sea."

"Who is it that wishes to harm me?" the pope asked tentatively.

"If anyone at all, it would be your strongest opponent."

"Cardinal Albertini?"

"I would say so."

"Without support, he will do nothing. You, my friend, will be there to watch him." The pope stood up slowly. "Albertini may be ambitious, but he is not evil. He is also aware that, should anything happen to me while we are all on the same boat, his credentials would come under scrutiny. He is not popular with everyone."

"I have asked Captain Roberto Silva to join us on the boat to keep a reliable eye on things," Pollini announced. "I trust him implicitly."

"Good; then it is settled," smiled the pope. "What possible harm could befall me under your careful supervision and Captain Silva's protective arm?"

* * *

Although Cardinal Albertini was currently sitting on a wooden bench in the Church of Saint Pellegrino inside the southern perimeter of the Vatican in an attitude of prayer, his mind was far from any thoughts of holy worship; it was focussed on the disconcerting report that he had received from Mento that the lawyer Stendardi had accompanied Michael Frost on board the *Bella Mare* for sea trials. It was bad enough he was communicating with Frost at all, but developing a strong bond of association did not augur well for the plans he had in mind. The lawyer had strong suspicions of his involvement with the Rochi fraud case and was certainly privy to the pope's incredible secret. It had all started with his visit to the pontiff a few months earlier.

Albertini had formulated a plan to expose the pope's secret that he was of Jewish birth and permanently sully his papacy and force him to resign. The last time a pontiff bowed out in disgrace was in 1046, when Gregory VI was accused of financial impropriety, but a heritage issue was not a strong enough cause. If he could put the cruise to good use, however, he might be able to spare the church any embarrassment. Of course, Mento knew what was required of him without having

Stan Miller

to be told, so it would leave his own conscience clear if anything bad happened to Pope John Pietro I.

* * *

Fabio Mento had no conscience; he sat at his desk plotting a murder with the same relish he would an exciting game of chess. The very thought of killing such an important personage served only to enhance his enthusiasm and raise his adrenalin level. He leaned back in his chair and looked up at the ceiling. What an immortal act it would be. His name would be spoken in the same breath as Napoleon, Mussolini, and Hitler for centuries to come; a little boy born on the bad side of town in Zurich achieving such notoriety. He sighed audibly. Of course, it wouldn't come to that; he had no intention of being caught, however appealing the notion of infamy was.

The plan was simple in design but difficult to implement. The pope would be most vulnerable while on board the yacht. Being a relatively small boat, there was not enough room for a large contingency of security personnel, but the small number of people on board would make him one of the prime suspects, together with the others. He wasn't sure if the clandestineness of his private activities would stand up to strict scrutiny. However, surviving an attack on the boat with injuries would put him above suspicion; being wounded in the course of duty while trying to save the life of the Holy Father would focus attention on the others instead. He had no qualms about self-inflicted wounds if it saved him from a lifetime in prison. He was pondering those thoughts when the phone rang.

"It is ready," the voice said in his ear when he picked up the phone.

"Will it stick securely in place?"

"Like a dog to the tail of a bitch in heat!"

"Excellent."

"One word of warning; it might not hold longer than twelve hours, especially if the sea is turbulent."

"I won't need that long."

Chapter 44

Santa Margherita

Captain Roberto Silva was waiting on the pier when the *Bella Mare* arrived back in port. No sooner had she berthed than the Vatican police officer bounded up the companion ladder and confronted Michael on deck. His identification badge was already in his hand and he showed it immediately to Michael.

"The Vatican has already sent their security chief," Michael told him blandly. He couldn't understand the need for another security check days before the cruise was due to begin, and he was eager to get to Milan and arrange the supplies from the special list of requirements he had been given.

"At Cardinal Pollini's insistence, I am to join the cruise," Silva announced, "and I'd like to see the layout of the boat for myself."

"Welcome aboard, captain," Michael said, feeling a little bit of relief. "It will be good to have one of Cardinal Pollini's men with us during the cruise. I'll have to make special arrangements. All the decent accommodation is taken."

"Any berth will do, Mr. Frost," Silva said in a pleasant tone. "Regard me as one of the crew. This is a letter from the cardinal explaining everything. He does not wish to leave the pope's security in the hands of only one man. I'm sure you'll understand and find a place for me, although I probably won't be sleeping much that night."

"I'll make a plan."

"Good. Now may I inspect the cabin the pope will be using?"

"You will find the main cabin extremely comfortable."

Captain Silva smiled. "I'm more concerned with the pope's safety than his comfort. We are dealing with a man whose spirituality far exceeds any desire for luxury."

"Point taken," Michael conceded.

Just then, Isabella emerged from Michael's cabin. As usual,

she looked stunningly beautiful, in a floral dress falling just above her knees. She smiled at the visitor and held out a hand. "I'm Isabella," she said before Michael could introduce her.

"*Buon giorno, signora*," he said, taking hold of her hand and bowing courteously. "Spending so much time in the Vatican, I had forgotten how beautiful some women can be."

"The cabin, Captain Silva," Michael urged, pointing the way.

Silva nodded and reluctantly let go of Isabella's hand. He followed Michael down the passageway. "It is indeed luxurious," he remarked on entering the main cabin. "I'm sure the pontiff won't mind," he smiled affably and proceeded to examine the layout.

Silva examined the cabin carefully before looking up at Michael. "This boat is a nightmare when it comes to security," he exclaimed, waving his arm in an arc to indicate the whole area. "So many places for a saboteur to set up shop."

"This is not a military vessel, captain," replied Michael, "and that guy from the Swiss Guards seemed satisfied with what he saw."

"Mento," snarled Silva. "That, my friend, is exactly the problem. The pope should not be allowed to sail on a boat as vulnerable as this one."

"That's precisely what I told the previous security guy, but he was adamant. Said arrangements couldn't be changed."

"As much as I hate the idea," said Silva, "there's nothing I can do to influence the clergy to cancel. In fact, Cardinal Albertini was quite adamant that the cruise take place as planned. That is why I am here, to ensure that nothing goes wrong. Of course, I will need your help."

"My help? What can I possibly do? I will have my hands full sailing this vessel."

"For some reason, Cardinal Pollini trusts you," said Silva with a shrug, "and who knows every nook and cranny on this boat better than you do?"

"What will you have me do?" asked Michael.

"Observe everything that goes on and report anything suspicious to me."

"That's a very wide brief."

"Hopefully it will be a routine cruise and nothing will get down to specifics."

"If our boat comes under attack, how the hell are the two of us going to protect the Holy Father?"

"Our only concern is what happens on board," said Silva. "We are not totally imbecilic. There will be a flotilla of naval vessels around us."

* * *

Two hours later, Captain Silva disembarked feeling more apprehensive than when he arrived. The boat did not meet with his security criteria for a safe voyage. It was too confined for the pope to remain aloof from those around him, and his instinct was to recommend that the trip be cancelled or redirected to a military vessel. The only redeeming factor was that there wouldn't be too many people on board to keep an eye on. He would state in his report that the third crew member be replaced by one of his own men with sailing experience. Captain Frost and his girlfriend had passed the preliminary security checks run by his department, but the murder of her husband on the boat and the fact that the two of them were an item so soon after her husband's death sat uneasily on his logic.

He looked around before climbing into his car but failed to see the figure of a well built man watching him from behind a parked van on the other side of the road. He tapped the accelerator and eased into the middle of the road, his thoughts now shifting to the beautiful image of Isabella in her short, floral dress.

Chapter 45

Milan

The reservation at the La Perla restaurant was for one o'clock. Michael and Isabella strolled through the Galleria looking at shop windows and using up some of the time they had in reserve before their table was ready. They had completed the acquisition of supplies for the Vatican cruise that morning and were due to collect everything the following day before returning to Santa Margherita.

"There's someone following us," Isabella suddenly announced in an undertone. "Don't look now, but he's standing at the curio stall reading a newspaper."

"Blue shirt and an Inter Milan cap?"

"I told you to be discreet."

"I also noticed him a little while ago while we were crossing the road by the La Scala Opera House. It may be nothing, but if he's watching us, I'd like to know why." Michael looked at her. "Maybe it's you he's interested in. Every other member of the male species has been ogling you wherever we've gone."

"I'll put that down to your jealousy causing a misjudgement," she said, finding it difficult to be jovial under the circumstances. The man behind them worried her.

"Let's go to the restaurant. If he's keeping an eye on us, we'll know soon enough."

They sat at a corner table on the veranda, which gave them a vantage point from which to observe anyone entering their restaurant or any of the others in the vicinity. Michael ordered a bottle of white wine and polenta.

"Surely you're not going to eat that stuff?"

"I'm a simple peasant."

"That's what I've been trying to tell you all along," said Isabella with a wry smile. She looked around. "Do you see him?"

"He's at a table by the window of the restaurant across the way."

The Papal Secret

"What did I tell you!" said Isabella raising her voice in alarm.

"Relax," he smiled. "Enjoy lunch and we'll see what he does when we leave."

"We should get up and go as they serve his main course. If he abandons his meal, we'll know for sure that he's interested in us."

"The trouble is, I'm starving," said Michael consulting the menu. "Let's not jump to conclusions."

She gave him a cold stare and opened the menu. Her appetite was stimulated the moment she saw what was available. They dined on seafood and forgot all about the mysterious stranger who had been following them, until they noticed he had gone.

"You see; you were neurotic for nothing," Michael told her.

After their meal, they left the restaurant and crossed the road to the Duomo—the Gothic Cathedral of Milan which dominated the piazza with its unique magnificence. They glanced up in amazement at the forest of pinnacles and spires set upon delicate buttresses on all sides of the roof. Atop the main spire, they saw the sculptured figure of the *Madonnina*, a baroque, gilded bronze statuette that looked out majestically over the piazza. The outer structure of the cathedral had been recently cleaned, and it gleamed like a fantasy in marble.

They entered through the main door and waited for their eyes to adjust to the dim interior lighting. They paused to look at the Altar of the Madonna of the Tree and admire the three stained glass windows framing it, all thoughts of their stalker dismissed from their minds.

It was not until they were sitting and resting in one of the pews that they became aware of his presence again. "I don't like it," said Isabella. "He's making me scared."

Michael took her hand and they made their way to the altar of Saint Catherine in the left-side transept. The area was deserted; most of the visitors present had congregated around the western apse to gaze at the illuminated windows against an afternoon sun. They waited behind one of the columns to see if the stalker was following.

Isabella sucked in her breath as she saw the man coming toward them. Feeling the victimization of his own privacy, Michael crouched behind the pillar, preparing to challenge the man as he drew alongside. He wasn't sure what he was going to do, so he just waited for the stalker to show himself.

The man rounded the pillar, not expecting anyone to be

Stan Miller

waiting for him. He was taken totally off-guard as Michael grabbed his arm and pulled him into the niche behind the pillar.

"What do you want from us?" Michael hissed. He was close enough to smell the garlic on the man's breath and see the tautness of his small mouth.

The stranger's reaction was totally unexpected. Instead of countering with a corresponding display of force, he tried to back away and escape Michael's grip on his arm. "You have nothing to fear from me, Mr. Frost," he said. "I'm not your enemy."

Michael loosened his grip but did not let go. "Who are you and why have you been following us?"

The man looked around as if he himself feared he had been followed into the cathedral. "Let's find a place where we can sit and talk." He indicated a row of seats at the back which looked secluded enough.

Michael kept hold of the man's arm as they walked up the aisle. They slid into a pew and the man leaned forward so that he could address both of them.

"The pope's cruise next week may not be a coincidence," the man finally said.

"Are you another Vatican security officer?" Michael asked, wondering when all this cloak and dagger stuff would end.

"No," the man said cutting Michael short. "I suppose you could say I'm with Internal Affairs, only not with the police."

"You're speaking in riddles," Isabella found her voice, "and what has that got to do with us?"

"I suppose it's time that I introduced myself," the man answered. "My name is Marco Vincento." He withdrew a card and handed it to Michael. "I'm a private investigator representing the insurance company of the bank which your late husband so cleverly defrauded." He looked at Isabella and quickly added. "Not that we suspect you had anything to do with it, of course, but we're trying to recover as much as we can, and I have to follow every lead."

Isabella suddenly felt cold. She wasn't sure if the account opened by her husband for her in Australia contained his personal assets or part of the illicit fortune he stole. As far as she believed, the money put away for her was legitimate and transferred into her account long before the crime was committed. In any event, she decided to be cautious and say nothing. She leaned back to listen.

"In fact, the money your late husband embezzled was in

turn stolen from him by Dr. Umbretti, the bank's representative sent to uncover the crime. Unfortunately, both are now dead and cannot shed any light on the investigation. Subsequently, the third member of the team, Mr. Martini, also died under mysterious circumstances. Only you have survived, Mrs. Rochi." He looked at her waiting for a response. When none came, Vincento continued. "It seems the syndicate behind these murders is not interested in you, signora; otherwise you, too, would be dead. Who am I to disagree with such powerful people?"

"Stop trying to intimidate her and tell us what you want," Michael said gruffly.

"It has come to my knowledge that someone in the Vatican has a finger in the pie, so to speak," said Vincento.

"You found evidence of this?" asked Michael.

"Not exactly," admitted Vincento. "Have you ever seen this before?" He handed Michael a piece of paper with an emblem printed on it.

Michael froze for an instant as he recognised the Vatican symbol he had asked Cardinal Pollini about.

"No, I don't think so," he lied.

"Look at it very carefully."

"What makes you think there's a Vatican connection? Where did you come across this?"

"The same place you did, Mr. Frost," he smiled knowingly. "On Umbretti's computer. It was used while transferring a large sum of money out of his account into the account of the person bearing this emblem."

"A clergyman?"

"A Vatican citizen is all I know."

"Shouldn't you direct your enquiry at the Vatican?"

"No point," Vincento answered. "You already have, with no results."

There was also no point denying it. The investigator seemed to know everything. "All I could establish was that it is a secret symbol used by only three cardinals for internal correspondence," Michael told him. "Anyway, the matter has nothing to do with me, and Isabella has already been cleared by the police."

"I believe two senior cardinals will be accompanying the pope on the cruise," said Vincento. "All I need you to do is to keep your eyes and ears open for a slip of the tongue, anything that could help us."

"Neither one is likely to say anything incriminating in my presence, even if one of them is the man you want," countered Michael. "You're wasting your time if you're relying on that to happen."

"We suspect that one of them is the man we're seeking, and if that is the case, he will be an extremely dangerous passenger to have on board."

"What should we fear from this man? He's not interested in us," Isabella said.

"You had the unfortunate experience of having been kidnapped recently, signora. Held on a boat, I believe?"

"So?" asked Michael.

"Someone obviously thinks you have information that could be harmful to him. I also know that Cardinal Albertini commissioned your boat on behalf of the Vatican. The same boat on which a murder was committed over the money we're investigating. And need I remind you it's the same money that was transferred into a mystery account bearing that secret symbol. This is not the first time the Vatican has been implicated in financial scandal. Prior to the death of Pope John Paul I, The Banco Ambrosiano, of which the Vatican was the main shareholder, was alleged to have been involved in laundering Mafia money for a commission. Large sums of money were diverted to foreign banks until the scandal was exposed when the bank collapsed in 1982. Of course, the Vatican as an institution was not to blame. Licio Gelli and his group of corrupt individuals controlled the scheme." Vincento cleared his throat and changed the subject. "I beg your pardon, but aren't there bigger and better yachts the Vatican could have chosen for such a cruise? Why yours? Have you asked yourself that, Mr. Frost?"

Isabella shuffled uncomfortably in her seat. "I have to agree with Mr. Vincento. It does seem ominous."

"It's not the cardinals we should be worried about," suggested Michael. "More than likely it will be one of the security guards carrying out the dirty work, and I think I know which one."

"I know who's behind all of this," Vincento clasped his hands as if in prayer. "I know the name of the cardinal who used the privy seal. All I need is proof."

Suddenly, Vincento's head jerked forward hitting the back of the wooden bench in front of him. Michael recognized the sound of a bullet striking flesh and he felt blood splatter over his arm like warm milk. There was blood on the back of Vincento's head where the bullet had entered. The man's eyes were still open.

Michael acted instinctively. He pushed Isabella to the floor and fell on top of her. There was an assassin lurking somewhere behind them and he had no doubt that they would be his next target.

"Crawl forward," he breathed heavily into Isabella's ear," and keep your head down!"

They edged forward, using the rows of seats to cover their progress, and crawled toward a group of tourists who were standing near the altar listening to their guide explaining the significance of the crypt's design. A few of them looked down in bewilderment as they crawled past and joined the group on the other side. Michael smiled sheepishly by way of an explanation and told Isabella to remove her jacket. He didn't want the sniper to identify her in the crowd.

"Stay with the group until they leave the cathedral and make your way across the road to La Rinascente and meet me upstairs in the men's department."

"Where are you going?" The timbre of her voice told Michael that she was still in shock.

He was reluctant to leave her alone but she stood a better chance if she separated from him and remained among the group. "I'll leave through one of the emergency exits and lure him away from you," he said softly.

"Be careful," she warned.

Michael stripped off his bloodied shirt and hoped the assailant wouldn't recognize him in the t-shirt he had on underneath. As the group passed one of the exits, he detached himself from them and slipped out into the sunlight.

He was in one of the side streets on the other side of the Duomo from the department store. There were only a few people walking around and he began running toward the piazza hoping that he would round the corner before the gunman emerged through the same exit. He ran without glancing backwards lest he tripped and fell, half expecting to hear the same sound as before and feel the pain of a bullet in his back.

It never came. He dropped his shirt in a bin and made his way into the store. He rode the escalator to the second floor and waited at the top to see if the gunman was following. He used the time to purchase a new shirt and only relaxed when

Stan Miller

he spotted Isabella coming up the same escalator he had used five minutes earlier.

They went upstairs to the coffee bar situated outside on the roof to wait for a reasonable time to elapse for the killer to realise he had lost them and leave the area.

"Are you okay?" Michael asked, taking hold of her hand.

She nodded and gave him a weak smile. "What was that all about?" she asked.

"Somebody wanted to silence Vincento before he could talk," said Michael, looking around to make sure no one was listening, "and if they think he did, we may be next."

Chapter 46

Santa Margherita

The deck of the *Bella Mare* took on an air of foreboding. Instead of feeling comfortable being back on board, Vincento's warning and murder had introduced a sombre tone to the forthcoming cruise. Usually Michael was happiest when at sea, but this was going to be a journey of tension. It was always going to be a difficult cruise with the pope present, because it was his responsibility as captain of the vessel to protect the holy entourage, and he wasn't sure he could do that. What worried him even more was that Vincento's killer knew they had to return to the boat and, if his contract was to kill them, he had ample opportunity to fulfil his mission.

Isabella's spirits, on the other hand, had returned in the tranquil atmosphere of the pleasure yacht. She had busied herself cleaning the cabins and getting the living quarters ready for the important visitors who were arriving the next day. Michael was pleased to see that her frivolous charm had returned and hoped his own mood would lift. She looked lovely in her shorts and t-shirt, and all the deck-hands on neighbouring boats had their heads turned in her direction. The surrounding yachts bobbed in the water, causing ripples in the harbour as crewmen scampered toward the sides of their boats closest to where the *Bella Mare* was berthed.

"I should warn my fellow seamen that this delightful show is about to end," said Michael, waving angrily at them.

"Jealous again, my love?"

"No, but we'll soon have to don clothing of a more conservative style if we are not to offend the men of the cloth when they arrive."

"Then perhaps I should remove my top now and give these sailors a final show to remember," Isabella teased.

"Don't you dare. That show is for my eyes only."

Michael had received instructions to move the yacht to a

private berth away from the prying eyes of outsiders, and he walked down the companion ladder and crossed to the other side of the harbour to inspect the pier designated for the *Bella Mare*. The pathway from the parking area had been cordoned off by a solid barrier flanking the full length of the pier, giving privacy to anyone boarding the boat and preventing a sniper from having a clear shot at any of the passengers as they arrived.

His Holiness was not due to begin the cruise here, as the initial stage of the journey would only have the philanthropist and his family on board, but it was better to take full precautions during all stages of the cruise. Fabio Mento, whose function, at this stage, was to ensure the Holy Father's cabin remained out of bounds at all times until the pontiff joined the cruise, would also be aboard for the initial stage of the cruise. Dottore Alessandro was rich enough to own a yacht double the size of the *Bella Mare*, and Vincento's words came floating back into Michael's mind. Why did they choose his boat for such an important cruise? Was there an ulterior motive, as the investigator had suggested?

Michael dismissed these thoughts. There was nothing he could do about it anyway. The Vatican had chosen him, and if all went well, it could be a tremendous endorsement for future bookings. The *Bella Mare* would attract dignitaries and film stars from all over the world so they could boast having slept in the same cabin the pope had occupied.

On a sudden impulse, Michael knelt down to look under the pier. It was a wooden structure stabilized by struts and girders underneath with ample opportunity for an assailant to hide and strike through the floorboards. He made a mental note to check the pier the pope would be using at their next port of call; all the trouble to provide protection on the pier would be wasted because there was a security flaw underneath it.

That night, sleep was out of the question. After he had raised the companion ladder, Michael positioned himself under the steps leading to the bridge. From there, he could see the whole length of the deck and would spot anyone trying to board. He tried not to think that anyone boarding from the seaward side could do so unseen. He offered a prayer of thanks that the sea was calm and the boat steady in her moorings. He would feel the slightest tilt of the deck should anyone try climbing over the side.

Michael was sitting on a wooden box containing the life vests, willing his eyes to stay open. His eyes were adjusted to

The Papal Secret

the darkness but it was beginning to induce sleep. He glanced at the luminous dial of his wristwatch and saw it was fifteen minutes past three. He had been in this position for over five hours and dawn was still a few hours away.

Suddenly, a surge of adrenalin sharpened his senses and he felt for the automatic tucked in his belt. It wasn't the noise that alerted him; it was the slightest shift in the angle of the deck beneath his feet. He peered up and down the deck and saw nothing. Someone was using his blind side to gain access. He shuffled under the stairway and, with his back against the bulkhead, edged his way to the seaward deck. Michael froze. A figure in a black wetsuit was climbing over the railing. Michael's initial instinct was to shoot the intruder before he could do anything. There was no doubt in his mind it was the same man who had shot Vincento. Who else would be after them?

But Michael was a lawyer, not a trained combatant, and it was not in his nature to take such drastic action. He watched and waited. In order to get to the cabins, the intruder would have to pass the spot where Michael had positioned himself. Any threat to Isabella and he would kill the intruder without hesitation. His knuckles went white with the intensity with which he was gripping the gun.

In a crouched position, the intruder was coming toward him. Michael stepped further back into the shadows. He managed to remain hidden until the man in the wetsuit was upon him. With the full force of his arm, Michael brought the butt of his gun down on the man's head.

Momentarily stunned and taken by surprise, the intruder fell to his knees. Michael would have had the advantage if the gun hadn't slipped from his grasp and fallen out of reach. The initial blow had struck the man's diving mask, which he had hoisted onto the top of his head. Michael saw the evil grin on the man's face when he realized Michael was disarmed.

"An elusive quarry you turned out to be," the man hissed, "but the hunt is over. First you will die and then the woman."

The unmistakable sound of a gun being cocked rose above the sound of the water lapping against the hull. In reflex reaction, Michael stepped backward into the shadows and grasped for the fire axe hanging from its mounting behind him. "Who sent you?" he asked, trying to buy some time.

"Someone you could destroy with the knowledge you possess."

"Kill me and the cruise will be cancelled. Does your mentor want that?"

"A change of crew can be organized very quickly, Mr. Frost. What do you care what happens tomorrow? You won't be alive to know."

Keeping his body between the assailant and the axe, he tightened his fingers around the handle and steadied himself for an opportunity to strike. The assassin began to raise the gun toward Michael's chest. He had no more time to deliberate. He swung the axe in a sideways arc and buried the shaft of the axe in the man's torso. The point went in deep, perforating the lungs and striking the bottom of the man's heart. Blood spurted everywhere.

Taken by surprise, the assailant stared into Michael's eyes with such intensity that he thought he had missed the target. When he heard the sound of the gun hitting the deck, he knew he had found his mark. Moments later, the intruder dropped to his knees and collapsed on the deck, lying completely still in the increasing pool of his own blood.

Michael shivered when he looked into the dead man's open eyes. The hatred was still there. He removed his clothes so he wouldn't get any blood on them and dragged the body to the side of the boat. He lifted him by the shoulders and dropped him over the side. He heard a splash as the body hit the water and he watched the dead man slowly sink beneath the surface. He knew it wouldn't be long before someone discovered the body, but by then the boat would be at its new mooring on the other side of the harbour. He cleaned the axe and replaced it on its mounting. Then he hosed away the blood until the deck was clean. Picking up the would-be-killer's gun carefully with his handkerchief, he went up to the wheelhouse and locked the gun in the safe in case he was later implicated in the assassin's killing and had to prove it was self defence.

He decided to spend the rest of the night lying on the bunk in the wheelhouse. He didn't want Isabella to know anything of this and didn't want to upset her any further. He remained awake the rest of the night, unable to explain to himself his own actions. As a lawyer, he knew he shouldn't have covered up the killing, even if it was self defence. The right thing was to have reported it immediately to Inspector Conti at police headquarters, but the police chief would have applied for an interdict to have the boat impounded and the cruise cancelled. It seemed to be the best option under the circumstances, but Michael was sure that the only way to trap the man behind all of this was during the Vatican cruise.

* * *

"I thought you told that idiot to hold off on any further action until notified? One impulsive mistake could have ruined everything," Albertini sighed wearily.

"I did," Mento said slowly. "He probably thought that with the captain out of the way you could appoint your own man to take over."

"If I wanted to do that I would have said so. You sure he's dead?"

"Yes. I saw the captain kill him myself," Mento chuckled. "I never thought he had it in him."

"At least we know he's a dangerous adversary."

"He'll get what's coming to him, I promise you that." Mento replaced the receiver. *Shit*, thought Mento, *if they discover the body before we sail, the cops might cancel the cruise. That would infuriate the cardinal even more. No choice but to find the body and drag it somewhere else.* He stripped to his underpants and eased himself quietly into the water.

Chapter 47

Santa Margherita

At the first hint of dawn, as the night sky lightened, Michael moved the boat to its new mooring place. In the light of day, he thoroughly re-examined the spot on deck where he had killed the assassin, to make sure he had cleaned up properly during the night. Then he went below and took a hot shower, remaining under the cathartic flow of water until he felt revived. He was in the galley preparing breakfast when Isabella came in.

"You're up early," she said.

"And you're half naked," he replied, when he saw she had nothing on under her slightly open gown.

"If you had come to bed in time, I might have thrown some of this your way," she said, opening her gown all the way. She looked into his eyes. "You look tired. Are you okay?"

"Of course I am; just stayed out on deck too late."

"I told you there was nothing to worry about."

"You are always right," he told her, and took her in his arms.

* * *

The passengers began arriving at two o'clock. Fabio Mento and Cardinal Albertini boarded together and then, fifteen minutes later, the Alessandro family. Mario was below deck helping the cardinal settle in, and Isabella was taking charge of the later arrivals. At precisely three o'clock, Mario cast off and Michael steered the *Bella Mare* out of the harbour. He took a quick look behind him as they cleared the marker buoy at the harbour entrance and was pleased to see that everything looked normal; the body had not yet been discovered. From behind his sunglasses, Michael saw Mento glance in his direction. He did it several times before turning away.

The Papal Secret

"Something wrong?" asked Michael.

"Of course not," replied Mento. "Why should there be?" He walked away with a faint smile on his lips.

Michael disliked the man even more.

Isabella was a wonderful hostess, taking care of everyone's needs and prancing around in her tailored white suit. It left Michael free to navigate the boat and ponder what to do next. Cardinal Albertini had not appeared on deck since their departure, and the family enjoyed themselves on the pool deck reading or playing games.

Mento kept his distance and watched everyone like a cat getting ready to pounce on a defenceless mouse. Michael, who was standing at the helm, did not escape his watchful eye either.

It was late afternoon and everyone had retired to their cabins to rest, when Dottore Alessandro entered the wheelhouse. "Is this what you do for a living?" he said to Michael, "Sit at the wheel and gaze out of the window all day at an empty ocean?"

"Somebody has to do it," replied Michael, not liking the inference.

"I believe you are a non-practising lawyer?" the philanthropist asked. "Why did you give it up?"

"I had my reasons," answered Michael. "And I find more satisfaction in looking over the water than into some client's messy life."

"But that's what you accepted when you read for your law degree."

"I changed my mind." He didn't want to disturb his happiness with Isabella by going over the tragic circumstances that had robbed him of his family.

Alessandro did not push any further. Instead, he changed the subject completely. "You must be quite an accomplished sailor, Captain Frost, if the Vatican chose you as the pope's mariner."

"I don't know what criteria they based their choice on but, of course, I'm flattered."

"Ever crossed the Atlantic?"

"No," Michael confessed. "The only time I sailed through the Straits of Gibraltar was to deliver a vessel to its owner in Southampton."

"Crossing the Atlantic would be the true test of a mariner's skills, would it not?"

"I'm not interested in proving myself to anyone," Michael said. "I'm happy with my life on the Mediterranean, the most beautiful coastline in the world."

"Tell me, captain, do you think the pope will be safe aboard this boat?"

"Safer than driving the streets of Rome in his pope-mobile." Michael said it more out of sarcasm than in jest.

Alessandro let out a hearty guffaw loud enough to warn any ship within a two-nautical-mile radius of their presence. "I like that," he added. "Pope-mobile, indeed. I've seen it. The holy seat encased in bullet-proof glass." He turned to Michael sharply, as if a sudden thought had crossed his mind. "What concerns me, however," he added, "is that you couldn't prevent the murder of an ordinary man on this very vessel."

"I think you should return to your cabin, Dottore; drinks will be served shortly on deck."

"My wife and child are also on board this boat, captain. Excuse me for being concerned with their safety. You are obviously incapable of giving me any such guarantee." He waved a finger at Michael. "You are cohabiting with the widow of the man who was murdered on this boat not so long ago. It does not augur well for your credibility. You are not above suspicion and I hold you personally responsible for the well-being of my family."

"Is that a threat?"

"Good Lord, no! I never threaten. I'm a man of action." He turned his back on Michael and walked out of the wheelhouse.

Once more the peacefulness of the day returned but could not penetrate into Michael's mind; he was disturbed over the encounter and wondered what had provoked it.

* * *

One thing Cardinal Albertini was certain of was that the clue to Dr. Umbretti's numbered bank account in Switzerland was somewhere in this cabin. He had spent the better part of two hours searching everywhere for a sign that would unlock the mystery of Umbretti's cash cache. So far, he had come up with nothing and was beginning to suspect that the information he had been given was contrived to ensure a bonus payment under false pretences. He would deal with his informant some other time. He still had a half an hour until dinner and continued methodically with his search.

He was ready to give up and soothe his aching back under a hot shower when he found it. It was cleverly concealed on the inside of the cupboard door at the bottom where it was almost impossible to see. But there it was—the number he was looking for. He shined the small flashlight on the spot and copied the number into his pocket notebook.

Umbretti was dead, so there was no rush trying to access the account. He would deal with that problem once back in his office. With the number safely recorded in his book, the yacht was now expendable. The plot to assassinate the pope could proceed without hindrance.

* * *

The passengers and crew gathered on the aft deck where a large table had been prepared with the finest crockery and cutlery, comparable to any five-star hotel. Isabella had decorated the white tablecloth with a sprinkling of flowers to give a spectrum of colour to the banquet table. The orange glow of the setting sun served to enhance the ambience.

The boat was ploughing through the water on auto-pilot and the alarm would only sound if an obstacle in their path was detected by the radar scanner. It enabled everyone, including Michael, to be seated at the table safely assured that the boat would not collide with anything. Isabella acted as hostess, with Mario assisting her. A meal of grilled prawns on rice was served, with a choice of wine to please any palate. Even Cardinal Albertini was savouring the succulence of the crustaceans, something he never got in the Vatican.

Mento noticed the cleric was in a good mood and, without anything needing to be said at this stage, knew that the plan was on schedule. He tucked into his meal with even greater relish, aware that when the pope boarded, the meals would become unappetizingly austere.

"My dear," Alessandro addressed his wife, "the Holy Father will be joining the cruise tomorrow for our business discussion, but arrangements have been made for you and the kids to tour Rome and spend the night there in one of the finest hotels until our return the following day."

Sophia smiled sweetly, knowing that any complaint would meet with a stern scowl from her husband and severe ramifications for her later. "I am looking forward to seeing Michelangelo's *Pieta* in Saint Peter's while in Rome," she said excitedly, wanting to please her husband.

"Did you know that the sculptor was only twenty-four years old when he created that masterpiece?" said Albertini with an air of reverence. "After all, it was the Reverend Cardinal of San Donigi who commissioned the work for the Vatican. Surprisingly enough, he only received a price of four hundred and fifty golden ducats from the papal mint in 1498, a pittance even then."

The conversation was light-hearted and meaningless and, not wishing to appear rude, Michael feigned interest befitting that of captain and contributed a remark or two whenever necessary. Isabella sensed his boredom and laid a hand on his leg beneath the table.

"Later," she whispered in his ear.

Michael smiled, but couldn't help wondering if this was the calm before the storm.

Chapter 48

Fiumicino

The coastal town of Fiumicino is situated in the Province of Rome, Lazio, about fifty kilometres from the Vatican. It is home to the largest airport in Italy, the Leonardo da Vinci International Airport; but it was to the yacht basin that the pope's convoy was heading. The town is low-lying with many sandy beaches and seaside hotels. The harbour is situated a little upstream along the waterway where a handful of uniformed policemen were stationed at the entrance to the pier, preventing unauthorised personnel from coming too close to where the *Bella Mare* was waiting for its holy guest. A few townsfolk had gathered outside the La Antico Molo Ristorante opposite the entrance to the car park, waiting to see what was going to happen.

Fifty kilometres away, in Rome, the side gate of the Vatican opened and three automobiles emerged in single file and turned into a side street. Their windows were tinted and no one from the outside could see the white robed figure sitting in the back of the middle vehicle. A few heads turned to look in mild interest at the cavalcade as it passed, but no advanced publicity had been announced of any travel arrangements by any VIPs from the Vatican, so the three limousines continued their journey onto the A-91 Rome to Fiumicino motorway unimpeded.

The convoy arrived without fanfare in Fiumicino, turned into Via Delle Gomene, carried on until Viale Traiano, and turned right into the entrance of the harbour. By the time those watching realized that the figure emerging from one of the vehicles was someone important, the pope had already boarded the yacht.

Michael was standing at the top of the companion ladder as the Holy Father stepped on board.

"Ah, you must be Captain Frost," the pope smiled. "How long will it take for these frail legs to become sea-worthy?"

"The weather report is favourable," replied Michael, bowing slightly, "and a calm sea is predicted, Your Holiness."

"Excellent. Then I shall do my best to enjoy the outing."

"We have set up a canvas enclosure on the aft deck where lunch will be served prior to our departure, Your Holiness," said Michael. "For your privacy, of course," added Michael quickly.

"You mean, to shield me from some crazed sniper?" the pope quipped.

"Who would want to harm you, Your Holiness?" said Isabella, standing next to Michael.

The pope turned to look at her, and smiled. "Some agnostic, my child, if for no other reason than to prove it can be done."

"Come, Your Holiness," Cardinal Albertini interrupted. "Let me show you to your cabin."

"I see, Vittorio, you have already become one of the crew." The pope took hold of his arm. "Lead on."

Michael took the opportunity while the holy entourage was below deck to examine the wharf to satisfy his own sense of responsibility that the police had made a thorough search of the space beneath the pier. The pillars and struts afforded an ideal place for an intruder to conceal himself. He walked along the horizontal beams shining his torch over the dark areas as he made his way to the end of the pier. When he got there, he crouched down to touch the hull of the *Bella Mare*. Instinctively, he began brushing away a dirty mark on the white hull, and then paused. His own hands were blackened with the dirt of rotting wood from where he had touched the wooden beams. He pressed his palm against the hull and saw that it left a similar mark. He shone his torch further down but all he could see was the slope of the hull disappearing into the water. He shrugged his shoulders; there was nobody hiding under the pier.

* * *

After a leisurely lunch served under the canopy on the aft deck, Michael gave the order to cast off. He steered the boat out of the harbour and turned sharply to port to enter the canal leading out to sea. He was relieved that the pope had retired to his cabin immediately after lunch so that he would not be visible from the high rise buildings they had to pass on the starboard side before reaching open waters, an ideal location from which a sniper could take a shot. Once the *Bella Mare* passed the breakwater, and the shoreline receded behind them, Michael turned to the instrument panel. The two naval gun ships were waiting a kilometre out to sea. The one positioned itself about a hundred and fifty metres ahead of them, which Michael was to use as the bearing for the course they would take. The other slipped in somewhere behind them at a similar distance.

Michael kept the radar screen active, although he had been given instructions that the escorting vessels would ensure that no other boat intruded into range of the flotilla. Free of any navigational obligations, Michael left Mario at the helm and went to check on the passengers. He found Isabella on deck ensconced in a deck chair reading a book. No one else was there.

"I'm glad I didn't employ you as a deck hand," he looked at her with raised eyebrows.

"I'm here in the capacity of your fiancé doing you a favour by keeping the holy entourage happy," she replied, mischievously.

"I'll be in our cabin if you need me."

"Do you want me to join you?" she said, her eyes twinkling.

"No, I think we should wait until tonight when everyone's asleep."

"You're rather presumptuous," she teased.

"The offer still stands," he retorted. "See you later."

Isabella was so engrossed in her book that she never saw the figure approaching her until he was standing in front of her. She looked up in astonishment to see the pope looking down at her.

"My apologies, Your Holiness," she said, jumping to her feet. "I didn't see you."

"Please, my child, it was not my intention to startle you." The pope smiled at her. He drew up a chair and sat down. "Sit," he said. "Perhaps we can talk for a while, before the cardinals come along and take me away from such beauty." He looked at the book she was reading. "*Exile*," he read. "The book is an excellent account of the dilemma between Israel and the Palestinians." He paused as if to gather his thoughts. "I believe your grandfather was Jewish?"

"Yes, he was," she replied, somewhat shocked at the question. "How did you know, Your Holiness?"

"To be quite honest, my child, my security staff did a

thorough check on everyone on board." By way of apology, he quickly added, "You know, they even wanted to check out President Bush's credentials before we first met." He smiled. "I don't mean to pry."

"I was brought up Catholic," Isabella said.

"Don't regard it as a fault. Being part Jewish, I mean. Even our Saviour had Jewish blood." The pope looked deeply into her eyes. "Do you ever feel an affinity toward your Jewish heritage?"

"I've never given it any thought," answered Isabella. "Of course, my grandfather taught me a lot about Judaism. They have some wonderful concepts and it is remarkable that their observance to God and their ritual hasn't changed in three thousand years."

"Yes, they are to be admired. Be thankful that you possess some Jewish blood. Jesus gave his blood to absolve our sins; the Jews passed on theirs to future generations to ensure their continuity." The pope rose. "I didn't mean to disturb you," he said, and went back inside.

Isabella tried reading again but she couldn't help wondering what had provoked such a strange conversation. She saw Cardinal Albertini and the Surveillance Corp officer named Mento come out on deck and move to the side railing amidships. Their voices didn't quite carry to where she was sitting but it was apparent that they were discussing something important, as their heads were close together. Perhaps they were behaving suspiciously only because of her dislike of them. The cardinal had a sombre aura around him, not at all like Cardinal Pollini, who had such a pleasant demeanour. It was also obvious that Pollini and the pope enjoyed a strong relationship. She couldn't help noticing the friction between the two cardinals when the papal party came on board. She put it down to jealousy. She turned back to the page she was reading.

Mento had seen Isabella reclining in the deck chair. "Keep your voice down, Your Excellency, the captain's woman is nearby."

"Is everything proceeding as planned?" Albertini enquired.

"Yes, I've received word that the explosives have been attached."

"What about us?"

"I have two lifebuoys ready. We must debark at precisely one a.m. After the explosion, we will be picked up by one of the escort vessels, praising the miracle that left two survivors."

The Papal Secret

"The cardinal electors will meet ten days after the pope's death," said Albertini. "I have to be back in Rome during the papal interregnum. I will use the time of *sede vacante* to canvass support for the full vote of the Sacred College of Cardinals. With Pollini out the way, the ballot should go in my favour."

* * *

Isabella's encounter with the pope left her with mixed feelings; that the pontiff was comfortable speaking alone in the company of a woman augured well for his progressiveness, but focusing the content of his dialogue on the Jews seemed a little strange coming from the Holy Father himself. She mentioned the conversation to Michael when they were alone in the wheelhouse.

"I think you're trying to conjure up an intent that isn't there," he told her. "His outreach program to the Jews is well documented."

"I don't know," said Isabella still feeling puzzled. "He gives me the impression that his strong attraction toward Judaism goes beyond policy."

Michael shrugged. "It's a very interesting faith," he said. "And if he could bring Christianity, Judaism, and Islam into empathetic alignment, the world would be a better place."

"I suppose so," conceded Isabella.

Michael measured the distance between the *Bella Mare* and the naval craft ahead of them and pulled slightly back on the throttle; he wanted to maintain the maximum distance allowed. He wasn't happy being hemmed in between two military vessels like a pirate ship being escorted into captivity, but he remembered why they were there.

"Our only concern is with the wellbeing of the papal entourage and getting them safely back to Port Fiumicino."

"What could possibly go wrong on such a sedate cruise?" asked Isabella.

Michael shrugged, but he was reminded of the Rochi cruise, where he had the same opinion as Isabella had just expressed.

* * *

When Cardinal Albertini entered the pope's cabin, he found

the pontiff kneeling at the foot of the crucifix which had been placed on the table, his hands joined in prayer. He waited for Bandini to stand up before proceeding toward him.

"I think we should talk," he said succinctly.

"I think we should," Bandini replied, taking a seat in the easy chair. He indicated to the cardinal to do the same in the remaining chair. "What do you wish to speak to me about?"

"This, Your Eminence," he said, handing the pope a letter.

Pope John Pietro I spread out the piece of paper on his desk and picked up his reading glasses. There was silence in the cabin while his eyes scanned the familiar words in the letter. He paled as he read his own words on the document, but showed no outward display of emotion. "This is a private letter which you have misappropriated by illegal means," he said slowly.

"It doesn't really matter how I came to possess it," Albertini replied. "Only what it proclaims."

"The words contained here reflect my private thoughts. You have intruded into my privacy."

"It's your confession that intrigues me, Pietro. Rather damning circumstances."

"Being born a Jew does not alter my commitment to the church, Vittorio."

"But maybe it will alter the way the Holy See views you."

"My role as pontiff has in no way been compromised by my accident of birth."

"You are still living a lie, and that cannot be tolerated by the Holy See." Albertini stood up for effect. "I recommend that, upon returning to Rome, you announce your resignation from the papacy due to ill health. What's more, you will endorse my candidacy as the next pope and, in return, I will not reveal the contents of this letter, if only for the sake of the Church."

"Are you blackmailing me, Vittorio?" the pope asked, rising to his feet.

"I wouldn't call it blackmail, Your Holiness," said Albertini sarcastically. "I would rather refer to it as an exchange of favours."

"You are not worthy of the cloth you wear, let alone that of a pope. You are a disgrace to the Vatican and I will do all in my power while I still live to see that you never progress beyond what you are."

"I was hoping it wouldn't come to this," said Albertini,

grabbing the letter off the desk. "I was so hoping to spare the Holy See this embarrassment." He turned and strutted out of the cabin, shaking his black cape edged in red like a bull fighter tormenting a bull.

* * *

Michael had told Isabella and Mario to keep aloof from the passengers and to hover on the periphery of intrusion until summoned. This was no ordinary cruise, where holiday-makers usually enjoyed interacting with members of the crew. The papal cruise demanded discretion and privacy. The cruise was an official outing designed to please a generous philanthropist and the patron of his generosity. A great deal of money was going to change hands for the benefit of some of the pope's favourite charities and it was the intention of the Vatican to flatter the benefactor with the honour of the Holy Father's exclusive attention.

As a result, Isabella and Mario had retired to the galley to prepare the evening meal while Michael remained on the bridge steering their course and keeping a watchful eye on the papal party sitting around the conference table he had set up for them at the bow.

The pope and Dr. Alessandro were engaged in what appeared to be cordial conversation, with smiles on both faces, while the two cardinals listened intently on either side of them. The two officers of the security detail sat at the bar, a discreet distance from them just below the bridge. Although they were speaking in an undertone so as not to draw any attention to themselves, it was evident to Michael from their hand gesticulations that they were in conflict with one another. He moved onto the deck above them, straining to hear what they were saying. Luckily, the little wind there was flowing over the prow carried their voices sufficiently enough to be audible.

"You may carry the favour of Cardinal Albertini," Roberto Silva was saying, "but the Pontifical Swiss Guard that you so nefariously represent is merely ceremonial."

"And the Corpo della Gendarmeria, my dear captain, that you represent, is purely for the enforcement of crowd and traffic control," said Fabio Mento sneeringly.

"You conveniently omitted criminal investigation as well."

"No crime has been committed here, so you are wasting your time."

"Well, it is my responsibility to ensure that none is," Silva added.

"On board this boat and with a military escort not too far away, your duties may as well be ceremonial," Mento rejoined dryly.

"Just don't forget who's really in charge here."

"If it boosts your ego, then think what you like. I also have my instructions and will do everything in my power to satisfy the trust of Cardinal Albertini, who commissioned me."

"Then I think a thorough search of the cabins while the meeting is in progress is in order," suggested Silva.

"I'll start with the pope's," volunteered Mento eagerly.

"We will conduct the search together. Albertini may trust you, but I don't."

The two men went below, more wary of each other than any intent of finding anything suspicious. Of course, for Mento, it was merely pretence. He knew that whatever they were looking for was safely out of sight beneath their feet.

* * *

The limpet mines attached to the underside of the *Bella Mare's* hull, like two melanomas that would prove fatal if not removed, were set to explode in another nine hours. They had been secured in place by two divers who had waited at the marina exit for the yacht to depart. They knew they only had five minutes in which to secure the explosives before the yacht cleared landfall at the end of the canal.

As the boat passed them, they kicked upward and attached the suction grips to the sides of the hull, each diver positioning himself on either side of the boat. They worked quickly but carefully. When the charges were in place, the one diver moved around to the swim platform at the stern and secured a third charge to its underside. Then both divers waited until the yacht reached open waters before letting go and diving deep toward the beach a kilometre away. It took them fourteen minutes to reach the rocks, where they emerged from the water talking excitedly so as not to arouse suspicion that they had done anything other than look for oysters.

The two saboteurs went directly to their vehicle parked at the side of the road and drove away quickly. The car had been stolen that morning and they were eager to dump it before it could be traced with them still in it. They had kept their faces and heads covered with their diving suits to ensure they wouldn't be identified once the investigation started after the pope's assassination. No one could possibly pick them out of a line-up, if it ever came to that, but with the advances made in forensic science, one could never be too careful.

Michael stood at the helm of his boat unaware of the danger they were in.

Chapter 49

Bella Mare

The sun hung low on the western horizon, channelling a fan of golden light over the calm sea. Michael was not alone in the wheelhouse; Captain Silva had joined him a few minutes earlier and the conversation had swiftly turned to matters of security.

"The sun will set in another two hours," said Silva thoughtfully, "and I don't know whether to regard darkness as an ally or an enemy."

"The two naval vessels will prevent anyone from intruding into our space," said Michael, throttling back slightly to maintain position behind the leading boat. "If we are to persist in our paranoia, the only threat can come from someone aboard this boat."

"Cardinal Pollini is a close friend of the Holy Father and I trust him completely."

"It is common knowledge that Cardinal Albertini has ambitions to be the next pope, and that could cause him to stray off the path of righteousness, but why would anybody aboard contemplate murder at sea when everyone on board would be suspect? What do you know of Mento?" added Michael.

"Not much," admitted Silva. "Our respective services run separately from each other; one ceremonial and the other law enforcement. He is not content with passive duty. Being a big cog in a small wheel doesn't suit him, but his credentials must have passed the stringent testing of the Swiss Guard's Intelligence Section. He and Albertini have formed a close working relationship."

"A strange juxtaposition of bedfellows," mumbled Michael.

"Exactly," agreed Silva. "I work closely with Cardinal Pollini, but we respect each other's disposition. I don't intrude into his spiritual reality and he doesn't embrace my secularism."

The Papal Secret

Just then the door to the wheelhouse burst open and Isabella stepped through the hatchway. "Mento . . . that fucking bastard . . ." she began, breathlessly. When she saw Silva standing there she put a hand up to her mouth as if to stop any further profanity. "Oh, I'm sorry Captain Silva. I though Michael was alone."

"No problem, my dear," Silva smiled. "But a fitting epilogue to the man we've just been discussing."

"What did he do?" asked Michael.

"Peeked up my skirt while I was climbing the steps, the perverted little man!"

"That vision ought to keep him preoccupied for a while."

"It's not funny, Michael!"

"I think I'd better leave," interjected Silva. "It's going to be a long night for all of us."

* * *

Cardinal Albertini was not a man of the ocean; he preferred closed places. Perhaps it was the years he had spent in the Vatican surrounded by high walls. He did not like open space. It lacked the constraint of discipline, and he sensed the danger of his soul being enticed into infinity. Surrounding himself with walls helped, so it seemed, to prevent his soul from straying. Looking out to sea, he felt vulnerable again, like his soul was attempting to escape from his very being to skim across the waves to get away from him. He knew the illusion was caused by a guilty conscience.

"What am I doing?" he asked the sea. "Have I slipped so far from righteousness that I could contemplate complicity in the murder of the Lord's holy representative on earth? Is it worth attaining the Throne of Saint Peter in the company of the devil?" He stared down into the water and watched the waves slapping against the hull. Then he quickly looked at his watch. It would soon be time for the explosion that would guarantee his entry into hell. Would the glory on earth as the next pope be worth eternal damnation? He thought of Dr. Faustus and the turmoil he went through as his day of death approached and the devil waited eagerly to claim his prize.

But he would be doing the Holy See good service by ridding them of the Jew who had usurped the throne. He saw himself as the holy purgative bringing order back into the church. Perhaps his soul could still be redeemed. All God wanted was for the sinner to turn from his evil ways. Confession and repentance was all that was required. And what about all his good deeds? They must count for something? As for the murder itself, how could he be held accountable for just turning a blind eye and doing nothing to prevent the course of events? Someone else would be committing the sin.

Albertini looked down into the water again and consulted his watch for the second time. The explosion would silence the secret of Pope John Pietro's Jewish heritage forever and the church would be spared the embarrassment. Albertini suddenly saw himself as the redeeming angel. He would allow the plan to proceed without any intervention.

Michael was watching the strange behaviour of the cardinal leaning against the railings and staring down into the water. At first, he thought he must be praying, but his gesticulations were more appropriate to a man having an argument, in this case with himself. Something in the water seemed to be bothering him, but it was improbable he was contemplating suicide. He saw the cleric suddenly move away from the edge and hurry inside.

* * *

Captain Silva had not planned to sleep that night. He had ensconced himself outside the door of the pope's cabin and, armed with a flask of strong black coffee and his faithful Colt .45, settled down in the chair he had taken from the galley. He was being overly cautious, he knew, but he had been entrusted with the Holy Father's safety and he was not going to shirk his responsibility by allowing himself the luxury of a good night's sleep. He had kept vigil throughout the night on many previous occasions of less importance, and he wasn't going to fail on this one. He took little comfort knowing that Frost would also be getting no sleep in the wheelhouse, but felt reassured that he was close enough to help if the need arose.

Michael was standing at the forward rail of the bridge. He could see the bow wave making a V of white foam in the dark water. The convoy was not due to make a course change until daybreak and the controls were set to maintain their present course without having to make continuous adjustments. He loved the stillness of the sea at night, especially when the weather was perfect, as it was now. The sound of the swell lapping against the hull filled him with a tranquillity that only a mariner could appreciate in calm sailing conditions. However, there was something about Cardinal Albertini's behaviour earlier that evening that bothered him. Something was not right.

Michael lengthened his gaze as he looked further ahead at the lights of the leading vessel, a hundred and fifty metres ahead of them. Behind, the other escort vessel was following at the same distance. He would have preferred a tighter formation at night, but radar scanners would warn of any other ship straying within two nautical miles of their safety zone. Nevertheless, he decided to contact the commodore and suggest they close in.

He stepped back into the wheelhouse and crossed to the communications table. He was surprised to see a hand towel covering the radio transmitter. It was not like Mario to leave things lying around before he went off duty. He lifted the towel and his skin went cold. Somebody had been fiddling with the transmitter. He switched it on but nothing happened. Then he saw that the back had been ripped out and all the wires cut. It would take hours to fix. Someone had sabotaged the radio. Then he realized what was bothering him. It was the way in which Cardinal Albertini kept looking down into the water and then repeatedly at his watch. Almost as if he was expecting something to happen. Instinctively, he looked at the clock above the window. The luminous dial showed it was half past twelve. Perhaps it was time to carry out another check. He left the bridge and went to find Silva. He found him sitting vigil outside the pope's cabin. He told him of his concern.

"We'd better check it out," said Silva reluctantly. He was loath to leave the door of the cabin unguarded, but if something was bothering the captain it was best to attend to it.

They inspected each side of the hull and found nothing wrong.

"What if there's something below the waterline?" asked Silva.

"We'd have to drop anchor for me to dive down and inspect the hull," Michael informed him.

"Let's inform the commodore."

"I can't," said Michael. "Someone has smashed the radio."

"I don't like this." Silva looked worried. "Something's going on and we'd better find out what it is before it's too late."

They were standing at the stern when Michael looked down at the swim platform. He thought he saw a silver object in the water through the wooden slats.

"What's that?" Silva had also seen it.

"I'm not sure, but it's not supposed to be there, whatever

Stan Miller

it is. I should be able to reach it if I lean into the water. Take hold of my legs." He extended his arms under the platform and groped for the object. His fingers brushed against a metal surface but it was still out of reach. "There's a diving mask under the bench by the steps. Maybe I'll be able to see what it is."

Silva went over to the bench and brought back the mask. Once again, Michael put his head under the water. The current was quite strong but as long as he faced the direction they were going in, the pressure wouldn't rip away the mask. What he saw sent shock waves through his body. He emerged from the water coughing and spluttering.

"What is it?" asked Silva not liking the expression on Michael's face.

"It looks like a limpet mine. This boat is rigged to explode!" Michael yelled, struggling to his feet.

"Catch up to the escort vessel so we can transfer the passengers," said Silva. "They'll be able to disarm it."

"Too late for that," shouted Michael. "I saw the timer. It's set to go off in seven minutes!"

Chapter 50

Bella Mare

Fabio Mento felt he was cutting it a bit fine. The minute hand on his Rolex was approaching the top of the hour when all hell would break loose. It was time to abandon ship. He had warned Albertini not to jump too soon; otherwise his rescuers might view with suspicion that he was picked up too far from where the *Bella Mare* went down. No point casting doubt about how the two of them managed to survive the explosion by abandoning ship long before it happened. What worried him even more was Albertini's presence on deck already. He seemed to be too nervous and impatient to get off the boat. If seen preparing to jump overboard by Frost or Silva they would wonder what the danger was and get the pope transferred to one of the escort vessels and the whole plan would come to nothing. He was supposed to wait for his signal.

In fact, Albertini had not waited for Mento to give the word and was standing against the rail on the starboard deck contemplating his evacuation. He had spotted Frost and Silva doing some sort of search of the hull and had moved back into the shadows as they passed. He had hoped it was just a routine inspection and not because they were on to something. He looked at his watch. Still seven minutes to go. He wasn't prepared to wait much longer. There was no sign of Mento on deck and he knew nothing about explosives and how accurate their timing devices were. What if it detonated before one o'clock? He didn't want to hang around to find out. He climbed onto the rail and steadied himself on one of the uprights. The sea below looked daunting. He wasn't a good swimmer, but Mento had told him that the life jacket would keep him afloat for hours, if necessary. He pulled the cord of the jacket and he felt it tightening around his chest. Then he closed his eyes and jumped.

* * *

Stan Miller

It was time to leave. Mento opened his cabin door and peered into the passageway. He was holding his silenced Beretta in front of him, expecting to see Silva guarding the pope's door. But the corridor was empty.

Strange, he thought, *for the post to be deserted*. He felt a little disappointed that he wouldn't have the satisfaction of killing Silva himself. He edged out slowly, not wanting to make any noise; no telling who might still be awake. He was about to turn left and ascend the few steps to the hatchway of the aft deck when he heard the sound of muffled voices coming from somewhere to his right. He glanced at his watch and saw that he still had a few more minutes, so decided to go and check it out. The voices were coming from an open hatch leading to the foredeck. When he got there, he saw Silva blocking the way.

"Going somewhere, Mento?"

Mento looked past Silva's shoulder and saw Frost lowering a lifeboat. He couldn't see who was in it but he knew it must be the pope and the other passengers. What had gone wrong? He had to get past Silva so that he could shoot them all. Their bodies would be obliterated by the explosion, so the police wouldn't suspect they had been shot. He lifted his gun to the firing position and aimed it at Silva.

As he pulled the trigger, Silva threw himself to the side and the bullet struck his arm. Ignoring the pain, Silva rushed at Mento before he could aim again. Both men crashed to the deck and the gun was knocked out of Mento's hand and slid out of reach against the bulkhead. Silva had to delay Mento at any cost, even if it was with his life.

The wrestle was an uneven contest, as Silva had the use of only one arm. Mento broke free and made a grab for the gun. He stood up, eager to shoot his opponent at point blank range. He managed a cruel smile as he lifted the barrel. Suddenly, Mento fell forward with glazed eyes. The gun dropped from his hand and he collapsed next to Silva.

Silva looked up and saw Michael standing there, holding the metal casing of a fire extinguisher.

Michael flung it aside and shouted. "Quick, take my hand, we only have minutes left." He helped Silva to his feet and pulled him by the good arm to the side railing. "Jump!"

"What about the pope?" he cried.

"They're all safe in the lifeboat; now jump!"

Both men hurled themselves over the side. Michael was hoping that the speed of the boat would give them the

The Papal Secret

necessary distance to survive the explosion. Swimming was pointless. He looked around for Silva. He couldn't see him in the darkness. "Roberto, where are you?" he shouted.

"Over here," came the reply.

Michael looked in the direction of the sound and saw Silva a few metres away. "Hold on, I'm coming." He swam to the policeman and grabbed his arm.

"Thanks," choked Silva. "You saved my life back there."

"You saved us from the madman's gun," replied Michael.

* * *

Albertini held his breath waiting to hit the water. When nothing happened, he opened his eyes and found himself dangling helplessly over the side of the boat. There was a terrible pain as the life jacket tightened over his chest, constricting his breathing. He saw that the jacket had impaled itself on the vertical post he had been leaning against. He tried moving his hands toward the release clip in front of him, but his arms were pinned to his side by the weight of his body on the life jacket. He cursed himself for having inflated it prematurely.

"Mento, help me!" he called. They were the last words he uttered before his body was blown into oblivion.

A few metres away, lying on the deck, was his trusted accomplice who could not save him. Mento had managed to get to his knees, but the concussion had left him groggy. He tried to stand but his legs buckled under him. He started dragging himself toward the side. The last thing he heard was the plaintive cry of the cardinal; and the last thing he saw was the dark sea seven metres below him.

* * *

The explosion turned the dark of the night sky into a brilliant orange light. Debris from the burning ship fell close to them, but the *Bella Mare* had sailed too far for any wreckage to reach them on the lifeboat. Michael watched his beloved yacht vanish into the sea, and soon even the fragments of ember burned themselves out and darkness once more claimed the sea around them. He unclipped his waterproof torch from his belt and began flashing the international SOS code, the signal of extreme distress, to alert one of the escort vessels of their position.

Chapter 51

Naval Boat

Michael and Captain Silva were escorted below deck for debriefing. They had swapped their wet clothes for Navy tracksuits and were eager to meet with the other survivors who, they were told, were waiting in the officers' canteen. Pope John Pietro I and Cardinal Pollini were resting in the captain's cabin.

"Your stories match," announced one of the officers, after he had interrogated each of them separately.

"What did you expect, that we are lying? We were together most of the time toward the end," Michael told him again.

"You and Captain Silva are to be commended," the officer smiled. "Through your alertness, you saved the Holy Father and the other passengers. Cardinal Albertini and Fabio Mento are still unaccounted for. We've searched the area thoroughly, so it looks like they never survived the explosion. Now we'll never know the reasons behind the assassination attempt on the pope's life, or who else may be involved."

Michael's main concern was being reunited with Isabella. All the time in the water, his only thought was for her safety. When he entered the canteen, Isabella rushed into his arms.

"Thank God you're safe," she sobbed happily. "I was so worried when the lifeboat pulled away without you."

"Silva and I had a little tidying up to do before we abandoned ship," Michael said.

"Sorry to interrupt," one of the officers interjected, "but His Holiness would like to see you and Captain Silva." He led the way to the captain's cabin and knocked softly on the door.

"Enter," Cardinal Pollini called.

The pope was sitting in a chair next to the writing desk. He looked rather sprightly in spite of his ordeal, and was wearing his white vestments as if they had just been freshly laundered. He listened intently to what Michael and Captain Silva told

The Papal Secret

him about the discovery of the bomb and what had subsequently happened to Mento as he tried to stop them from abandoning ship.

"We owe the two of you our lives," began the pope, "for which I express, on behalf of all of us, my grateful thanks." He turned to Pollini for continuation.

"The Holy Father," began Pollini, "wishes to keep Cardinal Albertini's involvement in the assassination attempt away from the media. It is sufficient to allocate the blame entirely on Mento, who was not part of the clergy, in order to spare the church any embarrassment. Albertini will get his rightful judgement when he stands before the Almighty and renders his accounts to the God he should have served more righteously. It is my opinion and that of Cardinal Pollini that it will serve no purpose desecrating his name here on earth and bringing the church into ridicule." He shifted uncomfortably on his feet. "It is our intention to announce his demise and hold a memorial prayer in memory of the good deeds the cardinal performed during his lifetime. There is no need to draw too much attention to him, and it is best if he is forgotten quickly."

"We will honour your request," said Silva. "My investigation and that of the police will focus on the role Mento played. He does seem to be the key figure in all of this and it will be to our advantage conducting a secular investigation."

"Thank you," replied the pope.

* * *

It had been difficult for Michael and Isabella to sleep during the remaining hours of darkness. They stood on deck when the sky began to lighten with the approaching dawn. Both naval vessels sailed in tight formation, heading directly for the port of Fiumicino and they watched the other ship cut easily through the swells.

"What are you going to do now?" asked Isabella, searching Michael's eyes.

"Marry you," he answered quickly.

"I mean, about your boat?"

"Unfortunately, I don't have one anymore," said Michael sadly. "She was a good craft. I'll miss her."

"The insurance will pay you out, won't they?"

"I guess."

"Will you get another one and continue with your life in the same way?"

"Since I met you, my life is not the same anymore." He turned to face her. "The only thing that matters is being with you."

"Let's get married as soon as possible and to hell with what people may say." She pressed herself against him and kissed him on the lips. "There's plenty of time to consider the future. I have enough money for both of us until you decide what you want to do."

"Until we decide what we want to do," he corrected her.

"I just want to spend the rest of my life with you, Captain Frost," she said adoringly.

"And I want to spend the rest of my life with you, Mrs. Frost."

The sun peeped over the horizon at them and, seeming to like what it saw, continued to rise until it was fully exposed at the edge of the sea, bringing warmth to the new day.

EPILOGUE

Vatican City

Between the tower and the palace, in the area now occupied by the Cortile di San Damaso and the Palace of Sixtus V, lay the *hortus segretus*, or private garden. The pope had chosen the location to meet with Cardinal Pollini not only because of its beauty, but mainly for the privacy it afforded. No one could eavesdrop on their conversation without being seen.

The Holy Father stooped to examine the petal of a delicate flower, taking the utmost care not to disturb it. "Such a beautiful specimen of God's wondrous creation," he said, looking up at Pollini standing beside him. "I love being surrounded by flowers and shrubbery. Even those arches covered in such fine greenery look like the portals to heaven, our own Garden of Eden."

"The folly of Adam to have ruined such a place of serenity," Pollini added.

"Cardinal Albertini must surely fall into that same category. I don't like talking ill of the dead, but he was such a sad soul, misguided by ambition."

"Your letter of confession died with him, too, Pietro," Pollini reminded him. He was hoping the Holy Father had suggested this meeting to tell him he would lay the matter to rest. "It was a wise decision not to attach any blame to Albertini. It is better for the world to believe he was an unfortunate victim of the explosion. Knowledge of his involvement would serve no purpose, and a scandal of this magnitude would have had disastrous results for the church. We have suffered enough scandal through wayward bishops. Let the media crucify Mento for the attempt on your life, if I might put it that way."

"And I suppose confessing to the world that their pope is Jewish would also complicate matters?" said Bandini with a twinkle in his eye. "I suppose it was fortunate my letter went down with the ship. A divine sign, perhaps?"

"No one must ever know of its contents," said Pollini.

"But withholding the truth of my Jewish birth will be perpetuating a lie."

"Withholding the truth is not lying," said Pollini, laying a gentle hand on his friend's shoulder.

"I don't see the difference, Angelo."

"Maintaining your silence, in this case, is for the protection of your flock and the church you have dedicated your whole life to uphold and serve. You are not concealing the truth for selfish reasons. To speak a lie, on the other hand, is deceitful."

"You should have been a lawyer, my friend."

"Heaven help us then!"

"I know I'm a Jew and God knows it. I can't just bury my head in the sand and ignore the fact."

"The media has acclaimed you as the 'Pope of Wisdom,' Pietro. You are regarded as one of the best pontiffs to have ever occupied the Throne of Saint Peter." Pollini couldn't help pleading. "The church needs a man like you. Please don't throw it all away and abandon the people who love you."

Bandini sighed. "I am a Catholic, yet I am also a Jew. How do I decide?"

"God has already decided, my friend," Pollini said quietly. "He saved you, after all."

The pope looked at him quizzically, waiting for an elaboration.

"God spared your life from the Holocaust," Pollini continued slowly. "He also spared your life on the boat. Do you put your survival down to chance? Don't you see God's plan in all of this?"

"I would like to believe I'm worthy of divine interest," said the pope.

"Of course you are," affirmed Pollini. "The Lord consumed the only two people who could betray you. Isn't that proof enough of God's will?"

"Which is?"

"Your destiny is to influence mankind to grow toward perfection," said Pollini, knowing this was his final attempt at persuasion. "The mission of the Jews is to be a light unto the nations. They project moral values that everyone should aspire to, and you are one of them. Your papacy is advocating exactly the same thing, but from a different perspective. Your Jewish blood has proved to be an advantage; don't regard it as a burden." Pollini felt drained. It was difficult asking such a great man to perpetuate such a secret for the good of the church.

Pope John Pietro I remained silent for a long time. When he spoke, he waved his arms over the garden as if blessing the foliage. "Very well, Angelo," he said in an undertone. "I must agree; it would be a shame to destroy such a beautiful place."

END